PRAISE FOR RAISING A DEMON

Selection of Five Star Reviews from Goodreads

I loved it! The characters were funny and likable. I found that it was an easy reading story and I hope to see more of these characters.

This is my first book by Amy Cissell and I really enjoyed it...in fact it was hard for me to put down. I loved the references to the shows Supernatural and Lucifer...both favourites of mine.

I loved this book, it is entertaining and the characters are pretty awesome. Evie is a single mom, who is sent into a crazy "revelation week" from hell (pun intended) and we discover that there is a lot more that meets the eye in sleepy Eden Valley. I'm curious about the other characters and what will happen next in the series. I just found a new series to look forward to and I think if you like fantasy, urban fantasy and hotness everywhere, this book is just for you.

I thoroughly enjoyed Evie's story. A fresh new take on a midlife crisis! All of the characters are so well developed and a joy to read. I loved Evie's friends and family and Lily especially is a precocious little girl. Even Luc's brother and sister were fun to read. I am definitely looking forward to the next book in the series!

RAISING A DEMON

AMY CISSELL

BROKEN
WORLD
PUBLISHING

RAISING A DEMON
Amy Cissell

A Broken World Publication
PO Box 11643
Portland, OR 97211
Raising A Demon
Copyright © 2021 by Amy Cissell
ISBN 978-1-949410-22-8 (ebook) ;
ISBN 978-1-949410-23-5 (paperback)

Cover Design: Cissell Ink
Edited by Suzanne Lahna, The Quick Fox
Edited & Proofread by Christopher Barnes, Cissell Ink

Eden Valley

Raising a Demon
Devil and the Deep, Blue Lake
Valley of Angels
Guardian of Eden

Eden Valley World Novellas

Match Made in Hell
Fall From Grace
Hell's Bells
Heaven Sent

For Liana
my very own demon child
Fucking Fine

ACKNOWLEDGMENTS

So many thanks to my advance readers! Y'all are beyond fantastic.

I'm grateful to my editors Suzanne Lahna of The Quick Fox and Christopher Barnes of Cissell Ink for their feedback, plot hole discoveries, comma rehabilitation, and insistence that I add some descriptions and character emotions (ew).

Mostly, though, I want to thank my daughter Liana. She is the real inspiration—language and everything—for Lily.

CONTENT WARNING

This book contains a depiction of a near child drowning and a child abduction.

CHAPTER ONE

Evelyn Addams stood in the small bathroom and gripped the sink. It was the last day of peace and quiet before her friends and parents descended on her house for her daughter's tenth birthday party, and she was grabbing every minute of solitary silence she could.

"Mooooooommm! Where are you?"

Evie sighed and opened the bathroom door and stepped out into the downstairs hall of the too-large farmhouse she'd taken over when her parents had retired to Hawaii.

"I'm in the bathroom, demon child!" she yelled back.

"Ugh. You're gross," Liliana said, thundering down the stairs. She was wearing black leggings with tiny pink skulls polka-dotting them, a tunic-length orange shirt, and beat-up black sneakers—typical Lily—and had pulled her black hair into a messy ponytail. She regarded her mother with light brown eyes that lately were perpetually rolling. Her darker features—gifts from her dad—contrasted with Evie's lighter skin and brown hair.

"Did you need something? Help with your homework? A chore to do? Or did you just want to come bask in my beauty?" Evie stopped the grimace that tried to accompany the last question. Four decades of life and one as a single mother had added more gray to her hair and lines on her face than she liked to think about. She wanted to want to age gracefully but hadn't quite captured the spirit yet.

"Whatever, Momster. I just need more screen time." Lily rolled her eyes at her mother and stuck her lower lip out in an exaggerated pout as she held out her iPad towards her mother.

"Lily, you've had more than enough screen time today. Go outside. Play. Be free! It's a gorgeous day, and you need to get some fresh air."

Lily heaved a sigh and fixed her mother with a glare. "You'd better be nicer to me when I'm ten."

"Not a chance, child," Evie said. "As soon as you hit those double digits, it's the Cinderella life for you. I'll have you scrubbing the hearth every morning before dawn, doing the laundry by hand, and sewing all your own clothes." Their banter did nothing to erase the abstract panic Evie felt every time Lily's imminent birthday came up. It was one thing to have a child, but ten felt too close to teen which was way too close to growing up and moving out.

"You do that, and I'll bring in field mice to help," Lily said. "And not just mice. Rats. Big ones. And tarantulas. They're great at sewing."

Evie laughed. "You're the worst."

Lily laughed and threw her arms around her mother, banging her iPad against the back of Evie's head. "You love me."

"From here to the ends of the universe and back," Evie agreed, dropping a kiss on her daughter's head, which was just a few inches below hers now. They were already sharing shoes, and it wouldn't be too much longer before her daughter's height surpassed Evie's. "Now go play. Grandma and Grandpa will be here tomorrow to help you celebrate your birthday, so it's your last chance to play without senior citizens trailing you around the lake yelling at you to be careful."

Lily rolled her eyes. "Even when I'm ten?"

"Until you're fifty, probably," Evie said. "Stay out of the lake, though."

"I know, *Mom*," Lily said. "The lake is dangerous, even for strong swimmers, and I'm never to go in without adult supervision." She mimicked Evie's voice so well that Evie blinked in surprise before laughing.

"Exactly. I'm so glad you've listened to at least one thing I've said in the last almost ten years."

"Whatever. I'll go out. Cerberus needs a walk anyway." Lily whistled shrilly. "C'mon, boy! Get in here. It's walksies time!"

Lily stood, staring expectantly up the stairs towards her room, then petted the air in front of her in three different places. "Someday, someone will invent a better leash," she assured the imaginary three-headed dog. She stuffed her iPad in her backpack, then opened the door, ushered Cerberus outside, and ran off.

Evie shook her head and walked towards the door. Lily'd never had an imaginary friend before, but her stuffies had always had very active lives, complete with more weddings than she could count, even though Evie had officiated most of them. Cerberus was new—he'd shown up a couple months ago—and for now, Evie was going with it. Anything that kept Lily a kid for a bit longer was good.

She started to close it but paused when she saw Lily make a stop in the garage. Evie closed the door and watched through the small window as Lily came back out of the garage with her backpack stuffed to the gills with something Evie couldn't make out. Lily looked around furtively, then jogged towards the small stand of trees at the edge of the property.

Evie slipped out of the house and followed. She normally trusted Lily—her daughter had a good head on her shoulders, and although she liked a good prank, she'd been a pretty decent child—so far. But something about the way Lily was sneaking—she was usually such an out-in-the-open child—rang Evie's alarm bells.

Things hadn't always been easy. It was tough being the daughter of a single mom, especially in a town like Eden Valley where everyone knows everything about everyone…and when they didn't have the details, they made them up. But Lily was bright, happy, and relatively well-adjusted.

Everyone knew about Evie's summer fling with the devastatingly handsome Luc, son of a real estate developer—or so the rumor mill said—who'd come to town looking for something. All he found was Evie, though, and he hadn't stayed.

Whether it was because he didn't want to settle down, because she was damaged goods—already divorced once—or because she'd scared him off by being too forward, the residents of Eden Valley were evenly split.

Evie'd shrugged off everyone's speculations, insinuations, and whispers, and finally, after more than ten years, she didn't feel like her life choices were on display anymore. Her only regret was that he'd left before she'd had a chance to tell him she was pregnant.

Lily had been the best and most challenging thing that'd ever happened to her. The challenges were often enough to make her want to tear her hair out and were responsible for most of the lines on her face and at least eighty-five percent of the gray hairs scattered on her head. But Lily had never been a troublemaker, which made her surreptitious raiding of the garage even more out of character.

❦ ❧ ❦

EVIE HEADED towards the "witch's clearing" that she and her friends had made when they were Lily's age. It was nothing more than a small area in the middle of the wooded area abutting the property where no trees or bushes grew. Evie and her best friends Beverly and Vivian had spent endless summer days cleaning up the space and decorating it with items swiped from their doll houses, matchbox car sets, and Lego builds until they had a small village overseen by a terrifying but benevolent witch.

When she was too old for magical dollhouses, Evie had redecorated with repurposed deck furniture and an old tent, making a reading nook, and later, a place to sneak a couple beers. It was where she'd sworn a blood oath with Viv and Bev to stay sisters forever, where she'd lost her virginity, where she'd come to cry after finding Jeremy in bed with Brandy, Evie's former boss, and where she'd hidden away from the world when all she had was a positive pregnancy test and a broken heart.

Lily had found the spot the summer before and had dragged her best friends—Kevin and Shelby—to fix it up. It's where her daughter hid when she was scared or overwhelmed, when she was angry with her mom, and when she needed privacy—something that'd been more and more common the closer she got to ten.

Evie paused, the clearing just out of sight. Lily was speaking, and Evie didn't want to interrupt in case something innocuous was going down, and Lily'd just been grabbing snacks for an impromptu meeting of the top secret "no grown-ups allowed" best friend's club.

Instead of giggles and the sound of junk food wrappers, she heard Lily chanting.

"Daemon esta subjetive volunteer me. And ligandum eros partier eros coram me."

Evie tilted her head in confusion as Lily repeated herself. It sounded vaguely like Latin, but not like anything she remembered studying during her one semester of Latin at the community college. She crept forward, careful not to disturb her daughter, and peered into the clearing.

Lily was sitting in the middle of the clearing, a Ouija board in front of her, birthday candles stuck into the ground at regular intervals, and the rock salt Evie scattered on the sidewalks when it was icy poured in a circle around the candles. An old can of spray paint Evie had once used to mark the underground utilities in her yard was on its side a little ways outside the circle. Inside the salt was a large box of matches and a pile of spent matches on Lily's right side and a dusty bottle of wine on her left. Evie peered at the wine, but it was unopened—which was maybe not the most worrisome thing in the clearing, but the easiest fear to dismiss.

Evie stopped trying to be silent and walked towards her daughter. Lily was cross-legged in the circle, palms together in front of her chest, and staring intently at a huge, ornately bound book open on her lap. Her iPad was on top of the book, an eerily familiar image clearly visible over the pictures of two men.

Was that...Sam and Dean?

Lily repeated the incantation, this time with impatience threading through her voice. Evie stood back, hands on her hips, and waited to be noticed.

After a third attempt with no apparent results—Evie wasn't sure what they were waiting for—Lily set her iPad on the Ouija board with the utmost care, then slammed the book shut and yelled, "Fucking fine! I'll wait."

Evie was so startled by Lily's cursing—more so than by her ritual—that she burst out laughing. Lily spun around in the dirt and stared up at her mom. Her eyes widened into an expression Evie knew only too well—there were about to be tears. Maybe an elaborate explanation about how none of this was technically against the rules. A denial of any culpability. A touch of blame-shifting to whoever had given her the book. And an absolution of any lingering guilt.

"Mommy," Lily said through newly formed tears. "I'm so sorry. I was trying to make Cerberus real so you could see him. It really hurts my feelings when you call him an imaginary dog and look at me like I'm lying to you. Even if he was imaginary, I don't think that's a very kind way to treat your daughter, is it? And I didn't do anything you've ever told me not to. I just found this old Ouija board and the paint and wine in the garage—they weren't being used. I'll buy new birthday candles from my allowance, I promise. It's Kevin's book, not mine. It was his idea to see if I could make Cerberus real. And no one was supposed to hear me say the f-word. You only heard it because you snuck up on me, something I'm not supposed to do to you, and you were spying. I have a right to privacy, and you broke your promise."

Evie was impressed. "That's some top-notch blame shifting, Lily-bear. I don't care about the swearing—as long as you save your curse words for when there aren't any other grownups around, especially at school. I'd rather you learn what the words mean and how to use them—and *when* to use them. But let me ask you this...if you thought you were so blameless and not doing anything wrong, why are you trying so hard to talk me into it?"

Lily stood up and brushed off her backside, then scuffed a break into the salt circle and walked towards her mother. "Mo-om, I'm sorry." She tipped her head back—although she didn't have to tip very much—and pointed her big, mournful puppy dog eyes at her mother.

Evie looked around Lily and saw the painted pentagram on the ground where Lily'd been sitting. "Turn around, monster," she said.

Lily turned, and Evie took a step back. Sure enough, fluorescent pink paint adorned the back of Lily's jeans. She sighed. This kid went through more clothing than seemed humanly possible.

"Next time, wait until the paint is dry before sitting in it," she advised. "Now clean up your mess—and give me that wine. I'm gonna need that after today."

"Yes, Mama," Lily said. She fetched the wine and her iPad and handed them to Evie. "I suppose you're taking away my screen time for the rest of the day?"

Evie looked at the wine, trying to remember where it'd come from and why it was in the garage. Oh. *Oh*. This was the last bottle of wedding wine that was supposed to be opened on hers and Jeremy's tenth anniversary—eleven years ago. Unfortunately, she'd spent that day in a lawyer's office signing divorce papers instead. Her chest tightened for a moment, as it always did when she thought about her divorce, and she turned her attention to the iPad before the tears pricking at the corners of her eyes had a chance to fall.

Sam and Dean Winchester caught her eye first—it was definitely them. Before she even had time to wonder what her daughter was doing with screenshots from a show no longer on the air that she was too young to watch, the rest of the page caught her eye—incantations used on the show to summon demons.

"Were you... Were you trying to summon a demon based on something from a TV show?" Evie asked, not even sure she wanted the answer. "And how do you know about *Supernatural* anyway?"

Lily stared at the ground. "I didn't understand the words in the book—they don't look like any letters I've ever seen. But I know there are demons on the show, so I Googled it. And you watch the reruns all the time after I go to bed."

"Key words: after you go to bed."

Lily shifted back and forth on her feet. "Sometimes I sit on the stairs and watch with you when I can't sleep. It's relaxing."

Evie closed her eyes and counted to ten. Then twenty. "An adult horror show about killing monsters is relaxing?"

"It's not as relaxing as when you watch true crime, but it makes me feel close to you. And I like monsters."

Evie shook her head. "I've totally ruined you. Not even ten years old and ruined for life."

Lily looked up at her mom through her ridiculously long eyelashes to gauge the seriousness of her mother's words. "Are you joking with me?"

Evie smiled. "Yes, monster. I'm joking. I'm going to take the wine, your iPad, and Kevin's book and head back to the house. I want you to clean up the rest of your mess—and that means toss the candles and put the Ouija board, salt, and paint back where you found them, then come into the house so we can have a chat about demon summoning."

"Yes, Mama," Lily said. "Do I have to put the salt I poured out back in the bag?"

"Not right now, baby girl," Evie said. "See you at the house." She grabbed the book and walked back through the woods. Inside, she made herself some tea and sat at the kitchen table to wait for her kid. Discussions about demon summoning hadn't been in the parenting handbook. Who did you even call for this? It was harmless—probably. A little amusing. Slightly concerning that Lily went for the dark arts to make her imaginary three-headed hellhound corporeal instead of writing to Santa or God or something. She exhaled forcefully and took another sip of tea. Maybe it was a mistake not attending church. Any church. Or maybe the real mistake was allowing her to read anything she wanted up to and including all the mythology books she was currently obsessed with.

Evie looked at the book Kevin had given Lily. It was huge—at least a foot tall and almost as wide. It was bound with cracked, black leather, and the gold embossed title was illegible from age and wear. She opened it up and a sheet of paper with Lily's scrawly handwriting slipped out.

Wish List for Demon
1. Mama to see Cerberus and buy him food
2. Meet my dad
3. Mama to be happy more

Evie tipped her head back and inhaled deeply. So much being said in fewer than two dozen words. She hadn't realized Lily even thought about her dad that much. Or Evie's happiness. Lily had asked about her dad a couple times when she was just starting kindergarten but seemed to accept Evie's explanation and didn't bring it up again. Damn it.

She turned her attention back to the pages of the book. Whatever language it was written in, it wasn't English. Or even Latin. Nothing Evie recognized. It looked like a hybrid of Arabic script, Greek, and Old Norse runes. She paged through, not surprised that Lily had given up on reading the sophisticated wingdings when something grabbed her attention. A page with only one "word" on it. She'd seen that before, and hadn't expected to see it again, especially not in a book.

Luc—her summer fling and Lily's father—had this symbol tattooed on his left shoulder blade. She'd asked him about it all those years ago, but he'd shrugged it off as a family symbol, then rolled over, pulling her on top of him, and drove all questions about his tattoos out of her mind.

CHAPTER TWO

Evie sat in the corner booth of Ambrosia, sipping her mimosa and waiting for her friends to show up. She'd dropped Lily off at the library where she usually stayed for a couple hours before wandering the half mile home.

Evie and her friends had been having brunch at Ambrosia once a month for the last twenty-five years—since they'd graduated from high school. Even when Beverly and Genevieve headed off to college after high school, they still drove back monthly from Spokane and Seattle to keep up the tradition. Bev had moved back to Eden Valley after college, but Viv had declared she would never return to the sleepy town she'd been too happy to escape. Small towns weren't always forgiving of differences, and Viv was different enough to feel uncomfortable all throughout high school.

Once Viv had moved on from working for others and had started her own graphic design firm, she'd started joining Bev and Evie for their monthly brunches. She was back in town now for Lily's birthday to fulfill her role as "Fairy Godmother Number One."

Evie scanned the menu the server had placed in front of her, even though she knew she'd order the same thing she'd ordered every month for the last twenty-five years.

Bev slid into the booth next to her, threw an arm around her shoulder, and squeezed Evie in an enthusiastic side-hug. "You look great, Evie!"

Evie rolled her eyes. "I have dark circles under my eyes, streaks of gray that my drugstore hair dye won't cover, and more crows' feet than the murder of crows Lily insists on feeding in my backyard."

Bev punched her friend in the shoulder. "You're forty-three. You have a ten-year-old daughter. You look amazing. Not twenty-five. Just good. And that dress makes your tits look amazing."

The smile that spread across Evie's face was genuine this time. "Thanks, Bev. You, look good, too, and I don't even want to start comparing boobs. You know I've been jealous of yours since middle school when you had cleavage, and I had the same A cup I'm sporting now. And if I didn't know better, I'd put you closer to twenty-three than forty-three. How do you keep your skin looking like that; you're as much a single mom as I am!"

"Decades of avoiding the sun while you and Viv slathered yourselves with suntan oil, skincare and makeup routines I've been performing religiously for fifteen years, and a thick layer of fat that smooths out my wrinkles. Oh, and I pay Heather a fortune every month to cover my grays. So, same as every time you ask."

Evie shook her head and looked at Bev through lowered lashes. "I just keep hoping that if I ask often enough, you'll be compelled to reveal the location of your portrait. I'd guess attic, but you don't have one."

Bev laughed. "You have always been good for my self-esteem, Evie. I hope we're still trading compliments when we're eighty."

Viv dropped into the booth opposite Bev and Evie and sighed dramatically, turning the other women's attention to her.

"Sorry I'm late," she said. "You would not believe the morning I've had."

Evie grinned. Viv was always late, and there was always an amazing reason. Viv's ability to spin a yarn and make everyone come along for the ride was one of her most amazing traits and why she was so successful as a graphic designer. She could make her clients *feel* her thought processes.

"What happened this time?" Bev asked. "Were there other people on your freeway again?"

"No one likes the snark, Bev," Viv said, sticking her tongue out at her friend. "And yes. There was a lot more traffic than I'd anticipated, especially for a Wednesday morning. But that's not what I was talking about. You will not *believe* the why." She paused dramatically and leaned forward. "A sinkhole opened up in the middle of the exit ramp to Eden Valley. Traffic was diverted to the next exit, and I had to take a long detour to get back to find out what'd happened."

"Or, and hear me out," Evie said, attempting to keep the amusement off her face, "you could've taken the next exit and driven straight here, adding only a handful of miles and less than fifteen minutes to your trip."

"But then how would've I known *why*?" Viv widened her shockingly blue eyes dramatically.

"I want to let you in on a little secret," Bev said, leaning forward and dropping her voice into a conspiratorial whisper. "There is…" she looked around, checking to make sure no one else was nearby, then lowered the volume even more, "…something called Google. From what I understand, you can look things up on it, even breaking news, and you can do it all on your phone from your seat at Ambrosia while sipping a mimosa."

Viv laughed. "But this way, I can bring you the news direct, which is more fun."

"For who?" Evie asked, taking another sip of her drink.

"Me, obviously."

Evie relented. "Tell me more about this sinkhole."

Viv leaned back to allow the server to set down her mimosa. They placed their orders—same as every month for each of them—and then pulled out her phone. "Look at this pic. It's too weird even for Instagram." She showed them a photo of the offramp from I-94 to Eden Valley. The entire road was gone and an almost perfect circle that had no discernible bottom was in its place. It would take three of the long firetrucks blocking the exit to span the diameter.

Bev looked skeptical. "I didn't know there was anything too weird for Instagram."

Evie pulled out her own phone, tapped the Instagram app, and scrolled through her feed. "There isn't." She held up the post of Viv's photo—it'd already garnered a few hundred likes.

"Fine. You caught me. Anyway, here's the next pic—and I didn't post this one." She scrolled to her next pic and passed her phone to Bev.

"That is weird. How would that even happen? Is it aliens?"

"Don't be ridiculous," Evie said, holding out her hand for the phone. "There's no such thing as aliens, and even if there were, why would they take out the off ramp to Eden Valley?" Bev handed her the phone. Evie glanced down at the photo and nearly dropped the phone.

"What is it, babe?" Viv asked. "You're almost as white as Bev."

Evie looked at the photo Viv had taken from above—likely the overpass. The sinkhole was deep, maintained its shape and size down to the bottom, and at the bottom, glowing red and fiery, was the same symbol she'd seen in Lily's book—the same symbol Luc had tattooed on his back.

She looked at her friends and handed Viv back her phone. "I have to tell you something, and it's gonna get weird."

"Fantastic," Viv said. "There is nothing I like more than weird. Tell us everything."

Evie drew in a deep breath, but before she could start talking—not that she knew where to begin—their food arrived. Evie looked up to thank their server Emily, one of Lily's favorite babysitters and a senior at Eden Valley High. Instead of Emily's cheerful smile, she met Brandy's eyes.

"Surprise," Brandy said, simpering at the three women.

"What the hell are you doing here?" Viv asked. She was never one to mince words, and she'd always had more than a few choice ones for Brandy since Evie had walked in on her ex-husband in bed with Brandy. The same ex-husband who'd not only cheated but lied about the vasectomy he'd gotten before they were even married, only revealing the truth when Evie'd started divorce proceedings. Being a mother was all she'd wanted and finding out at age thirty-three that all the promises Jer had made about trying for a baby as soon as the farm turned a profit went up in smoke—along with her marriage.

"I work here now. Didn't Evie tell you?" Brandy smiled.

Evie rolled her eyes. "Your employment status is so far below my radar that I'd forgotten you worked here five minutes after seeing you in here last time."

Viv laughed. "I don't know what you want, Brandy, but you're not going to get a rise out of us today. Run along now—and make sure you don't try to scoop up Emily's tip."

Brandy's grin faltered a bit, but then her gaze hardened. "I heard your bastard's tenth birthday is next week. How does a single mom even throw a party... Oh, that's right. By getting your daddy to destroy my business out from under me and pay for your 'lifestyle.'"

"Jer was as bad at hiding his secret income as he was about hiding his secret side-piece," Evie said. "It's hardly my fault—or my father's —that the divorce settlement gave me enough cash to buy your struggling bar and turn it into the most successful business in Eden Valley. Don't you think it's about time to let go of whatever rivalry you think we have? We're not competing for the same man—we never were. You got Jer, and I got freedom and Lily. We're both winners. The only thing that would make me happier at this point is if you'd walk away from this table and let me brunch with my friends in peace."

Brandy glared at Evie, then turned and stomped away.

"What was that?" Viv asked.

"She's been real weird lately," Bev said. "After almost a decade of getting to pretend she doesn't exist, she's suddenly all up in our business. She was in the school pickup line the other day talking to Lily, Shelby, and Kevin when I showed up to pick them up, and she's suddenly decided to switch banks, something she can't possibly do without consulting the branch manager multiple times a day. I am this close to doing a murder. Or quitting my job with no notice. Banking is boring anyway. I'm thinking of leaving it all behind to become an international pop sensation."

"You didn't tell me she was talking to the kids," Evie said.

"I forgot," Bev said. "The instant they saw me, all three kids were in the car yammering away about Lily's birthday party, why I never waited for Lily's imaginary dog to get comfortable before driving off, and the cluelessness of all adults everywhere. By the time I got everyone home, it'd slipped my mind. Sorry."

"It's no big deal," Evie said. "Just weird. It's weird, right? Why is Brandy suddenly everywhere?"

"Maybe there's trouble in paradise?" Viv suggested. "Ten years might be the shelf life on Jeremy Kantek."

"Way past the expiration date," Bev agreed. "That's spoiled milk left in the sun territory."

"Hey!" Evie protested. "I married him."

"We all make mistakes when we're young," Bev said. "Look at Viv's track record."

Viv stuck her tongue out at Bev. "You're lucky I can't reach you right now, or I'd pull your hair."

Evie laughed. These ladies really were the best of the best.

"No more speculation about Brandy," Bev said. "Let's get on with the weird stuff Evie wants to share."

Evie shoved a forkful of biscuits and gravy into her mouth to delay a little longer, trying to decide where to start. She chewed slowly, then swallowed and put down her fork.

"Okay, like I said. This is weird, and some of it is completely unbelievable. I just need you guys to trust me. Or at least hear me out."

"Of course," Viv said.

"Always," Bev agreed.

"You remember Luc?"

"The hotter than sin guy from your summer of love who left before you could tell him you were pregnant with his child? That Luc?" Bev asked. "Yeah, we remember."

Evie grimaced. "I started having dreams about him last summer—right around the tenth anniversary of the night we met."

Viv narrowed her eyes over a forkful of syrup-soaked pancakes. "Right around, or on the anniversary?"

"Fine. They started ten years to the day I met Luc."

"What kind of dreams?" Bev asked. "I hope they were dirty dreams. I never have them, but I understand they can be fun."

"We can dig into that more later," Viv said. "Let's hear about Evie's sex dreams first."

"They aren't sex dreams," Evie protested. "Well, at least not all of them. Sometimes they're...just mundane dreams where I'm watching him go about his daily life, talk to his siblings or his dad, go to work, that kind of life stuff. There's just one thing...in all of those, everyone calls him Lucifer, not Luc. And he has wings. Big ol' bat wings."

"Okay. That is weird," Viv said. "But I'm not seeing the connection between your subconscious trying to convince you that the absent father of your child is a literal demon and the photo of the sinkhole. You might want to run that first part by your therapist, though. And run some of the details of the sex dreams by us, so we can tell you if those are normal."

"That's just the beginning of the weird," Evie said, looking down at her hands. "Right after the dreams started, I noticed that...things were starting to happen around me. I'd be cooking dinner and wish that I'd grabbed a missing ingredient at the store, and when I opened the cupboard, it was there. Which is easy to explain away—maybe I had gotten it and just forgotten or whatever. But it was happening more and more... I'd wish for an item, and when I turned around, I'd have it. The other day, I wished I had some sexier lingerie—I haven't bought myself anything nice in years—and when I opened my drawer, I had three Agent Provocateur bras—all completely impractical and basically high-end fetish wear—with matching barely there thong panties. I can't explain that away by pretending I'd grabbed them on my last trip to Safeway; I've never even been to a store that carried that brand, and I've certainly never dropped a couple thousand bucks on underwear."

"Okay, you're right. That is weird. So you're basically a psychic shoplifter?" Viv asked, quirking up one perfectly manicured eyebrow.

"Oh my god. I *am*. I'm a criminal." Evie clasped her hand over her mouth and stared at her friends in horror. "I need to find out where my stuff is coming from and pay for it."

"Whoa, whoa, whoa," Bev said. "Simmer down a bit. You are not a shoplifter. We could call every store in the country that carries Agent Provocateur to see which one is missing bras in your size, but as much as any of this makes sense, it's more likely you're wishing things into existence not stealing already existing items, right?"

Evie opened her mouth, then closed it again. Nothing made sense anymore.

Bev continued, "Either way, I don't think anyone in loss control anywhere would be interested in hearing you confess to psychic shoplifting. Get a grip, Evie."

Evie took a breath. "Okay, okay. You're right. I would like to find out if I am accidentally stealing, though, so I can stop wishing for stuff."

Viv counted off on her fingers. "One, you're having dreams about Lily's dad that started ten years to the day after you met him, and in these dreams he's a demon. Two, you're making unconscious wishes, and they're coming true. Anything else?"

"I followed Lily to the witch's clearing yesterday. She was sneaking—poorly, I might add—and I was curious. I found her trying to raise a demon. She had a big-ass book she said Kevin had loaned her, but when she couldn't figure out how to read it, she tried a spell from the internet instead—a Supernatural fan page, in fact. She'd written down three wishes. The first was that I'd believe in Cerberus, the second that she'd get to meet her dad, and the third that I'd be happy."

"Oh, wow," Bev said, hand at her throat. "That catches you right in the feels, doesn't it? They're not supposed to know we're lonely."

"Damn kids, way too perceptive. Were we that perceptive?" Viv asked.

"I don't think so," Evie said. "I was a pretty oblivious kid. But the fact that Lily doesn't know the difference between demons, genies, and Santa isn't the weird part. I paged through her book and found that symbol—the one that's at the bottom of the sinkhole. Also Luc has that same symbol tattooed on his back."

"Let me see that again." Bev held out her hand for Viv's phone.

"I'll do you one better," Viv replied. Seconds later, Evie's and Bev's phones pinged, announcing incoming messages. "Now we can all stare at this mysterious symbol at the same time without endangering our cocktails."

Bev stared at the image, squinting and turning it around to examine it from every angle. "I could swear I've seen this before."

"Maybe you were creeping on Luc ten years ago," Viv suggested. "After all, he stayed with you that entire summer. It'd make sense you'd see his back from time to time."

"He was not *staying* with me," Bev protested. "He was renting the cabin. The cabin that is not in eyesight of my house. The only way his back would've come into view is if he'd showed up topless to drop off his lease agreement and the rent. Which he did not, FYI. No, this is something else." She resumed her study of the image. "I can't put my finger on it, but I know I've seen this before. Let me think about it… I'll figure it out."

"Of course you will," Evie said. "You always figure everything out. It's one of your best traits, next to your infuriating refusal to age like the rest of us."

"Speak for yourself," Viv said, tossing her blue-streaked black hair and revealing her undercut with two overlapping, point-down triangles shaved into the side.

"Nice hair," Bev said. "Your mom is gonna freak out."

"I am almost forty-four years old, and I can do whatever I want to my hair," Viv said, injecting a note of petulance into her tone and sticking out her lower lip.

Evie laughed. "You tell your mom that when she sees your hair. But make sure you're filming. I wanna see her reaction."

"Maybe I'll show her my Instagram pics first to distract her… After a glowing hellmouth, perhaps my hair won't seem so bad," Viv suggested.

Butterflies formed in Evie's stomach and quickly turned to bats.

She was a big believer in coincidences, and that was all this was. Lily's demon summoning. Evie's wish fulfillment. And a hellmouth opening that bore the mark of the man in her dreams. The mark she'd—

"Another drink, ladies?" she asked before she could finish her thought. "I think we're gonna need it."

❧ 🐾 ☙

WHEN THEY WERE FINISHED with their next round of drinks, and Emily brought the check, Evie handed over her credit card to pay for brunch. Viv and Bev protested half-heartedly. It was part of the ritual. They took turns paying and protesting—and had for twenty-plus years.

"How long are you staying in town, Viv?" Evie asked. "Please say longer than a week. It's been ages and ages since you've hung out. And don't give me that crap about needing to get back to the city for work. We all know you haven't set foot in an office building in years."

"We-elll…" Viv prevaricated, not making eye contact with either of her friends. "I have an important business meeting on Tuesday."

Bev snorted. "You're seeing someone new, aren't you?"

"Why would you say that?" Viv asked, hand on her chest in mock affront. "I am practically a nun. And if I had decided to date someone, I'm sure I would've told my two best friends about it before a third date."

Evie narrowed her eyes. "Name?"

"I am shocked that you don't believe me. Really, my heart is broken… So much distrust."

Bev rolled her eyes. "You might as well just tell us what we want to know. There's no way you'll be able to keep it a secret for an entire long weekend."

"Fine. Her name is Scottie, and she's adorable."

"How old is she?" Evie asked.

"Thirty-seven. I only dated someone too young that one time, and I didn't even know how old he was at the beginning. Men are the worst—so full of lies."

"You're not wrong," Bev said. "It's why I avoid them at all costs."

"That's not why," Viv said. "Your celibacy has nothing to do with your distrust of men. Or at least not much. You're punishing yourself for Shelby."

Evie opened her mouth to intervene in the old argument that came up every time they got together and change the subject to Viv's latest conquest, but movement near the front door caught her eye. She closed her mouth with a hard click and made a strangled noise.

Viv and Bev immediately turned their attention away from their bickering and stared at Evie.

"Are you okay?" Bev asked, reaching out and touching her friend on the shoulder.

Evie couldn't say anything. She pointed towards the restaurant entrance with her chin where a tall, mahogany-skinned man with close-cropped hair and a tight body that was evident even from this far away had just walked into the restaurant. No wings, though. She bit back her laughter, certain it would contain more than a note of hysteria, and sunk lower on her seat as if trying to slide under the table.

Bev and Viv turned to see what Evie was looking at.

"Is that..." Viv started, then trailed off.

"...Luc?" Bev finished. "Holy cow. What's he doing here, and after all this time?"

"Do you think people will know who he is, make the connection?" Viv asked. "Because you might want to go talk to him before someone asks him if he's back in town for his spawn's tenth birthday."

"Noooo," Evie moaned softly. "I might *not* want to talk to him. In fact, I would like to go into hiding. Through the floor. Why isn't The Secret working for me right now? This is so much more important than cumin."

The women watched Luc as he scanned the restaurant, obviously looking for someone. Evie dropped her purse and dove under the table to retrieve it when his gaze swung their way.

He looked past them, and Evie breathed a sigh of relief and started to sit up again when he pivoted for a double take at their table.

Luc started towards them, but his attention was diverted when two other people joined him in the waiting area.

"Cover me," Evie said. "I'm heading to the bathroom and out the backdoor."

"Cover you?" Viv said. "This isn't a cop show. I have no idea what you mean."

"I don't know," Evie said, a note of desperation in her voice. "Just… make a diversion or something. Anything. He can't see me. I don't want him to recognize me, but even worse, I don't want him to see me and not recognize me. I have to flee."

"You owe me," Viv said. "But you'll have your diversion."

"Thank you," Evie replied, sliding to the end of the booth. She waited until Luc's attention was on the hostess, then stood up and walked towards the back hallway housing the restrooms and an unalarmed emergency exit. She heard a crash behind her and Viv's too-loud voice expressing alarm and remorse for "accidentally" bumping Brandy's full tray of dirty dishes and knocking everything to the ground.

As soon as Evie was in the hallway and out of sight of her fellow diners, she picked up the pace and jogged to the back door, pushing it open and stepping out into the narrow alley that ran behind the restaurant.

She wrinkled her nose against the smell of garbage and sulphur, then paused for a moment. Did she dare take the time to get her car from the street right outside the front door, or should she leave it for later and power-walk home? It was only a couple miles, and she was wearing her Chucks.

Mind made up, she strode towards the end of the alley, eyes down to avoid stepping in anything unsavory. Two feet entered her line of sight, but she didn't register them soon enough to stop walking, and she crashed into the person who was standing in her way.

She looked up, prepared to give whoever this was a piece of her mind for not getting out of her way like a normal person, and stared directly at the stupidly handsome and unfairly unlined face of Luc Morgenstern.

24

"Oh," she said.

"If I didn't know better, I'd say you were running away from me," Luc said, his honey-warm voice curling around her body and bringing her to attention. "Just like old times."

"Oh," Evie repeated, trying to break eye contact and look anywhere else besides the deep pools of his dark brown eyes framed by the ridiculously long lashes Lily had inherited. She tore her gaze away and looked down, down past his long, straight nose. Down past his full, ruddy lips. Down to his shoulders and chest that were highlighted by the tight-fitting t-shirt he wore.

Stop it. Evie told herself. *Do not look any further.*

Evie's eyes had a mind of their own, though, and kept moving down—past his taut abdomen to his narrow hips encased in dark denim. Her gaze caught there—between his hips—and she hoped he thought she was staring at the ground.

Luc reached out and caught her chin, tilting her face up to meet his eyes again.

"Hi, Evelyn Grace," he said. "It's been a while. Miss me?"

CHAPTER THREE

Evie's breath caught in her throat. The last ten years disappeared—all the heartache, all the regrets.

A horn honking from the nearby street broke the spell, and everything rushed back. Evie took three steps back and drew a breath. "What are you doing here?"

"Aren't you happy to see me?" He sounded almost wounded.

"Not particularly," Evie lied. "It's been ten years. You left to get married, and I never heard from you again. I'd practically forgotten you even existed."

"Liar," Luc laughed. "If you'd forgotten about me, if I'd meant so little to you, you wouldn't have rushed out of the restaurant like a bat out of hell."

"Again, why are you here?" Evie pushed. "Why now?"

Luc shrugged. "I'm honestly not sure. It feels like unfinished business, but it was a bit of an unexpected journey."

"Was that woman your wife?" Evie asked. "What did she think about you rushing after me?"

Luc laughed. "Absolutely not. Sam is my sister. The other guy was my brother, Mat. I'm not married, Evie."

"Isn't that why you left? To take your betrothed home with you?"

"Yes, it is. And I did take her home to meet the family. Turns out she was just as excited about marrying me as I was about marrying her. We went through with it—it was expected by our families, after all, and neither of us believed we had any agency in the matter. But after a year together, we agreed that it was a mistake and informed our families that we were going to divorce. My father took it a lot better than I'd expected—he's big on dynasty. I didn't think he'd rest until I produced an heir, but he was surprisingly unbothered and hasn't mentioned needing me to reproduce in almost ten years."

Evie bit her lower lip. The timing was suspicious, but maybe Luc had overestimated his father's commitment to dynasty and desire to be a grandparent. Parents were often surprising. She smiled tightly at Luc and tried to think of a way to extricate herself from this conversation before she said something she'd regret.

"What about you?" Luc asked, taking a half-step closer to her. "Are you married? Do you have someone?"

"I'm not married, but I do have someone," Evie said. "And it's time for me to get home. It was great seeing you again. Enjoy your stay in Eden Valley." She held out her hand, but when Luc didn't take it, she dropped it to her side, turned, and walked away. Now that she'd been made, there was no reason to avoid her car.

"Wait!" Luc called after her. "Your someone... Is it serious?"

"We've lived together for the last almost ten years," Evie replied without turning around. "In fact, we're celebrating ten years Saturday."

"Oh," Luc said. "I mean, of course. I'm happy for you. Maybe I'll see you around, Evie."

"Maybe," Evie said. "Goodbye, Luc."

🌱 🌿 🌾

EVIE SAT in her driveway with her head on the steering wheel, trying to decide what to do. She hadn't expected him to ever come back. And now, when things were already weird... "AHHHHH!" She took a breath to calm her racing heart.

Her phone buzzed, and she glanced over at it. It was a text from Bev. Evie turned her phone off. Bev and Viv had been bombarding her with texts since she'd left Ambrosia, and she'd ignored every single one. She couldn't even explain to herself what'd happened, much less to her best friends.

A knock on her window made her jump and let out a shriek she hoped no one could hear. She raised her head and looked into the eyes of her daughter.

Evie sighed, pulled the keys from the ignition, and got out of the car. "Hey, monster. What's up?"

"Why are you sitting in your car like a creeper?" Lily asked.

"I'm just tired," Evie said.

"Where are Aunt Bev and Aunt Viv? I thought they were coming home with you after your grown-up lady brunch. When I'm ten, will I get to come to brunch?"

"Tween is not grown up enough for brunch," Evie said. "And I'd forgotten I was supposed to bring them by to see the birthday girl. Give me a minute and I'll find out where they are."

Evie turned her phone back on and scrolled through the messages in the group chat.

Bev: *Run! He didn't buy it! He's following you!*

Viv: *Don't run unless it's into his arms. He is looking gooood & hasn't aged a day. Bev probably shared her skincare routine w/ him when they were shacking up.*

Bev: *I kicked her under the table for both of us. Did he catch you? Did you talk? INQUIRING MINDS WANT TO KNOW!*

Viv: *Ugh. Brandy is on her way out, too. Want me to trip her & stuff her in the utility closet?*

Viv: *Evie? What's going on? It's been 20 minutes, Luc is back inside, & you haven't replied. Are you ok? Are you dead in a dumpster?*

Bev: *She's not dead in a dumpster. Her car is gone. We're coming for you. Be there in 10.*

Viv: *Luc is watching us leave. He looks sad. What did you say to him?*

Viv: *Brandy is trying to work her charms on the whole super-hot table. I think I saw the other dude roll his eyes when she turned away. I'm sending a pic. Do these people look familiar?*

Evie looked at the picture Viv sent. It was a little blurry—Viv was brilliant, but her surreptitious photography needed work. Evie zoomed in on the man and woman to Luc's left and felt the blood drain from her face. She'd seen them before—in her dreams. Luc's siblings.

"I probably saw pictures of them on Luc's phone or something," Evie said. "Eleven years ago when he definitely didn't have a smart phone. There has to be a logical explanation for this."

"Are you talking to me or to yourself? Or do you have a Cerberus that I can't see the way you can't see my dog? What are you looking at?"

Lily grabbed Evie's arm and tilted it so she could peer at the screen. "Who are those people? Who's Luc?"

"Someone I knew a long time ago," Evie answered.

Lily narrowed her eyes at her mother. "You know, I'll be ten in less than a week. Maybe it's time you started confiding in me. I can help you with all sorts of problems."

"Oh, yeah? Like what?" Evie retorted, mind still pinballing through all the possible explanations for her dreams.

"Liiiiike… How to return Kevin's book before he gets in trouble from his parents without admitting that you stole it from a helpless child."

Evie laughed and turned her full attention to her daughter. "Enlighten me, wise tweenager. How should I go about returning the book I so ruthlessly stole from a group of helpless children?"

Lily leaned forward and motioned for her mother to get closer. Evie bent down—although not very far anymore—and tipped her ear towards Lily's mouth to hear the great sneaky wisdom of her almost-ten-year-old.

"If you give me back the book, I'll return it to Kevin and no one has to know you stole it."

Evie chuckled. "Oh, sweetie… Your creativity is amazing. I just wish you could use it for good instead of evil."

"But the dark side has cookies, Mama. I saw it on a bumper sticker."

"I will consider your very wise advice regarding the book if you promise me you won't try to summon any more demons."

"I promise not to try to summon any more demons," Lily said, mimicking her mother's tone perfectly.

"I'll give you the book back Sunday so you can return it to Kevin at school."

Evie turned around as a car pulled into the driveway behind her. Bev and Viv were pulling up in Viv's red BMW convertible.

"Scoot, child," Evie said. "There's more grown-up talk coming."

"Fine, I'll scoot," Lily said. "After hugs. Aunt Viv always slips me some folding money when you're not looking."

"Folding money? Who talks like that?"

"I do, Mama. Duh." Lily darted forward as soon as Viv shut off the engine. Bev got a perfunctory hug—she didn't rate much more than a rushed squeeze since her presence was a near-everyday occurrence. Viv, however, rated a longer hug. "I missed you Aunt Vivi! When are you going to move back to Eden Valley and teach me your ways?"

Viv laughed and handed Lily a twenty. "When hell freezes over, Liliana. I'll buy you some skates and we'll hit the rink." It was the same answer she always gave the child, and it never failed to make Lily giggle. She gave Viv another squeeze, then took off towards the house.

"I remember my promise, Mama!" Lily yelled over her shoulder. "I will not *try* to raise any demons. There is no try!" Cackling maniacally, she disappeared around the house and into the woods.

"Letting her watch Star Wars seemed like such a harmless activity," Evie said, shaking her head. "I don't know where I've gone wrong with her."

"Should we follow her and make sure she doesn't inadvertently put her bio-dad on speed dial with a few candles and some Latin?" Bev asked.

"He's not a demon," Evie said. "That would be ridiculous and impossible."

"As ridiculous and impossible as your supernatural crime spree?"

Viv asked. "Because if I hadn't known you for more than thirty years, I wouldn't believe you."

"Maybe I'm sleep shopping. I've heard Ambien can do that to a person." Evie worried at her lower lip.

"Do you take Ambien?" Bev asked. "I don't remember you saying anything about having trouble sleeping."

"Well, not that I remember. Maybe I sleep-shopped that, too."

"You sleep-walked yourself to a doctor to get a prescription for Ambien then sleep-ambled to the pharmacy to fill it, and haven't come across your prescription bottle yet?" Viv asked. "That's pretty unlikely."

"More or less unlikely than Luc showing up with a demon family at the same time that my daughter is reading books with weird symbols that also decorate the bottom of local sinkholes as well as my ex's back?" There was a note of rising hysteria in Evie's voice, and she took a deep breath to tamp it down. "Let's sit on the porch," she snapped.

"Um, okay," Bev said, exchanging a worried glance with Viv that Evie intercepted.

"I am so sorry, guys," she said. "I don't know what's gotten into me. Would you like to join me on the porch? I wish I'd made lemonade or sun tea or something, but you'll have to settle for water."

"I, for one, would love some water," Viv said. "Sparkling mineral, if you have it. It's such a beautiful day—almost too nice for April."

"Water is just fine," Bev agreed. "Do you need help?"

"No. Go sit. I won't be a minute." Evie shooed her friends to the large wrap-around porch and headed inside for beverages.

Moments later, she walked through the back door. Viv caught sight of her first. "What is it, Evie? Are you okay? You look like you've seen a ghost."

"It happened again," Evie said. "Can you come inside?"

"Of course," Bev said.

Evie's friends followed her in. There, on the counter, were two large glass pitchers, one filled with lemonade and the other with sun tea. They were just beginning to show a little condensation on the outside of the etched glass.

"I have never seen those pitchers before in my life," Evie said. "And I certainly don't make my own lemonade. Country Time for life."

"Should we drink it?" Viv asked. "Is it safe?"

"Probably? None of the other cooking supplies have killed me yet."

Bev marched forward, got three tall glasses out of the cupboard, and added ice. She poured two glasses of lemonade and one of tea, handed the tea to Viv, and said, "Let's go outside. Some things are easier to deal with when you have a gorgeous view of the lake."

Evie followed her out, lemonade in hand, and collapsed into the white Adirondack chair her father had made over forty years before.

"I think something really weird is happening," she said.

CHAPTER FOUR

E vie watched the sun set behind the mountains. The reds and oranges reflected in the lake in front of her and disappeared into the gathering darkness of the deep, cold water. Stars were beginning to appear in the sky above her, and the air was taking on the nighttime chill of early spring.

She wrapped a blanket around herself, tucked her toes up and under her body, and grabbed her glass of wine. It was early enough in the year that mosquitos weren't a problem yet and late enough that the frogs were beginning to sing their evening love songs.

Spring was her favorite season. It came slowly in the mountains, in fits and starts between snow flurries, but by April, the crocuses were blooming, and the tulips were thinking about joining the show. The days were longer now, although they wouldn't be at their longest when the sunlight lingered in the sky until well after ten.

She took a sip of her wine. A noise from the house caught her attention and she sat up, ready to dash into action. It'd been years since she'd had to answer the endless bedtime calls of another story, another cuddle, another drink of water, and almost as long since she'd had to enforce lights out time or shoo her daughter back to bed. But somehow, the adrenaline-fueled reflex remained. She wondered if she'd ever get to a point where a noise didn't send her heart beating into her throat with the fear that something had happened... That Lily was sick or injured or...

She stopped herself. No use walking down that path. No good ever came of it.

When the noise didn't repeat itself, she relaxed back into her chair and had another sip of wine.

"Is this seat taken?"

Evie didn't look over—didn't look at him.

"What are you doing here? I thought I made it clear that I wasn't interested."

"You made it clear that you were involved with someone," he said. "But I have it on very good authority that the only person you live with is your child and you haven't dated anyone seriously since she was born."

Evie hoped he hadn't heard her sharp intake of breath. Did he know? Was he trying to push her to tell him? *Should* she tell him?

"Guess it's pretty hard to keep a secret like that in a small town," she said. "But I didn't lie. I never said I was involved, just that I had someone in my life, we weren't married, but we lived together. No lies."

"I have to admire that," he said. "It's not always easy lying with the truth."

"Why are you here, Luc?" Evie asked. "I don't want to banter with you. You've been gone eleven years. I've moved on with my life and there's no place for you in it."

"Arrogant to assume I want back in your life," he said. "I'm just back for a minute. I'm not trying to be in your life—at least not for more than a couple nights. We had something special—something I've never been able to replicate. The things you can do in the bedroom..."

"You're here for...sex? After eleven years, you walk back into my town, into my life, for sex?" Evie laughed. "You are the most unbelievable man I've ever met, and I have been on more Tinder dates than I care to admit in the last five years."

"Is that a no, then?" he asked.

"Get out of here, Luc. That was a no. It will always be no. Go away. Take your family and go home. Maybe stop back in another eleven years and see if I'm desperate enough then to repeat old mistakes."

Evie turned back to the water. Instead of leaving, Luc sat down next to her. "Mind if I help myself to some wine?"

"Very much," she snapped.

He set a wine glass down on the small table separating them and poured himself a glass.

"Boundaries, Luc," she said. "Time for you to respect mine. Where did you get the glass, anyway? Are you just a more adept psychic shoplifter?"

"Happened to have it with me," he said. "I had hopes about tonight."

"I don't understand you," Evie exploded. "What kind of person walks away without saying goodbye then reappears over a decade later and has 'hopes' about falling back into bed with the person whose heart they broke?"

Luc set down the glass. "I broke your heart? You said it was a summer fling, that I was nothing more than a good time."

"Yeah, well I lied," she said. Her breath hitched in her chest with the effort of not letting him see her cry. She took a large gulp of wine and let the cool, lake breeze dry the tears that were trickling down her face.

"Why? Why didn't you tell me how you felt?" Luc asked.

"Because it was just a summer fling, Luc. You were in town for a couple months before heading home to get married. What was I supposed to say? Should've I told you I'd caught feelings knowing you were leaving town with your fiancée? How would that have helped? Then, instead of being quietly heartbroken, I could be heartbroken and humiliated when you left anyway."

"I might not have gone," Luc said.

"Really? Can you look me in the eyes right now and say there was a chance in hell that you wouldn't have run off to do your daddy's bidding by marrying for money and status?"

"No," Luc said. "I can't tell you that."

Evie shrugged and poured herself another glass of wine. "And that's why I didn't say anything."

"I'm here now, though."

"Too little and way too late, Luc. That ship sailed a long, long time ago. I don't know what you're doing back in town and why your whole family is here, but I do know that you don't have to involve me in anything. I wish you'd just leave."

Luc didn't respond for so long that Evie was forced to glance over at him. His chair was empty, his half-full glass of wine still balanced on the arm.

"This is really getting out of hand," Evie said out loud. "I wonder if it'll work on Brandy?"

LILY SAT at the table in the sunny kitchen kicking the rungs of her chair and stuffing her mouth with syrup-soaked pancakes. "Mama, what time will Grandma and Grandpa be here?"

"Don't talk with your mouth full," Evie said without turning around from where she was flipping pancakes.

"Fine," Lily said, then swallowed. "What time will they be here?"

Evie glanced at the clock hanging on the wall. "Three hours. Their flight will just be landing, then they'll have to get their bags and their rental car, stop for lunch with Christina and Frances, stop again for pie at the roadside diner, then finally make their way here."

"Why couldn't we go pick them up like usual?" Lily whined.

"They didn't want us to. I think Grandma and Grandpa wanted to make all the stops without feeling like they were holding us up. They haven't seen their friends or their favorite pie in over a year."

"Whatever," Lily muttered. "I just think it would've been more polite to do what I wanted, since it's my birthday and all."

"Once they're here, it's all about you," Evie promised. "And, since they'll have a car, there could be day trips."

Lily brightened up. "Do you think they'll take me to see the giant hellmouth?"

"Hellmouth? What are you talking about?" Evie's heart was beating too fast in her chest, and it took all her concentration to flip the pancakes without flinging them onto the counter.

"I saw the picture of the weird hole by the interstate," Lily said. "It's all over YouTube."

Evie sighed. "You're not supposed to be on YouTube."

"It's not my fault, Mama. Sometimes it just comes on when I'm doing homework."

"Wow. Voluntarily doing homework during spring break? I am impressed."

"I am a model student," Lily agreed.

"Finish your pancakes. I want you to help me make Grandma and Grandpa's bed."

"Are Bev and Viv coming over tonight? With Shelby?"

"Absolutely. It's tradition at this point. How else could we welcome people back to Eden Valley?"

"Grandpa says the V Club is what makes this town special. Then he laughed and laughed. What does he mean?"

Evie closed her eyes. Her father had started calling them that in middle school to emphasize their similar names, claiming he'd heard it around town. At least he'd never shared it with anyone else. Until now. "It means he's a silly old man who doesn't know when to let go of an unfunny joke. He's been calling us that for thirty years, and it's just as not funny now."

"I'm gonna call you that. Grandpa said I should."

"If you do, I will call you Silly Lily in front of your friends and tell them it's your favorite nickname," Evie threatened.

"No you won't," Lily retorted. "You'd never embarrass me on purpose."

"Just wait until you start dating. Then you'll see how far I'll go to embarrass you."

"Really?" Lily asked, a crease forming between her eyebrows.

Evie brought a plate of pancakes and set them on the table before dropping a kiss on Lily's forehead and using her thumb to smooth out the furrow. "Of course not. That would be mean, and my only goal in parenting is to never be mean on purpose."

"And to keep me alive until adulthood," Lily added.

"And hopefully teach you enough that you can keep yourself alive after," Evie agreed.

Lily took another bite of pancake, swallowed, and asked, "Who was that man who was here last night? Was he your new boyfriend?"

Evie choked on her coffee. "No. Definitely not a new boyfriend."

"Was it Luc? Your old friend whose picture you were mooning over yesterday? Do you have a crush on him?"

"No one was mooning, child, and there are zero crushes. I can tell by the number of questions you've managed to ask that you are fresh out of things to do now that your pancakes have been devoured. Brush your teeth, wash your hands and face, and make sure your bedroom floor isn't a Lego minefield. I'll be up in a minute, and you can help me finish cleaning the bathroom and the guest room."

"When I'm grown up, I'm going to pay someone to pick up my Legos," Lily declared, carrying her dirty dishes to the dishwasher.

"Whatever makes you happy. Now scoot."

❦ ❦ ❦

EVIE CHECKED HER WATCH AGAIN. She'd played it cool in front of Lily earlier, but she was almost as anxious for her parents to arrive as Lily was. It'd seemed a relief when her parents had retired and moved to Hawaii, leaving her alone—more or less—in the house they'd left for her and Lily. It was the house she'd grown up in, and where she'd moved back to after her divorce. And once she found out she was pregnant and an impending single mother, it didn't make sense to move out again. Not with built in evening childcare, and—after her mother cut back on her hours at the library—daytime care as well, allowing Evie to go to college and later, work in the bar she'd bought —formerly Brandy's—with the financial settlement from her divorce.

She'd moved into the bedroom suite after her parents had moved out, and it'd only taken three visits from them plus a couple neighbors recruited for the heavy lifting when Evie was at work to make it happen. But even with that change, it didn't feel like home without them.

It'd been almost a year since they'd last visited, coming for two weeks in August and leaving with Lily who got to spend the last two weeks before fourth grade in Hawaii. The first week before Evie joined them was the longest she'd ever been away from Lily, and it had taken every bit of willpower to not change her ticket to an earlier flight. Only Viv's influence and highly detailed "single ladies on the town" schedule had kept her from plunking down her credit card and winging west.

"Mom! Mom! I see a car!" Lily shouted from upstairs.

There was only one window that had a decent view of the road leading to the driveway, and that was in Evie's room.

"What are you doing in my bedroom? You know you're not allowed in there!" Evie yelled back. "I will launch you into outer space!"

Lily ran down the stairs and slid across the hardwood floor in her stocking feet, bumping into the dining room table and rattling the overflowing fruit bowl. "I was the lookout," she said. "There are no bedroom rules when a sentinel is needed."

The sound of a car engine reached their ears, and Lily was out of the house before she could push back against Evie's toothless threat. Evie followed, albeit at a more sedate pace.

"Grandma! Grandpa!" Lily yelled, tearing across the lawn to the driveway. She skidded to a stop about three feet from the driveway and the car that was still in motion. She waited, vibrating from excitement and impatience, until the purr of the engine shut off and the passenger door opened. An older man—white skin tanned from the sun and salt and pepper hair that was mostly salt—got out. He opened his arms and nearly tipped over as Lily bowled into him.

"How's my favorite flower?" he asked.

Lily flung her arms around his waist. "I missed you so much, Grandpa," she said. "Why do you have to live in stupid Hawaii?"

"Your grandmother made me do it," he said. "She's a cruel, cruel woman." His brown eyes widened, and he frowned, blinking several times in a move that could almost be called eyelash fluttering.

"You're so silly, Grandpa," Lily said. "Grandma is never cruel."

A tall woman with snow-white hair trailing down her back in two long braids, light brown skin that hinted at her mother's Mediterranean heritage, and twinkling hazel eyes got out of the car. Other than the color of her hair, there was nothing to give away her age. She had smooth skin and a clear gaze that belied her seventy-one years.

She smiled at her husband and granddaughter. "It's all true, my Liliana. I forced him into the hellscape that is a tropical beach retirement community with endless golf, snorkeling, and hiking."

"You can do all of those things here," Lily pointed out. "Eden Lake is great for snorkeling."

"You don't go in the lake, do you?" Hope asked, suddenly very serious.

Lily rolled her eyes and looked back at her mother. "As if Mama would let me," Lily said. "Supervised boating trips only. Pools are for swimming."

"That's my girl," Hope said, opening her arms to Lily. "I've missed you, Liliana Addams."

Evie walked forward and threw her arms around her dad. "Thanks for coming, Daddy," she whispered into his ear. "I know this trip isn't easy anymore."

"Nonsense," James Addams replied. "Your mother and I love coming home, and I feel younger and stronger than ever." He flexed, causing Evie to roll her eyes. "Guess my chemo and radiation combo gave me some superpowers. Killed the cancer and made me even handsomer than before."

"I'm so glad, Daddy. Although I'm worried that you're *too* handsome now, and we'll be beating the single retirees off with a stick."

"Not just the single ones." James winked. "I create chaos and jealous husbands everywhere I go."

"Pay no attention to him," Hope said. "He's been full of himself ever since an octogenarian in the clubhouse tried to lure him away from me."

"What's an octogenarian?" Lily asked.

"Someone in their eighties," Hope answered. "Someone a lot older than me."

"Let's go have lemonade!" Lily said. "Mommy made lots and lots of it yesterday. With real lemons and everything."

Evie pasted a smile on her face. She'd almost forgotten about the mystery lemonade that'd shown up. She'd have to be extra careful about what she wished for—it was no longer a cliché, at least not for her. "I'll get your bags," she said. "Go have some lemonade with Lily. She'll explode if she has to wait too much longer."

Evie grabbed the two suitcases out of the trunk and headed back to the house, trailing after her over-excited daughter and the best parents in the west—or at least the Pacific Northwest. She caught up to them at the house, just in time to hear Lily say, "Mama has a new boyfriend, and he was here in the middle of the night last night. His name is Luc, and he is a blast from the past."

Evie shook her head. She'd seldom been able to keep anything from her mother before, but Lily's ill-timed snooping was taking away her ability to pick the times of her revelations. She trudged up the stairs, but not before she heard Lily giving an enthusiastic if completely inaccurate recitation of her conversation with Luc the night before.

CHAPTER FIVE

E vie stood in the middle of her kitchen, door closed to the noise of conversation outside. It'd been another beautiful April evening, and even though it was cold enough to elicit complaints from the tropical visitors, they'd elected to have dinner outside. Evie set up the propane heater for the elderly folk, as she teased them, and had set the table for nine. Viv brought her mom, who was a lovely woman when she could get out of her own head and small-town mentality. Unfortunately, it usually took someone besides Viv to force her to be her best self. But Guenevere spent too much time on her own, and had as long as Evie had known her, so Evie always suggested Viv bring her along to the larger family gatherings. It gave Viv a break from being the only person her mother had to criticize and gave Gwen a break from the self-imposed loneliness.

Bev had brought Shelby, of course, and had stopped to pick up Kevin on the way. Kevin's parents were always invited, and they always sent their excuses and their child. Evie tried not to let it bother her that Kevin's parents—Aurielle and Brand Jones—never reciprocated and that Shelby and Lily had never even been inside his home. And she was mostly successful. She was grateful that Kevin had a place to go and kids to play with. She didn't know the situation at home, but he wasn't being abused or starved or neglected as far as she could tell. Just raised by recluses who made sure his physical needs were met and didn't get in the way of his social needs. Evie'd always meant to get to know them better—it felt weird to not speak to the parents of one of her daughter's best friends, especially since she was so close to Shelby's adoptive mom.

Evie was so grateful to have all the people she loved best in one place, but it was also a lot. Most evenings she spent alone with a glass of wine and either Sam and Dean or Buffy. She'd come to relish the silence, or at least get used to it, and the cacophony of voices competing to catch each other up on the latest news and gossip could be overwhelming. Especially when her daughter insisted that the best gossip was her mother's non-existent love life and was trying to outdo herself by imagining more and more ridiculous scenarios about her mother's evening visitor.

She knew it was more than likely her parents had made the connection between the "Luc" Lily had mentioned as the middle-of-the-night visitor and the "Luc" who'd impregnated their daughter and left town almost immediately after, but she owed Bev and Viv so many margaritas for not forcing the issue, and her parents for waiting to bring it up in private.

"Ugh," she said to herself, knowing that she'd already taken too long to find whatever it was she'd told everyone she was coming in to look for. "I wish—" She stopped. Nope. No wishes. It was probably nothing. An over-active imagination or short-term memory loss. Maybe early onset dementia. That had to be it. It wouldn't explain Luc's disappearance, though, would it? "Unless I just made up his presence. But no, Lily saw him. So maybe I forgot when he left." She shook her head and did a slow circle, hoping something would catch her eye and alert her to the excuse she'd used so she'd have something to take back outside. "I wish I knew what was going on. And I wish I knew what I'd promised to bring out."

Another slow circle and her eye caught on the napkin holder in the corner of the kitchen. That was it—more napkins for the children. She grabbed the napkins and headed back outside, then stopped cold in the doorway. Luc was out there, sitting in the seat she'd vacated and chatting up her parents.

No no no no, her mind chanted as she forced herself to walk and not run to the patio. Maybe she could wish him away again—although she didn't want to make him vanish as abruptly as he had last night. That would raise even more questions she didn't want to answer.

Evie had never really internalized "stuck between a rock and a hard place" until now, but choosing between wishing away her boyfriend—ex-boyfriend, she corrected herself—in front of everyone or letting him talk to her parents like there was nothing weird going on was a lot more difficult than she would've guessed.

She widened her eyes at Viv and Bev and tried to tell them to make sure no one mentioned Lily's parentage. All the adults knew, of course, even though she wanted to pretend her parents had suddenly lost their quick wits. Even Gwen knew, and she'd be the most likely to say something out of turn. Not through malice, but because she might not realize that neither Luc nor Lily knew the truth of each other.

Viv and Bev widened their eyes back at Evie, and she could tell neither of them had any idea what she was saying. Telepathy would've been a lot more useful a gift than instant gratification.

Evie smiled tightly and set the napkins down with more force than was necessary. "Luc," she said through gritted teeth. "I didn't know you were going to stop by." She forced her jaw to relax. No one, least of all Lily, needed to know how pissed off she was right now.

"I didn't know you were having a party," Luc said, smiling up at her, the heat in his eyes finding an answering spark low in her belly.

Damn him to hell. This was not how life was supposed to go, and definitely not how her body should react to a man she hadn't seen in almost eleven years. A man she was still angry with this many years later. The spark warmed to a flutter, and she tried to squash it down. "Can I talk to you a minute?" she asked. "Privately?"

"Of course," he replied, standing up without waiting for Evie to move backwards. The entire long length of him was a hair's breadth from her body, and the electricity between them made it feel even closer. He looked down at her, and her breath caught in her throat.

For a moment, the whole world fell away until it was just her and Luc, the last ten years disappearing.

EVIE SHOOK HERSELF, closed her mouth, and took a step back before turning and walking away from the deck and house and into the woods. She didn't turn around to see if Luc was following—she could feel his presence behind her. When she judged they were both out of sight and out of earshot of the others, she stopped and looked up. She was in the witches' clearing, and it was obvious Lily hadn't tried hard enough to stop summoning demons. The candles had gotten a little more serious—five large, red pillar candles were in skull candle holders pilfered from the Halloween decorations—and there was a new neon orange spray-painted pentagram.

Evie took a deep breath and turned around to face Luc. He'd stopped close enough behind her that she could feel his body heat. She took a step back to put space between them and to cool her blood.

"Why are you here?" she asked.

"How old is Lily?"

Evie shook her head. "I asked first." She knew she sounded childish, but she didn't care. She didn't want to talk about Lily, didn't want him doing the math and connecting any dots. She knew he deserved to know, that she *should* tell him, but not now. Not like this.

"I felt the urge to visit," Luc said. "I don't often feel pushed into things like this, so it's always good to stick around and see what's going on."

"No. Why are you here? At my house. Today. I thought I made it clear last night—"

"Yes, let's talk about last night. I didn't get that glass of wine you promised." Luc crossed his arms and looked down at her.

Evie worried the inside of her lip. "I didn't..."

"Didn't what? Politely offer your guest wine or you didn't make me disappear before I could have a sip?"

Evie flattened her lips into a thin line, but couldn't stop herself from asking, "Where did you end up?"

"In the hotel room where we first—"

It was Evie's turn to interrupt. "You're staying in the same room?"

"No. Which made it exceptionally awkward and extremely difficult to explain. It took some quick talking to convince the couple who I inadvertently caught *in flagrante delicto* not to call the police. Fortunately, they were almost as unenthusiastic as I to avoid anyone else seeing them. I got the impression that the wedding rings they were wearing hadn't come as a set."

"Hadn't come as a set?" Evie wrinkled her brow before it hit her. "Oh."

"I answered your question; now you can answer mine. How old is your daughter?"

"Nine. It's birthday week." Evie hoped that Luc would assume she'd just turned nine and write himself out of the story.

"What day is her birthday?" he pressed.

Evie cursed inwardly. "The tenth."

"And she'll turn ten?"

"Yes," she bit out, turning away from him and staring back at Lily's makeshift summoning circle. A soft growl across the clearing caught her attention, and her gaze snapped up. There was nothing there—nothing she could see, anyway. They didn't often get wild animals in town, but it was known to happen, and early spring when the bears were coming out of hibernation but there wasn't much to eat yet would drive them closer to civilization. "Did you hear that?"

Luc took three large steps and placed his body in front of hers. "Why is there a hellhound here?"

"A what now?" Evie asked. "I don't see anything."

"There is a three-headed black, slavering dog on the other side of —" he gestured at Lily's demon-summoning materials "—this mess."

"Cerberus?" Evie asked. The growling stopped, and a happy woof echoed across the clearing.

"Cerberus?" Luc sank to his knees and stretched out a hand. "She named her hellhound Cerberus? That's not very original, is it?"

"She named her betta fish Mr. Fish," Evie responded dryly. "And all her stuffies have such original names as Kitty, Dragon, Sharkie, and

Monkey. Other than Chloe the Beaver, this is the most creative name she's come up with."

"If she's ten and has a pet hellhound, I don't think I need to ask, but I'm going to anyway. Who's her father, Evie?" Luc stood and crossed his arms, pinning her down with his gaze.

"I don't know—"

"What do you mean, you don't know?" Luc's angry outburst was punctuated by the resumption of growling noises that had caught Evie's attention before.

Evie's phone beeped and vibrated in her pocket, but she ignored it and glared at the man in front of her, his eyes fixed on something she couldn't see.

"You interrupted," Evie said. "I was going to say I don't know what a hellhound is, why there's one here, and why I can't see anything. It's a lot. This whole week has been a lot. The last nine months have been a lot, honestly. The dreams. The wishes. The hellmouth on the interstate. You showing up after ten years and seven months is kind of the cherry on top of the stress sundae."

"Evie, please," Luc said, rising to his feet and grabbing her hands. "Tell me."

"You already know."

"I need to hear you say it." The look in his eyes as he stared down into hers was enough to make a hardened secret agent spill state secrets. Evie didn't have a chance in hell.

"She's yours, Luc. You left before I could tell you, and I had no way to get in touch. I didn't keep her from you deliberately." Her phone beeped again, and she pulled it out of her pocket, silenced it, and shoved it back in, never taking her eyes off Luc.

Luc shook his head and ran his fingers through his hair. "I really made a mess of things back then, didn't I?"

"Yeah, you kinda did. But I was a willing participant. Even after you told me you were getting married, I didn't walk away. I should have. I'd like to believe I'm not the kind of person who'd stay in a relationship with someone who wasn't single, but apparently I am."

"It wasn't like I was engaged. Well, not really. It was an arranged thing, and I hadn't even met her yet. I wasn't cheating, and I was never dishonest."

"A little," Evie said. "You didn't tell me about her until I'd already fallen—" Evie blushed and broke eye contact, looking down at her shoes.

"Fallen?" Luc asked.

"Fallen into bed with you," Evie finished.

"Nothing wrong with falling. Some of the best people I know have fallen." Luc chuckled and bumped her chin gently upwards with his knuckles until she was looking into his eyes again. He inhaled deeply. "I have a daughter. A child. Tell me everything about her."

There was a crash behind Evie, and she spun around in time to see a small figure flee, braids trailing behind her. A second crash followed Lily, this one accompanied by excited barking.

"Oh no," Evie said. "Lily."

🌱 🌿 🌾

EVIE CHASED HER DAUGHTER, following the sound of the joyously barking dog she couldn't see. Lily veered away from the path that would take her back to the house and headed deeper into the forest. Evie wasn't too worried—she knew Lily was familiar with every square inch of the wooded area between their house and the county road that marked the boundary between their property and the National Forest—but if Lily had overheard, and there was nothing else that could've elicited a reaction like this, she shouldn't be left alone.

There were times to leave a child to sit with their feelings, but finding out the identity of your father was not one of those times.

The crashing noises ahead of her disappeared, and the barks gave way to heavy panting. Evie slowed her pace and sucked in air, trying to get her breathing to manageable levels. She put her hands on her knees and ignored the spots in her vision. She hadn't realized she'd lost so much fitness, but then she seldom had a chance or a reason to go on off-trail runs. As soon as she could breathe without wheezing, she stood up. Ignoring the stitch in her side, she walked towards the sound of the sobs nearly muffled by the low woofs Cerberus was making.

There was so much to process, but she didn't have the luxury of taking the time to do any of that. Lily came first. Evie's feelings could wait.

Lily was on the ground, knees drawn up to her chest, and her arms wrapped around... Evie squinted. For a second, she'd almost seen something shimmer, but when she blinked, it was gone. It was ridiculous to pretend there wasn't something there. Lily clearly could see the dog, and Luc had called it a hellhound. Besides, what else could be woofing in three-part harmony?

"Lily-bear?" Evie asked, squatting down beside her. "Are you okay? I don't know how much you heard, but..."

"Was that really my dad?" Lily asked, voice choked with sobs.

"It was, baby. I'm sorry. I didn't mean for you to find out like that. I wouldn't have had you hear that conversation for anything."

"You didn't want me to find out at all," Lily accused. "You could've told me today when I asked who he was. But you didn't. You lied."

Evie bit back the instinctive, "I did not lie." Everything was so black and white for Lily—for a lot of kids her age—and lies of omission and misdirection were not any less damning than straight up bald-faced lies.

"I'm sorry," Evie said again. "I should've told you, you're right. I have very good excuses for not telling you this morning, but I don't know if you want to hear them."

Lily let go of whatever she was holding onto and scrubbed at her face with dirty hands and arms, smearing dirt and snot and tears into a Pollock painting on her face. "Tell me your excuses," she commanded.

"I hadn't seen him, Luc, your father, in almost eleven years until yesterday. He showed up at Ambrosia with no warning, and then stopped by last night without being invited. I didn't know he'd come back again today, and I didn't know how I felt about it. About him. It's been a long time, and I can't make decisions in an instant."

"Would've you told me eventually? Would've you told him?"

"I don't know," Evie said honestly. "Probably. I never meant to hide your existence from him; he just left town before I could tell him. And I didn't mean to keep him from you, either. But I didn't expect him to ever come back."

Lily stood up, one hand palm-down just above waist level, fingers curling and uncurling slowly in a motion that looked exactly like one would expect head scratches to look like. "Does he want to be my dad?" Lily asked, voice so small and quiet Evie had to lean in to hear her.

"I don't know, Lily-bear," Evie said. "He found out he had a kid about the same time you found out he was your dad. It might take some time to get used to... I wish..." She stopped herself. She wasn't sure what she'd been about to wish for, but whatever it was, she didn't need it. Not right now. "Wanna head back to the house? You can wash your face, and we can sit back down to finish dinner. I think Viv and her mom brought cookies."

Lily visibly brightened when she heard the c-word. "I like cookies, and Nana Gwen makes really, really good cookies."

Evie stood and held out her hand. "Let's go then."

They started walking back towards the house in silence, the sounds of Lily's invisible dog padding beside them the only sound.

"What are you going to tell everyone?" Lily asked. "About why we were gone so long. Do they know that was my dad?"

"Bev and Viv know—they spent a lot of time with him when he was here before, and they recognized him immediately. Grandma and Grandpa and Nana Gwen probably know—for the same reasons. It might've been ten years ago, but he looks just the same. Kevin and Shelby don't know, so that can be your news. How do you want to handle things? We can go back, sit down, and pretend nothing happened. Or you can make an announcement. I'll follow your lead."

"Do you think he'll be there?" Lily asked. "I'm nervous."

"Do you want to meet him officially and talk to him before you talk to anyone else about it?" Evie asked.

Lily squeezed her mother's hand tightly and nodded. "Yeah. I don't want to tell Kev and Shel until I've talked to my dad. That sounds weird. I've never had a dad before."

"Do you want one?" Evie asked.

"I don't know. What if he's a dick?"

Evie's hand slapped over her mouth in a failed attempt to quell a burst of laughter before it broke free. "Where did you learn that kind of language, young lady?" she asked, using her best stern mom voice.

"I learned it from watching you, Mom. I learned it from watching you." Lily shook her head mournfully and looked up at her mother from under her lashes.

They emerged from the trees behind the house. Luc was standing in the middle of the lawn, halfway between them and the back door.

"What's he doing?" Lily whispered.

"Waiting for us, is my guess," Evie whispered back. "Do you want me to ask him to leave and come back later?"

Lily sighed, sounding fifty instead of nearly ten. "No. I guess I'll have to deal with him sooner or later. Might as well get it out of the way now."

She walked forward and held out her hand. "Hello. My name is Liliana Faith Addams. I'm your daughter, and you owe me ten years of missing birthday and Christmas presents. I'll accept cash, checks, or money orders, or you can buy me a pony. Make that three ponies— one each for my friends."

"Hello, Liliana Faith Addams. My name is Luc Morgenstern, and I'd love to buy you some ponies, but I might have to check with your mother first."

"She'll be cool with it," Lily said without looking at her mom. "Eventually. Besides, it's better to ask forgiveness than permission. That's what Grandpa always says when he's about to get us into trouble."

"Your grandpa sounds like a wise man," Luc said. "I'll have to get some tips from him."

"I'd like you to leave now," Lily said. "You make me confused."

"If that's what you'd like." Luc bowed and kissed the back of her hand. "May I take you to lunch tomorrow?"

Lily glanced back at her mom. Evie nodded slightly. "You may," Lily said graciously. "But my mom will come, too."

"Of course," Luc said. He let go of Evie's hand and stood upright. "Until tomorrow, then. I look forward to getting to know you." He turned and walked away.

Lily watched until he disappeared around the house, then looked at her mom. "I'd like those cookies now."

CHAPTER SIX

vie extended Lily's bedtime routine as long as she could.
They did two meditations, two chapters of the latest book
they were reading together, and then Evie exhausted her
repertoire of lullabies, something that hadn't been part of the routine
for years. Finally, exasperated, Lily kicked her mother out of her
room.

"Mama, I don't know what you're doing, but it's annoying. I'm
tired and want to go to sleep now. Please leave."

Evie sighed, kissed her daughter's forehead, and started the rain-
storm ambient noise track her daughter preferred to fall asleep to.
Then she took a deep, steadying breath, and headed downstairs to
face the music.

James and Hope Addams were in the large living room. There was
a fire burning merrily away in the fireplace—the warmth of the mid-
spring day had given way to a mountain evening chill.

Hope had decanted a bottle of Cabernet Franc and was currently
enjoying a glass of wine as she relaxed in the large recliner with a
thick crossword puzzle book. James had a glass of wine next to him,
but he was preoccupied with the latest knitting project. He'd taught
himself woodworking and knitting in his retirement and now spent

most evenings watching nature documentaries and knitting sweaters for the mermaids he carved.

"So. Luc." Hope fixed her daughter with an intense stare. "When were you planning on telling us?"

"I don't know," Evie said, pouring herself a glass of wine and settling cross-legged on the opposite end of the couch from her father. "He just showed up yesterday. I've hardly had a chance to talk to him, and I certainly didn't expect him to just show up today without notice or invitation."

"Does he know about Lily?" James asked, not looking up.

"He does now. And Lily overheard us, so she knows, too. I know it wouldn't have remained a secret for long, but I would've liked to tell her under my own terms."

"So what next?" Hope asked.

"The three of us are going for lunch tomorrow," Evie said, rubbing her eyes. "I never intended to hide them from each other, but…"

"Of course you didn't," Hope said. "It's not your fault he disappeared with no notice and without leaving you his phone number or a forwarding address."

"It's not really his, either," Evie pointed out, not sure why she was defending him. "It was just a summer thing; he made that clear from the beginning. I knew he was leaving from the night we met. He had a life to get back to. A wedding to participate in. A bride to meet and all that jazz." Evie clapped a hand over her mouth. She'd never told her parents that particular piece of the puzzle.

"He was engaged when you met him and yet you two carried on like hormonal teenagers?" Hope asked with what sounded like a choked laugh around cold steel.

"Not exactly," Evie prevaricated. "He was betrothed, but only in the sense that he'd been promised to someone he'd never met as an alliance between two powerful families." She wasn't sure if this was making Luc sound better or worse, but she plowed on anyway. "That's why he was here in the first place. One of the conditions of marriage was that he find the bride from where she'd been hidden."

"Let me get this straight," James said, looking up from the teeny blue and green striped sweater he was knitting. "Luc came to Eden Valley looking for a woman to marry, one he'd never met and whose family thought the best way to do an engagement was a larger-than-life scavenger hunt, and while he was actively searching for his bride-to-be, he hung out in the Valley for an entire summer and spent enough time with you to get you pregnant, but not enough time to decide to call the whole wedding thing off?"

Evie shrugged. "Summer fling, Dad. I seem to remember Mom bragging about the notches on her bedpost. And I never felt like either of us were betraying anyone. He hadn't taken vows. He'd never even met the woman. I'm not a home wrecker, and he wasn't cheating. If I hadn't ended up pregnant... We were being so careful."

Hope sighed and picked up her crossword puzzle. "Accidents happen. I wonder, though... Do you think it had anything to do with him being a demon?"

Evie paced back and forth in the kitchen. She'd fled there after her mother's casual question. There was no way to answer that didn't sound absolutely bananas. She took a big gulp of her wine and found another bottle to bring to the living room.

When she stood still long enough to slow her breathing and attempt to slow her racing thoughts, the sounds of her parents' voices drifted towards her.

"Do you think she didn't know?" Hope asked.

"How could she not?" James countered. "He doesn't hide it very well. He might as well have horns and a tail."

"I guess it's possible he didn't tell her, especially since they were just having a summer fling—no need to get complicated when it's not expected to last. I just assumed."

"Well, she has to come back in sooner or later," James reasoned, the rhythmic click of his knitting needles punctuating his serene voice. "And then we can ask her."

"This is my fault," Hope said. "I should've said something eleven years ago. Made sure she knew what she was getting into. Or at least when Lily started showing signs... I wonder if Evie got an aspect of the demon, too?"

"If she did, and she didn't know Luc was a demon, she's probably been freaking out about it and refusing to tell anyone in case they thought she'd lost her mind. You know how she internalizes everything. And, since she's eavesdropping right now, I'm assuming she'll tell us when she comes back with the wine."

Evie marched back into the room, brandishing her bottle of wine. "How did you know? Why didn't you tell me? Everything is ridiculous but at least you could've prepared me, given me time."

"You really didn't know," Hope said. "Oh, honey. I'm so sorry you had to find out this way. I should've told you when I found out, but I didn't want to butt in."

Evie collapsed onto the couch. "It's just a lot, Mom. Too much. I mean, I was having dreams, but they were dreams! Demons aren't real. At least, they shouldn't be."

"And Cerberus?" James asked. "I noticed he's a lot more solid than he was even a month ago over FaceTime. Is he not real?"

"Are you telling me you knew Lily's 'imaginary' three-headed dog was real?" Evie asked, punctuating her question with sarcastic finger quotes.

Hope stood and rescued the full bottle of wine from Evie's increasingly wild gesticulations. "Hand me your glass, Evelyn."

Evie handed over her glass and sat, stupefied, staring into the fire. When her mother handed back a glass full of wine, she took a slow, careful sip. "How did you know?" she asked again, cutting through all her questions to the one that seemed most significant now. "Why did you meet Luc eleven years ago and think 'demon?'"

Hope and James shared a long look before Hope turned back towards her daughter. "There are things about this town that you don't know. Things I should've told you. I almost did when you met Luc, but then he took off and I let it slide. Lily seemed so human for so long... But I had planned on telling you while we were here. Just not tonight. And not like this."

FOR THE SECOND night in a row, Evie bundled up and sat on the porch, sipping a glass of wine and gazing at the lake—or at least the reflections of the sky on the darkness where the lake was. Her parents had explained a little, although not enough to actually make any sense, and Evie'd made her escape before she went mad. There'd been too much information in the last two days, and she was about one more surprise away from a nervous breakdown.

"Ugh. I wish none of this had ever happened," she said aloud, then clapped her hand over her mouth. What had she done?

"So do all who live to see such times," Luc intoned from the chair next to her.

Evie shrieked, dropped her wine, and jumped out of her chair. "What are you doing here?" she whispered loudly. "I need to go check on Lily and make sure—"

"She's fine," Luc said. He'd caught Evie's wine mere inches from the ground, and he set the glass down on the side armrest of the Adirondack chair.

"You don't understand. I made a wish, and they always come true."

"It was pretty nonspecific, though. Wishing I'd go away is one thing. Wishing 'this' away isn't enough to grab onto. And some things are too big, even for demon powers. Changing an entire timeline isn't possible. It'd upset the fabric of time."

"Demon powers, huh?" Evie said. "You left out a few things when we met, huh?"

"I wasn't staying, it didn't seem necessary to get into it," Luc said. "It takes a long time to get past a human's skepticism about heaven and hell and everything in between, and even if I'm believed, the person I'm talking to either can't deal with the new world they've been tuned into or they can't keep their mouths shut and they end up shunned, or worse."

"So, at no point during that summer did it occur to you that I deserved to know?" Evie pressed. She already knew the answer, but she wanted him to say it.

Luc ran his hands through his hair, a familiar gesture of frustration she'd seen a hundred times that summer when he talked about not wanting to go home—wanting to make his own way. "I thought about it," he said.

Evie picked up her glass and took a long sip to hide her surprise.

"The timing was never right, and I didn't want to waste the short time we had together trying to convince you I wasn't a pathological liar with delusions of grandeur."

"My parents knew," Evie said.

Luc had the good manners to look guilty, and he squirmed under her glare. "They asked. I confirmed. It wasn't a conspiracy. We didn't band together to keep it from you. It was just..."

Evie's phone buzzed, and she ignored it. "I need to know more. I need to know what's happening to me. What's going to happen to Lily. I'm so angry right now. It sucked when I found out I was pregnant but didn't get a chance to tell you before you left town. And it sucked when you showed back up with no warning, and I had to introduce my daughter to her absentee father with zero notice. But the worst part is things have been happening. Things I can't explain, and part of me thought I was going mad. Or that Lily was taking some childhood games too far, and this whole time, you and my parents all had the answers."

Evie's phone vibrated again, then three times more in quick succession.

"You can get that if you want," Luc said. "I won't be offended."

"I don't care about offending you," Evie said. "I'm mad at you."

"I'll tell you everything you want to know," Luc offered. "I know it's a decade too late, but I wasn't deliberately trying to—"

Evie's phone rang. She pulled it out of her pocket to silence it and glanced at the screen. "It's Bev," she said. "And I have twelve missed texts."

"Answer it," Luc said. "What I have to say has waited this long, a couple more minutes won't make a difference."

Evie answered. "Hey lady, what's going on?"

"We need help," Bev whispered. "Please. Please come."

Evie stood up. "Of course. Anything. Where are you? What's going on?"

"We're at the exit. Viv wanted a couple more pics, and I wanted to see it. Please just come." The line went silent.

"I've got to go," she said. "I need shoes and my purse. Breathe, Evie." She stopped, pressed her finger and thumb to the bridge of her nose, and forced herself to take a deep breath to slow her quickly accelerating pulse.

"You can't drive," Luc said. "You're too amped and panicky."

"And this is my third glass of wine. *Dammit*. I guess I can wake up Dad."

"Or, and you can say no, you could ask me to drive you," Luc suggested.

Evie took a deep breath and tried to regulate her nerves. "That is probably the best idea. Let me leave a note for my parents. Do you have a car here or should we take mine?"

"I didn't drive." He sounded apologetic. "Your car would probably be easier. Where are we going?" He followed her inside and watched her scribble a note for her parents.

Evie grabbed her purse and slipped on a pair of shoes she had by the front door. "The Eden Valley exit off the highway. I don't know why, but Viv and Bev went back there this evening to take pictures."

"Pictures of the exit?" Luc asked, holding his hand out for the keys.

Evie handed them over, grabbed a jacket, and walked back outside. "Of the hellmouth that appeared. You must have heard about it. Or caused it."

"Why would I make a hellmouth? Why are you calling it a hellmouth?" Luc opened the door for Evie, then went around to the driver's seat and moved it back before getting in.

"It's a huge, perfectly round sinkhole in the middle of the off-ramp and at the bottom is a glowing symbol that perfectly matches the tattoo you have on your back. And the day it appeared, so did you. That's an awful lot of coincidences."

Luc started the car, pulled out of the driveway, and headed

towards town and the road that would lead them towards the highway.

Evie started a playlist through the bluetooth speakers and then read through the text messages she'd gotten from Bev over the last forty-five minutes. They started out poking light-hearted fun at Viv's Instagram addiction, bitched about the difficulty of finding a last-minute babysitter in a small town, and progressed to more and more frantic messages about car accidents, hellpits, and the sad lack of sexy slayers in Eden Valley, and ending with several pleas to come help or at least answer the damn phone.

After a few minutes, Luc interrupted her reading and increased self-recriminations for not checking her messages earlier.

"The symbol in the sinkhole looks like my tattoo?" he asked.

"Yeah. It was extra weird because I'd seen the same symbol in Lily's black magic demon summoning book, or whatever she was calling it."

Luc flexed his hands on the steering wheel until the leather creaked in protest under his grip. "Lily has a black magic book? That's what she was using to summon demons? How long has she had this and why were you allowing it?"

"Oh no," Evie said, thrusting her index finger towards him. "You do not get to show up here and question my parenting less than twelve hours after finding out you have a child. That is not how this works."

"I'm sorry," Luc said. "I'm just...surprised is all. Most fourth graders don't have access to demon tomes, and if it had this symbol in it, it's more than likely authentic—or at least close enough to cause problems."

"I don't know how long she's had it," Evie admitted. "I saw it earlier this week when I caught her making three wishes to a demon with some birthday candles, a Ouija board, and a Latin-esque summoning ritual she pulled off a Supernatural fan site. She said she got the book from her friend Kevin, but I didn't even think to ask when. I confiscated it, of course. When I was paging thorough it, that's when I saw the symbol. And then a couple days later, sinkhole and you." Evie shrugged. "You can look at it tomorrow if you want."

"Oh, I want," Luc muttered. "And then I might have to have a word with this Kevin character. He was the boy child at dinner earlier?"

"That was him. He's around a lot, so I'm sure you'll see him again." Evie reached out and touched Luc's arm, then flinched when a current of electricity shot through her body, heating her in ways she barely remembered were possible. "Turn here," she said. "It'll be faster."

They rode in silence again for a while, broken only by Evie's directions. She texted Bev and Viv a couple more times, letting them know they were on the way, but there was no response.

"Are you okay?" Luc asked when she jumped at the sound of the blinker turning on.

"Kinda freaking out," Evie replied. "It's weird that no one's texting me back. And it's weirder that they're out here at night. And it's weirdest that I am in a car with you going to rescue my friends. You're a demon. My daughter is a demon. Everyone's a demon." She heard the note of hysteria rising in her voice but couldn't stop the words from spilling out. "My whole life, or at least the last ten years of it, has been lie after deception after lie, and I don't know who I blame more —you or my parents."

"Evie, I'm sorry. But not everyone's a demon. It's only me. And Lily. And my siblings you saw in Ambrosia."

"Not now, Luc. Just get me to the hellmouth so I can rescue my friends from whatever's happening at a sinkhole in the dark—do you think I should call 911?"

"We're almost there," Luc said. "Maybe five minutes more, right?"

Evie peered through the darkness, looking for landmarks. "Sure. Five minutes."

"We'll get there. Evaluate the situation. And if necessary, we will call for backup. Don't you think if it was an emergency, Bev would've called 911 before calling you?"

Evie thought about it. Viv might've skipped the official channels and relied on Evie, but Bev was a rule follower. She trusted the police, more or less, and in Eden Valley it wasn't dangerous to do so. There was a Sheriff and two deputies who lived in town. Everyone knew them, and most people trusted them. Viv didn't, though, which is why she wouldn't call 911. Sheriff Mills had gone to high school with them, back when she was just Joanne Olson, and she'd been the one to out Viv to the school and to Viv's mom.

No way would Viv ever forget or forgive that. Evie didn't have much use for the Sheriff either. She might not be petty and vindictive anymore, but she'd wreaked havoc on Viv's life, and by extension, Evie's and Bev's, when Viv placed ahead of Jo in cross-country, securing herself a place on the all-state team. Viv had somehow talked the school into letting her skip the last semester of her senior year, giving up her almost assured valedictorian title, and with diploma in hand, she'd headed to UW in Seattle a semester early and had never really looked back.

Evie called Bev's phone again, but it went straight to voicemail. Viv's did the same thing.

"Almost there," Luc said, placing a hand over hers where it was resting on her thigh. "Everything will be okay."

"You can't know that," Evie said. "Can you?"

"No. I can't. Telling the future was never one of my gifts."

He took the last turn and pulled off the road at the top of the exit ramp. The sinkhole glowed slightly and was ringed round with yellow caution tape. Blinking barriers blocked the ramp, but other than that, there was nothing to designate the danger.

"I don't see another car, do you?" Evie asked, unbuckling her seat-belt and opening the door. She popped the trunk and grabbed a couple industrial sized flashlights, handing one to Luc.

"Do you always carry giant flashlights around?" Luc asked, flicking his on and off then on again.

"Flashlights, emergency flares, extra blankets, protein bars, snow chains, first aid kit… I could go on."

"No need. I get the picture. You sound prepared for anything."

"I wasn't prepared for you," Evie muttered under her breath.

"I might not be able to see the future, but I can hear extraordinarily well," Luc said. "I wish we could start over."

Evie flinched when he said the "w" word, then forced a grin, hoping it would reflect in her voice. "And do what, exactly? Are you telling me things would turn out differently if we did it again? How? Would you not buy me a drink when you saw me at the bar? Would I not go back to your hotel with you the night we met? Would I not have Lily? Because Luc, as messed up as everything is, I wouldn't change that for the world."

Luc took her hand and pulled her close. "I was thinking more along the lines of me not leaving. What if I'd stayed? Told my father I wasn't coming back. What if we'd tried to make a go of it?"

Evie shook her head and switched on her flashlight. "What ifs and maybes aren't solid enough ground to stand on. What's done is done, and there's no going back. I like my life. Sure, it's a little lonely at times, but I have great friends, a good job, and the best kid. I don't need to look backwards."

Evie pulled her hand out of Luc's and led the way down the steep hill, swinging the beam of light back and forth in front of her, looking for uneven ground and any hint that her friends were here.

"Bev! Viv! Are you here?" she called out.

Nothing.

She went closer, conscious of Luc's presence right behind her. "Bev! Viv!" she yelled. "Where are you?"

They were close enough to the sinkhole that the glow was almost brighter than the flashlights.

"Beverly! Genevieve! You'd better answer me right now or so help me, I'll tell everyone about the time you broke into the hotel pool and went skinny dipping with the youth pastor the summer after y'all graduated college!"

There was still no reply. Evie slowed her walk and crept to the edge of the sinkhole, then dropped to her knees and peered in. The symbol was even larger and more terrifying looking than it'd been in Viv's picture, and the stench of sulphur was almost overwhelming.

And there, at the bottom of the pit, were Evie's friends. Bev was sitting cross-legged on the ground with Viv's head in her lap and was glaring up at Evie. "If you tell anyone about the skinny dipping, I swear to god, I will take out a billboard on the freeway with the pics I took of you in Vegas on your thirty-fifth birthday."

"You wouldn't dare!" Evie said. "Are you okay? What happened? What's wrong with Viv?"

Bev sighed. "She just wanted pictures—better than the ones she'd gotten before. So we drove up here in her stupid little car, went around the barrier—there was no one to stop us, and we figured the yellow caution tape would show us where to stop. But as soon as we touched the tape, the ground...tilted, I guess, and the car rolled on in. Almost in slow motion. We got out when it hit the bottom—it was very dramatic—but the car landed square on this glowing bit and slowly disappeared like it was stuck in quicksand. The cell signal is crap, by the way. And you not answering the phone was crap, too."

Evie bit her lip as she considered the distance between her and the bottom of the sinkhole. It had to be at least thirty or forty feet down. "Is Viv okay?" she asked as she tried to remember how much rope she had in the back of the car.

"I don't know," Bev said. "She seemed fine when we bailed out of the car, but just before I finally got a hold of you, she passed out, and I haven't been able to wake her up."

"Why didn't you call 911?" Evie demanded. "I don't know how we're going to get you out of there."

"We?" Bev asked. "You brought help?"

Luc peered over the side of the sinkhole and waved. "Hi, Bev. If you hold on a minute, I think I can get you both out of there. Are either of you injured? Broken bones or nasty cuts or anything?"

"Luc?" Bev asked. "What are you doing here?" She clapped a hand over her mouth. "Oh. Oh! That's why you didn't answer. You two were..."

"Talking," Evie said firmly. She turned to Luc. "How are we going to get them out? Should I get some rope?"

"Are they going to freak out if I do something unexpected and not humanly possible?" he asked.

"Probably not, but no guarantees. It doesn't matter, though. Get them out. Please."

Luc stood and jumped down into the pit, landing softly beside Bev. Evie laid flat on her belly and watched.

"Beverly, I am going to pick Viv up now," Luc said. "It'd be best if you didn't watch this next part."

"Why? What are you going to do with her?"

"Is she always this suspicious?" Luc called up to Evie.

Evie shrugged. "When it comes to the people she loves, yes. I'm surprised you don't remember."

Luc sighed loud enough for Evie to hear. "Fine. Watch, don't watch. I don't care." He stood with Viv in his arms. Dark wings erupted from his back and stretched almost as wide as the pit was deep. He bent his knees then shot straight up into the air and landed gently beside Evie. "I think she's fine," Luc said. "But I'm not a doctor nor a healer, and I can't be sure. We should take her to a hospital if she doesn't wake by the time we get back to town, and insist that she go to a doctor tomorrow if she does wake."

He raced up the hill, and Evie heard the sound of a car door open and close. Moments later, he was back in the sinkhole, picking up Bev. "Meet you at the car," he said to Evie as he flew over her with Bev.

Bev's arms were wrapped around Luc's neck, and Evie squashed the ugly spark of envy she felt seeing someone else being held the way she wished he'd hold her.

No.

No.

That ship had sailed and gotten lost at sea almost eleven years ago. It didn't matter who Luc held and why. As long as it wasn't her. She wrapped her arms around herself and started the walk back up the hill. A dull ache formed in her chest, a faint echo of the crushing sadness she'd felt when Luc walked out of her life. Seeing him again had resurrected the grief she thought had been banished the first time she'd held Lily and seen the echo of Luc in her daughter's eyes. That was not a path she could walk down again.

CHAPTER SEVEN

Evie paced the length of Bev's living room, waiting for Bev to get back from driving Emily, Shelby's babysitter home. Viv was in the recliner, chugging water and giving the remote control the workout of a lifetime.

Luc had driven them back to Bev's and then offered to take Evie home, too, but she declined. And after he'd carried Viv in—under protest from the now awake woman—Evie'd shooed him away without meeting his eyes. She knew it was irrational to have the wings be the deal breaker at this point, after all, he'd already confirmed he was a demon and her daughter had an invisible but very real dog, but somehow seeing his wings—watching him fly—was the straw that broke her brain tonight.

"Tomorrow, then," he'd said. "I'll text in the morning, and we can figure out the best time for you and Lily to meet me for lunch."

When she hadn't replied, he turned and walked back out of the house, followed by Bev and Emily.

Evie's friends reeked of sulphur, and she knew her car would need to be aired out for weeks if it was ever going to be the same.

"Ugh," she said, then grabbed Viv's empty glass and took it to the kitchen for a refill. "How do you feel?" she asked, handing the glass back.

"About the same as last time you asked," Viv said. "And since that was less than five minutes ago, I'm sure you remember what I said then. I have a headache, I'm thirstier than I've ever been before, and I want a shower something fierce. I should really get home."

"I've already texted your mom to let her know you were staying with Bev tonight. I texted my parents, too. Gotta love a sleepover party, right?"

Viv smiled tightly and drained her glass. Evie refilled it again.

"What happened, Viv? Bev told me a little, but it's all so bananas. I just don't understand."

"I'm gonna go take a shower. Do you think Bev will mind if I grab a t-shirt and some sweats? These clothes stink." Viv pulled her shirt away from her skin and wrinkled her nose. She didn't meet Evie's eyes, though, instead focusing on a point a good three feet to the left of her friend.

"Of course not. The steam will probably do you a world of good."

"Thanks," Viv said. "When Bev gets back, we can talk. There are a lot of things to say. Back in ten."

❧ ❦ ❧

EVIE WAS CURLED up in front of the fireplace when Bev returned. She'd helped herself to a glass of Cardboardeaux Bev had on the kitchen counter and was distractedly playing one of the time-wasting games she'd installed on her phone mostly to distract Lily when she was required to sit still and at risk for terminal boredom.

"I'd like to grab a shower before we talk. I reek," Bev said. "Where's Viv?"

"She took a twenty-minute shower that ended a little bit ago, but she hasn't emerged yet. I checked on her, but she told me to go away and stop mothering her."

"Well at least she sounds like herself," Bev said, biting her lip as she looked toward the bathroom.

Evie flapped her hands at Bev. "Go upstairs and shower. It's really late, and I need to know what happened. If Viv is still hiding when you're done, we can drag her out by her ankles."

"I can hear you guys, you know," Viv called from behind the bathroom door. "I'll be out in a minute."

Bev jogged up the stairs. Viv emerged just as Bev turned the water on. She made a beeline for the kitchen and came out with a glass of ice water and one of wine, then settled on the couch as far away from the fireplace as was possible in the small room and set her drinks down on the adjacent end table. Evie snagged a super soft fleece blanket from the antique travel trunk that doubled as a coffee table and draped it over Viv.

"I thought I told you to stop mothering me," Viv said, sticking her tongue out at Evie before tucking the blanket around herself securely.

"It's like you've never met me," Evie chided. "I've been mothering you since you and your mom moved back to Eden Valley in fourth grade."

"Sometimes it feels like yesterday," Viv said. "We were the age that Lily is now, and I was so worried about being the weird one who wouldn't be able to make friends."

"You're still the weird one," Bev called from upstairs. She appeared at the top of the staircase, towel drying her hair and dressed in flannel pajama pants and a soft, gray tank top. After tossing her towel back into her bedroom, she came downstairs, tossed a second pair of pajamas at Evie, and made a pit stop in the kitchen for water and wine, then parked herself on the opposite end of the couch from Viv.

Evie grabbed two more blankets, and after getting Bev tucked in, wrapped the other one around herself.

"Okay. We're all here. You two are clean and cozy and hydrating. What the hell happened?"

"Hell happened, I think," Viv said.

Viv and Bev exchanged a look. Viv looked down at her hands, and Bev heaved a melodramatic sigh.

"Viv and I were texting at dinner, and she talked me into getting a sitter for Shel and going to get better pics of the sinkhole."

"But why?" Evie asked.

"I do it all for the 'gram," Viv said, looking up and flashing a smile at Evie.

"No, seriously. I know you're way more media savvy than me, but I also know you aren't an influencer. You have a decent following, but you usually use your account to showcase your graphic design skills and craft cocktails."

"Evelyn Addams, do you follow me on Instagram?" Viv placed a palm on her chest and widened her eyes.

"Stop deflecting. Why?"

"I don't know." Viv deflated a bit, her eyes back in her lap where she was twisting her hands. "I've been feeling this pull—almost a compulsion—to go back since I saw the symbol on my way here. It's been getting stronger, and I knew if I didn't pull someone into it with me, I'd still go alone. And based on what happened, I'm not sure I would've been able to leave. Even now, all I can think about is going back even though I know I won't be able to escape a second time."

"Wow. That's...full on banana-crackers," Evie said. "I need you to know I one hundred percent believe you, but—"

"It sounds completely unbelievable. I know. Bev just went along to humor me."

"I believe you," Bev said. "I'm feeling it, too. There's something about that glow. It felt like it was talking to me. I could hear voices—hundreds of them—crying out in pain."

"That's some next-level Alderaan stuff, Bev," Viv said. "I didn't hear any voices. But I could see..."

"See what? I love you both, but neither of you are making any sense."

Bev stood up, dumping her blanket on the ground and walking out of the room. She came back a couple minutes later with a giant bottle of aloe gel. "I'm trying too hard to get my thoughts together, Evie. Everything's all jumbled up. In the meantime, will you rub aloe on my left shoulder? I think I burned it or something."

"Me, too," Viv said. She pulled off her sweatshirt and twisted around.

Bev dropped the bottle of aloe. "Oh my god, Viv."

"What? Is it bad?" Viv twisted her head trying to look over her left shoulder. "What is it?"

"It's like a…brand," Evie said.

"What do you mean, a brand?" Viv demanded.

Bev reached forward and lightly traced the air above the fiery lines in Viv's skin. "This looks like the symbol in the pit," she whispered.

"Turn around, Beverly," Viv said.

Bev turned her back to her friends. Evie carefully pulled back the wide strap of Bev's tank top and revealed an identical brand on her shoulder.

"That's what's on my back?" Viv's eyes were darting between Bev's brand and Evie's eyes.

Evie nodded. "Yeah. Exactly the same."

"Didn't you say your boyfriend had this symbol tattooed on his back?" Bev leaned forward, pulling her shirt out of Evie's grasp and turning back around.

Viv grabbed her glass of wine and took a gulp. "We should call him. Maybe he knows what's going on. This is obviously some demon thing."

Evie took a breath and looked down at her phone. "It is so late, you guys. Can we call him in the morning?"

"If you don't call him now, I will," Viv said. "You'll forget by morning."

"What do you mean, I'll forget?" Evie asked. "My memory isn't that bad."

"You'll find something, Evelyn. Excuses, deflections, something urgent at home… Do it now." Viv winced as she put her sweatshirt back on. "If he doesn't answer or refuses to come back over, I'll drop it. Pinky swear."

Evie reached out and locked pinkies with Viv. "Fine. I'll call, but I doubt he'll answer."

"He will," Viv said. "And on the first ring, I bet."

Viv's prediction rang true, and Luc had answered on the first ring. When she explained what'd happened, he said he'd be there in ten and hung up before she could reply.

Ten minutes later, he knocked on the door, and Evie pulled it open. She tried not to gape at him. He looked even more attractive than he had last time she'd seen him, and the pull to walk into his arms was stronger than ever. She glared suspiciously at the wineglass in her hand before her gaze was pulled back to Luc.

"Hey, Evie," he said in a voice warm enough to melt her insides.

In the hour since he'd dropped them off, Luc had managed a shower and clean clothes—two things Evie was painfully aware that she hadn't.

"Can I come in?" He quirked an eyebrow up and grinned.

"If I say no, will you be stuck outside?" Evie asked, fear, exhaustion, and attraction blown away in an instant by prurient curiosity.

Luc rolled his eyes. "I'm not a vampire. And anyway, this isn't your house, and you have zero power to keep me out. I was just being polite."

"Oh." Evie felt a flush start in her chest and willed it to stay down where it belonged and not compound her embarrassment by staining her cheeks.

"So..." Luc drew out the "o" and gazed down at her expectantly. "Can I?"

This time, Evie was unsuccessful in tamping down her blush, and she ducked, hoped no one would notice, and stepped out of the way.

Luc walked into the living room and looked around. He raised his head and inhaled deeply through his nose.

"Sulphur."

"We know," Viv snipped. "We were at your backdoor and got hell stench all over."

"I can assure you that you have *never* been anywhere near my back-door, Genevieve Kane."

"Bite me, demon," Viv said, flipping him off.

"Charming. But I don't mean the sulphur odor that was in your hair and on your clothes—that's so faint now that I can barely detect it. Evie still smells, but it's different. Not wrong..."

Evie stood behind Luc, frozen smile on her face as she tried not to take it personally.

Luc stared at the ceiling long enough that the women started fidgeting.

"Do you want to know why we had Evie call you?" Bev finally asked, breaking the silence.

Luc looked at her, then his gaze intensified. "I really do," he said. "But I'm afraid I won't like what I'm about to hear."

Viv and Bev stood up and turned their backs to show him their matching brands.

"I need to call my father," Luc said. "Something has gone terribly wrong."

"You're not going anywhere or calling anyone until you tell us what's going on," Bev said. She pulled the strap of her tank top back into place, wincing as the material of her shirt rubbed against the angry red mark on her skin. She sat down on the sofa and wrapped herself in her blanket before grabbing her water and draining it in one go.

Evie took Bev's glass and walked into the kitchen to refill it. She placed the water on the counter, grabbed it with both hands, and leaned forward, dropping her chin to her chest and inhaling as deeply as she could to quell the rising ball of fear and anxiety that threatened to rise and take her ability to function away.

The last couple days had been a lot—too much—but she needed to maintain her strong façade, because what was happening to Viv and Bev was way, way more important. Calmed, at least for the moment, she picked up the glass again and turned around.

Luc was standing behind her.

Evie yelped, and the glass slid out of her hand. Luc reached forward and caught it before it could hit the ground.

"Nice reflexes," Evie snapped.

"Catlike, wouldn't you say?" Luc grinned.

"If you mean you also sneak around like a cat and need a bell, then, sure." Evie wiped her hands on the tea towel hanging above the sink and took the water glass back.

"Do you have one, too?" Luc asked.

"Water?" Evie asked, eyes wide with exaggerated innocence.

"Evie," Luc growled.

She half-smiled, not able to really get into it. "I didn't even go in," Evie said.

"Let me check. Please."

Evie put down Bev's water again and lifted her sweater up to her shoulders.

Luc's hands, warm against her cool skin, skimmed up her back and across her shoulders, his thumbs tracing the lines of her shoulder blades.

Evie's breath hitched, and she felt her heart accelerate—for like the one hundredth time that night.

"What are you doing?" she asked, her voice breathier than she'd intended.

"Looking for the mark." The rough skin on the tips of his fingers dragged along her upper back. "What's this?"

"Lilies of the Valley. I got that done shortly after Lily was born." Goosebumps rose in the wake of his fingers, and she suppressed a shiver.

"And this one?" His thumb brushed over the hint of ink visible on her low back, mostly hidden by the waistline of her jeans.

Evie blushed. She hadn't realized that one was visible at all. There was no way she was talking about it. Not now, and certainly not with Luc. After all, it wasn't a brand, and it hadn't appeared tonight. Probably just a coincidence. She tried for breezy. "After Lily was born—" last summer *was* after Lily was born "—I was feeling a little stuck in time and wanted to do something spontaneous. Make those bad decisions I didn't get a chance to make in my early twenties. So I got a tramp stamp. No big deal. I don't think anyone's ever seen it."

"No one has seen your lower back in the last ten years?" Luc asked, brow wrinkled. "How is that even possible? Not even Lily or your friends?"

"Do you think I walk around naked with my friends or kid?" Evie knew she was deflecting, but she hoped that Luc would follow the conversation she was having and not the thoughts she was sure were forming in his head.

"I think it's unlikely that in ten years, you've never gone swimming or had a sleepover or been half-dressed around anyone else." Luc dropped her shirt, and Evie tried not to sigh in relief.

"I will see your tattoo, though." Luc smirked. "You'll have no choice but to show me."

Evie picked up Bev's water and fled back to the living room before her imagination galloped out of control and created the sensation of his fingers on her skin, dipping low as he traced the lines on her body that matched the ones on his.

CHAPTER EIGHT

Evie woke up and rubbed the sleep out of her eyes before rolling over to look at her clock. Her eyes sprang open wide as the edge of the bed hit her midsection, and she flailed fruitlessly for a second before continuing her forward momentum and crashing onto the floor.

"Ow!" she yelled. The floor was an inch in front of her face and was the complete wrong color. Her bedroom floor was dark hardwood with an enormous, fluffy gray and pink rug taking up most of the space. This floor was bamboo. And there was no rug.

She rolled over and sat up. She was in Bev's guest room and had rolled out of the full-size bed that was significantly smaller than her own king bed. A light snore snagged her attention and she spun around, heart in her throat. Surely she hadn't...

Viv was still fast asleep on the other side of the bed closest to the wall.

Evie breathed a sigh of relief, grabbed her phone, and headed to the bathroom.

Morning ablutions taken care of, Evie followed the smell of coffee downstairs. Shelby was sitting at the kitchen counter eating a bowl of cereal and staring at her iPad.

"Hey, Shel," Evie said, snagging a bucket-sized coffee cup from the cupboard.

Shelby looked up. "Evie? What are you doing here? Is Aunt Bev okay?"

Evie could see the panic boiling up on Shelby's face. Her breathing sped up as she began to shrink into herself. Her shoulders were up around her ears, and she was starting to rock back and forth on the stool.

"She's fine. Just asleep. Bev, Viv, and I had a sleepover last night. Nothing is wrong. She's fine."

Shelby didn't often show any signs of the PTSD she still suffered from the car accident she barely remembered... The one that had taken her mother and grandparents, and nearly killed her, too. And even though she could tolerate being separated from her Aunt Bev for longer periods of time now, she still automatically went to the worst-possible outcome more often than a child should have to.

"Promise?" Shelby asked. Her shoulders were relaxing a bit, but her breathing was still too fast and too shallow.

"I promise," Evie said. "If you want to run upstairs and peek at her, you can. Viv's asleep in the guest room, too. Just an old lady sleepover."

"Swear on the River Styx?" Shelby demanded.

Evie cocked her head and regarded the girl. "Lily's got you all swearing on mythological rivers now?"

"You are myth-taken," Shelby said, a grin breaking out on her face. "It's real. Lily told me. Cerberus is really Cerberus, Junior, and his dad is the original Cerberus."

Evie wanted to laugh at the imagination of children, but after the last few days, she wasn't sure what was real anymore, and certainly wasn't going to argue about hellhound pedigrees with a nine-year-old. At least not before she had her morning dose of caffeine.

"You got me there," Evie said instead. "Did you make the coffee?"

Shelby nodded. "Aunt Bev loves coffee, and it makes her so happy to have it waiting for her when she gets up. I didn't know you and Viv were here, though, or I would've made more."

"It's fine. I'll make more once I've drained this pot. You're a really great kid, Shel."

Shelby ducked her head, a blush staining her cheeks. "Thanks, Evie. You're not too bad for an old person." A mischievous grin quirked up the corners of Shelby's lips, and Evie leaned back to enjoy her coffee. Crisis averted.

"I wish Bev took her coffee with creamer," Evie said. "I don't know how she drinks it black."

"I read that only serial killers drink black coffee," Shelby volunteered, not even looking up from the Minecraft video she was watching. "But I don't think it's true. Unless Aunt Bev is really good at keeping secrets."

Evie shook her head. "I'm sure it just means that all serial killers drink their coffee black, not that all people who prefer unadulterated coffee are serial killers." She opened the fridge, even though she knew there wouldn't be any. Front and center was a small bottle of her favorite creamer—caramel vanilla flavored, and full of so many additives and too much sugar. Everything else in the fridge was organic and whole food. Nothing with artificial color or flavor.

Evie grabbed the creamer and liberally doctored her coffee. It might be creepy, but wish fulfillment powers definitely had their uses.

She took her coffee to the back patio and sat on the wide swing, tucking her legs underneath her and wrapping her fingers around the cup to stay warm. Bev had a huge backyard that was mostly garden. The perimeter was lined with shrubs just starting to bloom. Lilacs stood tall in the corners, a smudge of purple starting to show along the dark green leaves. Hyacinths bloomed behind irregularly spaced clumps of yellow and purple tulips and irises. Later, dahlias and lilies would take over for the spring flowers, poppies would volunteer everywhere, and the annual sunflowers would compete in height among the salvia.

The main part of the yard was mostly dormant raised beds, although a small greenhouse with tables laden with starts took up most of the south side of the yard. Freshly dug dirt indicated that the first seeds were in the ground. Radishes, peas, and spring greens, probably. It was too early for much else. There was still a chance of a freeze before winter fully gave up its grip on the high mountain town.

Evie loved Bev's backyard. She might not have the lakefront view Evie did, but the garden was quiet and peaceful. Butterflies and hummingbirds flocked there in summer, although only a few of the tiny birds stayed over the winter.

She breathed in deeply, the scents of new grass and the wisteria blooming over the patio pergola.

"Hey," Bev said.

Evie jumped, spilling her coffee on her lap. Her startle reflex, mostly dormant since her divorce, was out of control lately.

"I'm sorry," Bev said. "I didn't mean to scare you. I thought you heard me come out."

"It's fine. I was just lost in the beauty of your backyard. I love it here. It's so peaceful."

Bev nodded and settled on the swing next to Evie. "It really is. Gardening—getting my hands in the dirt—is my happy place. And Shelby is really starting to enjoy it almost as much as I do. She asked to have one of the raised beds for herself this year. Apparently, it'll be a surprise. She took her bike and her allowance to the garden store last week and came back with a backpack full of things she refused to show me."

"That's awesome," Evie said. "So much better than surprise—and apparently surprisingly effective—demon summonings. You are definitely winning child-rearing right now."

Bev laughed, startling the goldfinches on the feeder hanging at the edge of the pergola between the hummingbird feeders. "Not bad, right? Especially considering I got a late start."

"So. Wanna talk about it?" Evie asked.

"Not really. You?" Bev's knuckles whitened on her coffee cup, and she stared at the ground in front of them.

"Not in the least. But I guess we should."

"Let's wait for Viv," Beverly said. "I don't want to do this more than once."

The door behind them creaked open. "Wait for me for what?" Viv asked. "By the way, thanks for the creamer. It's almost like you knew we'd be here."

"I didn't get creamer," Bev said, nose wrinkling in confusion. "Unless you mean the whipping cream I have for baking."

"That was probably me," Evie admitted. "I really wanted some this morning."

"Oh, you *wished* you had creamer?" Viv asked. "Handy."

"Sometimes. Still weird, though."

"About last night," Viv started.

"I'll get more coffee started!" Bev said, jumping up and running inside.

Evie and Viv looked at each other.

"She's wigging out," Evie said.

Viv shook her head and massaged her temples for a moment before responding. "Okay. First of all, no one says 'wigging out' anymore. Second—of course she is. I am, too. And if you weren't so stubborn, you'd admit how freaked out you are about all of this. Third, even if you aren't 'wigged out' about what happened last night, you're plenty 'wigged' about Luc falling back into your life. I saw the way you looked at him last night. The heat you two were generating was almost enough to replace the fireplace."

"You're abusing air quotes," Evie said, sidestepping Viv's third point. "I'm plenty freaked out, but it doesn't do any good to give into it. We're not gonna get through this by being scared."

"You know, Evelyn Addams, it's okay to not be strong all the time. I get you've worked hard at staying strong for Lily, and it's been a long time since you've let yourself really feel everything else that runs around in your brain, but it's still us, and you never have to put on a show of strength for us. Be brave. Be vulnerable. We don't need protecting."

Bev chose that moment to return, coffee carafe in one hand and the bottle of creamer in her other. "She's right, you know," Bev said, refilling everyone's coffee. "I know it's not easy. I struggle with it, too. But if you start shutting us out, you're not protecting us, you're isolating yourself. Don't make that mistake."

Evie sighed and set down her coffee. "There's one more thing I haven't told you guys. I got a tattoo last summer. I was feeling sad and old. I missed being young, not being a mom, and being able to go home with guys I'd just met."

"You did that exactly one time," Viv pointed out.

"Yeah, and I got pregnant, or maybe I would've made a habit of it," Evie retorted.

"Tell us about the mid-life crisis tattoo," Bev said.

Evie stood up. "It's a tramp stamp," she warned her friends. She turned her back and pulled down the waistband of her jeans. "It's just like yours..."

"No it isn't," Viv said. "Maybe you've forgotten?"

"What do you mean?" Evie asked, twisting around to try to look at her own lower back.

"Mind if I take a picture?" Viv asked.

"Go for it," Evie said. "But maybe don't Instagram it."

"Promise," Viv said. She pulled out her phone and took a pic, then handed her phone to Evie.

"Oh. Wow. That's...not what I had tattooed."

"Um. Of course it is," Bev said. "It's a tattoo. Those are permanent. That's like their whole thing."

Evie handed Viv her phone back and pulled her own out and scrolled through her photos. When she found the one she was looking for, she handed it over. "This is the tattoo right after I had it done."

Evie's picture showed an upside-down "A" connected to an upside down "V" by a circle with a vertical line running from the tip of the A to the tip of the V.

"This is just like the brands you both have, like the symbol in the ground. It's the symbol on Luc's back."

Bev snapped her fingers, pulling the attention of her friends off the photo and towards her. "I knew I'd seen this symbol before. I just couldn't place where. It's one of the portfolio photos showcased on the Tiger Lily Tattoo website. I can't believe that was your upper ass region."

"Ignoring all the weirder implications of Bev checking out tattoo websites and your tattoo not looking like it did nine months ago, you got a tattoo to match your baby daddy's ink ten years after he walked out on you? And you didn't tell us?" Viv asked, handing Evie her phone back. "That's…"

"Pathetic," Evie said. "I know. I was tired of being alone. Single parenting is no walk in the park, but I've gotten used to that. But I missed him. Missed that connection. And felt really stupid about the whole thing, so I got a tattoo to remind me of him."

"And it was right around this time that things started to get weird?" Bev asked. "You got a tattoo to match your demon boyfriend, and all of a sudden you could finally live your dream of being a first-class kleptomaniac?"

"That was never my dream," Evie said.

"I remember you wanting to be a high-end jewel thief, complete with black leotard, when we were in middle school. This is totally the safety school version of cat burglar," Viv said.

"I earned a parent-teacher conference for that essay," Evie said.

"Me, too," Viv confessed. "Apparently 'Warrior Princess with a hottie blonde *totally platonic* sidekick' is cause for concern, too. I was grounded for the rest of the school year after that."

"I was obsessed with the zombie apocalypse then," Bev said. "One of my cousins was staying with us then, and he was obsessed with death and Ouija boards and seances. Pretty sure I wrote about raising armies of the dead or something. And I'm equally sure that there wasn't a parent teacher conference for my essay. By then, all the teachers had given up on conferencing with my parents at all."

Evie held her hand out. "Let me look at that picture again," she said. Viv handed over her phone. The tattoo bore almost zero resemblance to the original. The lines and circle were there, and the style was the same, but instead of an A and V connected by a dissected circle, now she had an L marked with x's at the end points and where the two bars of the L joined. Halfway up the vertical line of the L, two parallel lines sprang out to the right and were crowned by a small circle.

"That's…"

"Does Luc know?" Viv asked. "About you getting a tribute tattoo?"

"No," Evie said. "I didn't get branded in a pit like you guys. I paid someone to ink me a matching tattoo—a matching *tramp stamp*—and I wasn't about to admit that. Neither of our egos could take it."

"You need to tell him," Bev said. "It means something. You saw how freaked out he was last night. He took photos of our backs—which he better not 'gram, either—and took off almost immediately. To do research. Or make a call. Maybe both."

Evie tipped her arm and looked at her watch. "Speaking of, I need to get home and get ready for brunch. Lily and I are meeting Luc in an hour, and I'd like to freshen up a bit. Viv, do you want a ride home?"

"Nah... I'll walk back to Mom's when I finish my coffee. And then call my insurance. Getting an unholy brand is one thing. Trying to file a claim on a car lost in hell without being accused of insurance fraud —or my mom finding out—is gonna be the real trick."

CHAPTER NINE

E vie pulled into the driveway at her house. Voices from the back deck overlooking the lake wafted her way, and she briefly considered going in the back door and heading upstairs before anyone could see her. It'd been a long time since she'd tried to sneak in, but not so long that she thought this would be the time it'd work.

"Evie?" Her mother's voice rose on the wind. "Come have some coffee as soon as you've changed. I'd love to hear about your impromptu sleepover."

Evie winced. Her mother had the uncanny ability to hear her coming from a mile away, know when Evie was trying to avoid her parents, and find just the right thing to say to make her feel guilty and rebellious at the same time.

"Sure thing, Mom," Evie called back.

"And don't think you can avoid us by taking an hour to get dressed. I put an outfit on your bed—a gift from us to you. Pair it with a cardigan, and you'll look amazing but won't show too much skin or get cold."

Evie rolled her eyes. Her mother had never stopped trying to pick out her outfits, even though it'd been more than thirty years since she'd gone with Hope's first choice. Evie had always favored a mix of frill and casual maxi dresses and Chucks, skinny jeans and stilettos, and not the floral prints her hippie mother was inexplicably fond of.

She ran up the stairs, washed her face and brushed out the braids she'd put in last night after she'd showered before bed, and walked into her bedroom. A light blue sundress with big, yellow sunflowers was laid out on the bed next to a black cardigan that almost perfectly matched the centers of the flowers on the dress. A pair of strappy espadrilles were at the foot of the bed, and a chunky amber and brown necklace with matching earrings were on the dresser.

Evie ignored the clothes her mother had laid out and opened her closet. She glanced back at the bed. She'd never hear the end of it if she wore the dress her mom'd picked out.

Evie stripped off the borrowed pajamas she'd worn home from Bev's and pulled on a pair of jeans and topped it with a tunic-length striped black and pink tank top. She glanced back at the bed, pursed her lips, then grabbed the cardigan her mother had chosen. Then she eyed the shoes... Those espadrilles, though... Evie slipped on the shoes, ignored her mother's jewelry, and put on a long, silver necklace with a rose quartz pendant and matching earrings.

She added some makeup—primer, foundation, mascara, and lip gloss—and checked her watch. Twenty minutes had passed. She didn't need to leave for at least another forty-five.

Damn. There was only so much she could do to procrastinate before it became obvious she was avoiding her family. It's not like she didn't want to spend time with them. She'd always been close with both parents, and Lily was the light of her life. It was just... There were questions she didn't want to answer. Questions she *couldn't* answer. Like what'd happened last night. How she felt about Luc. What was going to happen in the future.

"Pull up your big girl pants and spend time with your family," she said to her reflection.

Loins properly girded, she headed downstairs and out onto the deck. There was a large cup of coffee, deliciously pale with creamer, waiting for her, steam still rising from the cup.

"Mama mama mama," Lily yelled. "Cerberus has a new name."

"Oh yeah?" Evie asked, looking around a little nervously, afraid the three-headed hellhound might be lounging nearby. "What's his new name, sweetie?"

"*Her* name," Lily corrected. "She told me that she was really a girl and not a boy like everyone thought. Kinda like Shelby. Sometimes people make mistakes when people are born and say the wrong thing and it takes a while to sort out."

"That must have been hard for her," Evie said, nodding. "It'd suck to have people not knowing who you really were. What's her name, Monster?"

"Sprinkles," Lily said, with all the gravitas you'd expect when announcing Her Majesty, Liliana Faith Addams, by the Grace of God, of Eden Valley and Greater Washington State and of her other realms, both above and below, Queen of the Cascades, Defender of Hellhounds.

"Sprinkles?" Evie asked. She knew better than to laugh. Her daughter had a delightful sense of humor that accompanied her quick wit, but it all went out the window when she suspected—for any reason, valid or not—that she was being mocked.

"Well, that's not her *really* real name," Lily confided. "Her really real name is Princess Surma, of the Cerberina Surmas. But she likes to be called Sprinkles. More dignified."

"Well, if that's what she wants, that's what we'll call her," Evie said. It might've been her imagination, but she thought she heard a satisfied chuff from the far end of the deck.

"Lily, darling," Hope said. "If you're done eating, why don't you wash up and brush your teeth, then get dressed in the clothes I laid out for you. I want to talk to your Mama."

"About things you don't want me to hear," Lily added.

"You're absolutely right," Hope said, unperturbed. "You never know—it might be birthday surprise conversations."

Lily narrowed her eyes at her grandmother, but decided the risk wasn't worth it. She grabbed her plate and glass and went inside.

"So," Hope said. "What's going on?"

☙ ❧ ☙

EVIE SAT in the kitchen with her cup of coffee. Her mother had taken everything in stride, as she always did, and hadn't offered any advice —she was unusually fantastic about listening without advising. Hope was doing dishes and letting Evie sit with her thoughts.

Evie stared out of the picture windows into the still, dark water of Eden Lake and tried to figure out where everything had gone wrong. Was it when she'd decided to get the tattoo? When she'd gone home with Luc the night they'd met? Taking off work early to surprise Jer with an afternoon delight, only to find him in bed with Brandy? Marrying Jer fresh out of high school?

She sighed. She couldn't begrudge her relationship with Luc, however brief and possibly ill-advised. It'd brought her Lily, and she wouldn't give up her demon child for anything.

There was something, though. She couldn't put a finger on it, but there'd been a wrong turn. Now Luc was back, her daughter had an invisible three-headed dog, her friends wore demon brands, and she no longer knew which way was up.

An alarm on her phone chimed, and she glared at it. She'd set herself a reminder so she'd be able to tell Lily they were leaving in plenty of time to get out the door only a little late, but now that it was time, she didn't want to go.

"I'll get Lily moving!" her mother called.

"Thanks, Mom!" Evie replied.

James Addams walked into the kitchen. "You don't have to go if you really don't want to. He might be back and ready to be a father, but he hasn't earned it. Not yet."

Evie smiled, but knew it wasn't reaching her eyes. "I don't know what to do, Daddy. Everything is moving too fast after eleven years of glacial speed. I've created so many messes and don't have the first idea how to clean them up."

"The way I see it, you didn't create any messes at all. Lily isn't a mess. What you had with Luc that summer led to my granddaughter, so that's not a mess. And Viv and Bev are perfectly capable of getting themselves into their own messes. There's no need to take responsibility for their poor decision making. A lot of what's going on right now can be tied to you, but that doesn't mean you made it happen. You're the center of a vortex, one you probably could've avoided—or at least mitigated the effects of—if you'd had more information. That's on Luc, and on your mother and me."

Evie grinned, and this time it was genuine. "If I'm not to feel guilty, I don't think you should, either. Life isn't a straight road of cause and effect, is it?"

"If only that were true, darling girl. We'd have a lot better idea of where we're headed. It's more like a river delta. Any small change of current, any rock or branch or leaf can push us into a different course still headed in the same direction. There's no way to look back and see what one thing is responsible for where we are currently."

"Currently. Ha. River pun." Evie laughed.

James shrugged. "I'm glad you appreciate me. Your mother does not."

Hope walked into the kitchen, a sullen Lily in tow. "I appreciate you so much," Hope said, dropping a kiss on her husband's head. "But you have to admit your puns leave something to be desired."

Evie ignored her parents' flirtatious banter and focused on her daughter. Lily was dressed in a brand-new sundress Evie'd never seen before. It was pink with white flowers, was trimmed with lace, and was a *lot* of frill.

"Grandma?" she mouthed.

Lily nodded, looking for all the world like she'd been told she was grounded from her iPad forever.

"Wanna change?" Evie whispered.

Lily's eyes lit up. "Please?" she whispered back.

Evie glanced at her mother. She was currently involved in a heated debate with James about the merits of various forms of humor. Her dad looked at her and winked. Evie nodded at Lily. "Do it, but be extra fast."

Lily flashed a grateful smile at her mother and grandfather and disappeared up the stairs. Five minutes later, Evie heard her clattering back down.

"Time to go!" she announced to her parents. "See you later."

"Have fun, dear," Hope said. "Don't do anything I wouldn't do."

"It's brunch, Mother," Evie said. "I don't know what could possibly happen that would make that advice relevant."

"You never know," her mom said. "I remember this one time in Reykjavik..."

"No one needs to hear that story right now, dear," James interrupted. "Least of all our granddaughter."

Lily walked through the door, grabbed her mother's hand, and pulled her out of the house. Evie regarded her daughter as they walked to the car. She was no longer pink and frilly—instead, she was now dressed in black leggings with a skull print, a long purple shirt sporting a black rhinestone cat wearing a witch's hat, and black chucks. If she'd been allowed, she probably would've added smudged eyeliner to the ensemble, but Evie was holding out on letting Lily go full goth until she was thirteen.

"Feel better?" Evie asked.

Lily nodded. "I'm not a pink, lacy person," she said.

"Grandma spent so many years buying me tie dye and carpenter jeans that she's overcorrected with you," Evie said. "I like dresses and frills and pink sometimes. And it's AOK that you don't."

They got into the car. Evie rolled down the windows right away. It still smelled like sulphur and probably would for the foreseeable future.

"I don't mind pink as long as it's skulls," Lily said, buckling into the back seat.

"I know, baby girl. And grandma might get the memo by the time you're eighteen. Or forty."

"Mama? I'm nervous."

Evie glanced over her shoulder to check the driveway for obstacles and saw Lily twisting her hair around her finger and into her mouth—a self-soothing technique Lily hadn't used for years.

"About lunch with Luc?" Evie asked, already knowing the answer.

"Yeah. What if he doesn't like me?" Lily's voice was so quiet, Evie had to strain to hear her.

Evie paused before she could say, "Of course he'll like you." She pursed her lips. "I think he will like you—that he already does. But if he doesn't, it's his loss. You're pretty amazing, even when doing dark rituals without permission. And if he doesn't like you, he can get the hell out of town."

Lily giggled, as she always did when her mother used any salty language, then sobered. "What if he only likes you? And you like him back? Then what?"

Evie pulled out onto the main road that ran by her house and glanced back at Lily. The child was hunched in a way Evie seldom saw her. Lily was a happy-go-lucky child. She was pure summer—bright and sunshiny with occasional and quick-lived storms. "Baby girl. Liliana. There is nothing in the world more important to me than you. I don't care if he was the handsomest, richest man in the universe. If he doesn't like you, then I don't like him. You and me are a package deal."

"What if he had a Spanish Villa on the Mediterranean with a bottomless wine cellar and white beaches and palm trees and sangria and men in swimming suits to feed you tomatoes and fan you?"

"Tomatoes?" Evie asked, totally confused. "Why would they feed me tomatoes?"

"That's not the point," Lily said.

"Not even then, sweetie. Not for all the tomatoes in Spain."

"Swear on the River Styx?" Lily asked.

"Swear on the River Styx," Evie answered as she pulled into the parking lot of Ambrosia. "It's just like always. You and me. I love you to the moon and back."

"I love you to Uranus and back," Lily replied, then dissolved into a pile of giggles.

"I don't know what I'm going to do with you," Evie said, turning off the car and getting out. "C'mon, Monster. Let's go have brunch."

"With my dad."

"With your dad."

Evie fixed a smile on her face, hoped Lily didn't notice it was forced, and held out her hand to her daughter, as much for her own comfort as for Lily's.

CHAPTER TEN

L ily ran ahead of Evie and into the restaurant. Apparently the pep talk had worked.

When Evie made it in, Lily was hanging back, hiding behind the hostess station.

Evie scanned the room. Luc was in a booth at the far end of the restaurant—one of the booths that had a killer view of the lake and valley. The tight orange shirt he was wearing showed every contour of his muscular arms and chest, and for a minute, Evie forgot how to breathe.

"Mama!" Lily whispered urgently. "I need to pee."

"Do you need me to go with you?"

"No. But I don't want to walk by him by myself." Lily was shuffling back and forth in her own version of her nervous-pee dance.

"I'll walk with you to the table, and then you can continue on your own. Does that sound okay?"

Lily stood up, held out her hand, and dragged her mother forward. When they got to Luc's table, Lily dropped Evie's hand and darted towards the restrooms in the back.

Evie hung her purse and jacket on the hangers on the booth and slid in and around the u-bend at the back.

A server—whose name was escaping Evie at the moment, but who at least, thankfully, wasn't Brandy, dropped off two regular menus and a kid's menu with a cup of crayons. "Coffee, Evie?" she asked.

"Yes. And a large orange juice, please."

"You got it! Cranberry or grapefruit for the kiddo today?"

"Grapefruit!" a voice yelled from the back. For a kid who couldn't hear someone telling her to pick up her dirty socks, she sure seemed to have impeccable hearing at other times.

"You heard the lady," Evie laughed.

"Thank you, Katie," Luc said, smiling.

"Anything more for you, sir?" Katie asked.

"Another coffee would be wonderful."

"You got it!" Katie bustled off, stopping at several other tables to check on the diners, refill coffee, and pick up empty glasses in need of refilling.

"So," Luc said. "How are you this morning? Did you sleep okay? I felt bad taking off the way I did, but I had questions desperately in need of answers."

Evie's breath hitched as she settled her nerves enough to register Luc's question and come up with an answer. "I slept fine. Or at least as fine as one can when sharing a small bed with your best friend who takes up ten times as much space when sleeping than she does when awake. Did you find any answers? Do you know what's happening to Viv and Bev?" *And me?* she added silently.

"Not yet. Or at least, not enough to be certain. I don't want to be wrong." Luc steepled his fingers in front of his face and met her eyes. Then he tilted his head and stared past her, brow furrowing. "Do you know who that woman behind you is? She was my server at Ambrosia when I saw you the first time, and she's been staring at us since you got here."

Evie turned around and looked straight into Brandy's eyes. Brandy waved her fingers at Evie and smirked, then dropped something on her table and walked out of the diner.

"That's Brandy, Jer's...partner." There. That sounded diplomatic.

"I remember you talking about her," Luc said. "This has to be the third or fourth time I've seen her since I got back. Is she harassing you?"

"No." Evie reconsidered. "I don't think so, anyway. She's just been...around lately. I'm sure it's mostly coincidence, although it is starting to get weird."

Luc narrowed his eyes and stared at the door Brandy'd exited through. "I'll keep an eye on her. Something feels...off."

Evie opened her mouth to argue, but before she could tell him she was fine without him, Lily burst back into the room, skidded to a stop next to the booth, and then scooted in next to Evie, dipping her head down to hide her face with her hair.

"Hi, Lily," Luc said. The smile on his face looked almost as terrified as the grimace behind Lily's hair curtain.

If it'd just been Luc freaking out, Evie would've let it go, but it wasn't. "Hey, Lily. This is Luc Morgenstern. I knew him a long time ago, and he was pretty nice then, so I imagine he'll be nice now. And he's your father."

Lily peeked out between a gap in her hair and regarded Luc. He smiled at her, and she shook her hair back in front of her face.

Katie came back to take their orders before Evie could facilitate further conversation.

"Eggs Benedict with a side of hash browns," Evie said. She was living life on the edge today, breaking free from the norm, eating outside the box.

"I'll have the biscuits and gravy, also with a side of hash browns," Luc said.

"Do you want me to order for you?" Evie said.

"No," Lily said, scorn dripping from her voice. She parted her hair with her hands and looked at Katie. "Pancakes and bacon. But not from the kid menu. I'm almost ten, and I am going to have adult pancakes." She stared defiantly at her mother, who shrugged.

Katie smiled at Lily. "No problem. Adult pancakes and bacon for you." The server walked away from the table and Lily narrowed her eyes at her mother.

"Why are you letting me order adult pancakes? Is it because of *him*?"

"Honestly, it's mostly because you keep saying 'adult pancakes' and it makes me laugh," Evie said. "But I'm not gonna argue with you today. Partially because of *him*. And partially because you're old enough to make some of your own decisions. Food decisions, for sure. Maybe not Ouija board decisions, though."

Lily looked at her father, this time without the waterfall of hair obstructing her view. "You are very handsome," she said. "I guess that's why my mom did sex with you."

"Lily!" Evie gasped, trying to keep from laughing.

"What? That's how people get pregnant. It's not like it's a surprise to anyone here."

Luc lost his battle to keep a straight face. "Your mother is also a very good-looking person. That makes you super lucky, you know. Better chance of being attractive yourself."

Lily turned her scorn on Luc. "There are way more important things than being good looking, you know. Being smart is good. And willing to learn from mistakes. And having a good sense of humor. Only shallow people think good looks are the best."

"It's really amazing when the lessons I've been trying to drill in since you were little come spilling out all at once," Evie said. "And if you know all that, then you know that I wouldn't fall for someone based on looks alone."

"And did you?" Luc asked, gaze suddenly intense enough to make Evie tingle.

"Did I what?" she asked, hating the way she sounded breathless.

"Fall for me?"

Heat flushed Evie's cheeks as she tried to figure out a way to answer that question without lying or giving away too much in front of her daughter.

"Here's breakfast!" Katie announced, saving Evie from having to come up with an answer.

Conversation returned, and after a few awkward silences, Lily managed to catch Luc up on everything she'd done or thought or experienced in the last few years around mouthfuls of adult pancakes.

When Katie dropped off the bill, Luc grabbed it before Evie could. "My treat," he said. "I've missed too many years of picking up the tab."

"And way too many years of not giving your daughter birthday presents," Lily piped up.

Luc grinned at her, then leaned forward and put his hand up to screen them from Evie's view. "Expect me to do my best to make up for all the missed birthdays and all other present-giving occasions," he whispered. "Just don't tell your mom."

🌱 🌿 🌾

AFTER SAYING GOODBYE TO LUC, Evie and Lily got back in the car.

"Mama, before we go home, can we make a stop?" Lily asked in a hesitant voice.

Evie glanced over at her daughter. Today must really be shaking her confidence. Lily was never hesitant. She was more of a "full steam ahead" kinda kid.

"Depends on where. We're not making a stop in Seattle."

Lily laughed, sounding a lot more like herself. "That would not be a stop. That'd be a road trip. No. I want to see the sinkhole."

Evie drew in a sharp breath. "I don't think that's a good idea, sweetie. It's kinda dangerous there right now. Aunt Viv's car fell in last night."

"I don't want to get close," Lily argued. "Just...maybe from the overpass? Please. It's important."

"I know I'm going to regret this." Evie started the car, but instead of heading towards home, turned right and drove out of town.

When they got to the overpass, Evie pulled over and turned off the engine. The wind nearly ripped the door out of her hand, and she grabbed a jacket from the backseat. "It's cold. Zip your coat."

Lily rolled her eyes at her mother, but did as she was told. They walked toward the bridge over the interstate. The wind carried the stench of sulphur to them, and Evie pulled her shirt up over her nose.

The closer they got, the less the wind tried to knock them off their feet. Lily's hand slipped into Evie's, and Evie tried not to react. It wasn't often that Lily initiated hand holding anymore—certainly not in public. Evie squeezed lightly.

At the top of the small arch over the freeway, Lily stopped. They weren't quite over the sinkhole, but Evie judged they were close enough.

"It's beautiful," Lily breathed.

Evie looked down at her daughter. "Beautiful?" She turned her full attention to the fiery sinkhole below them.

The symbol glowed and appeared to be pulsing. It wasn't what she'd normally call beautiful, but now that she was staring directly at it, she could see what her daughter was talking about. It was alluring. She took a step forward.

"Mama!" Lily said, grabbing her hand again. "Don't get closer. It's hungry. Beautiful and hungry. Like a shark."

Evie shook her head and the spell dissipated.

"We should go, Lily," she whispered.

"Yeah. You're not strong enough to resist. That's probably why Aunt Viv's car fell in. She got too close and got caught in the tractor beam."

"What are you talking about?" Evie pulled her gaze away from the pulsing, glowing symbol in the ground and looked at Lily.

Lily shrugged. "I don't know how else to describe it. It's hungry, but it doesn't want me, so I don't need to get closer. But I think it wants you—just a little. And I bet it super wanted Aunt Viv because she's new, and it wants something new."

"It?" Evie asked, turning her back on the sinkhole and starting back toward the car.

"Hell," Lily said matter-of-factly, shedding her coat and climbing into her booster seat. "I already belong because of my dad. And you kinda belong, because of him. But Aunt Viv doesn't. At least not yet."

🌱 🌷 🌾

EVIE SAT in her car in the driveway of her house, staring at the lake that peeked around the corner. Lily hadn't said anything else about Hell having claimed her or Evie. Instead, she'd chatted about her birthday party, bemoaned the fact that Evie wouldn't let her have a fourth-grade sleepover party until it was reliably warmer and all the kids could camp out in the backyard, and contemplated how many cakes she actually deserved—ten, one for each year—versus how many Evie had agreed to provide—one.

Lily had dashed away the second Evie'd turned the car off, probably to try to sweet talk her grandparents into more cakes.

And Evie sat. She glanced down at her phone. She knew she should ring Luc and tell him what'd happened. What Lily had said. But she didn't. And if she was honest with herself, it was because she was afraid. Afraid to get confirmation that her daughter had been already marked for hell. That she and Viv and Bev might be marked as well. Afraid to find out what that meant.

She'd never been religious, but she'd never *not* been religious, either. It just wasn't a part of her life, and if you'd asked her point blank what she thought happened after death, she would've laughed, made a joke about worm food, and moved on with her life. Heaven and hell and souls were not ever anything she'd considered.

But if there was a hell, did that mean there was a heaven? If there are demons, are there angels? Is there a god? And is he the old dude with a beard and white robes, or more of a Chuck type?

She banged her head lightly against the steering wheel. She hadn't planned to have a theological crisis this year. She was going to deal with having a ten-year-old, consider dating more, possibly sell the house for something smaller and more practical for two people. Not welcome Luc back into her town, if not her life. And definitely not weather the effects of a hellmouth opening up in town.

"Where's Buffy when you need her?" Evie asked her car.

Her cell rang, and she jumped, dropping her phone between the seat and the console.

"Dammit," she muttered as she tried to fish her phone back out.

It'd stopped ringing by the time she grabbed ahold of it but started up again almost immediately.

Evie pushed the button to answer without more than a cursory glance at the caller ID. "Hello?" She knew she sounded curt and winced at her own rudeness. "This is Evie," she said in a much pleasanter tone.

"Evie, it's Luc. What happened?"

"What do you mean?" No way could he know about her crisis of faith. Or lack thereof.

"Did you go to the mark?" he asked, urgency vibrating his voice.

Evie hesitated. She wasn't sure why she didn't want to admit what she'd done to Luc, but the urge to lie was strong. "Yes," she said after a too-long pause. "Lily wanted to see it. We didn't get close, or anything. Just looked from the bridge."

"That was stupid," Luc said bluntly.

Evie's hackles rose, and for the first time since Luc had walked back into her life, she didn't feel confused at all about how she was feeling. "You don't get an opinion on my parenting decisions, Luc. You don't get to call me stupid. And you especially don't get to judge me when you won't give me enough information to make informed decisions. Unless you're ready to tell me what you know—and what you suspect—then fuck off."

"I'll be there in twenty minutes. Try not to put our daughter in danger between now and then."

Before Evie could yell at him, he hung up. Her phone vibrated with a text message. She glanced at the screen. It was from Viv. The preview read *Be careful. I have a really bad feeling. Stay away from L...* The rest of the message was hidden. Evie shoved her phone into her pocket and got out of the car. She didn't need Viv to tell her spending time with Luc was dangerous—at least where her heart was concerned.

"This is why I'm single," Evie said, getting out of the car and glaring at nothing in particular. "Men, whether human or demon, are infuriating."

CHAPTER ELEVEN

J ames and Hope were in full-on party preparation mode when Evie made her way back into the house.

"Mom, it's just a small gathering. There's no need to do all this." Evie gestured to the vases of cut flowers—lilies, mostly —fine china that'd been pulled out of storage that Evie hadn't even known was still here, and cloth napkins James was folding into swans.

"Pshaw. She's our only granddaughter, and she only turns ten once. Let me have a little fun." Hope opened the oven and pulled out two cake pans.

"Are you making cake? Why? I bought a cake from her favorite bakery already."

"I know, dear. But Lily said she wanted a second cake—for variety. And she told me you'd given her full control over all her food choices." Hope smiled serenely at her daughter, but there was a twinkle in her eyes.

"I just told her that this morning; there's no way these cakes have anything to do with letting her order 'adult pancakes.' You are enabling her poor dessert decision making." Evie set down her car keys and purse and washed her hands.

James chuckled. "She's definitely got a bit of the devil in her," he said.

Evie froze, hand in the knife drawer. She recovered quickly, but not before her father noticed.

"I'm sorry, Pumpkin," he said. "I didn't mean…"

"I know. And it's fine. It's true literally and figuratively. I don't know why it freaked me out so much." Evie grabbed the utility knife she'd been after and pulled a cutting board out of the cupboard.

"Because it's still new information. And not only new, but weird," Hope said, placing the cake layers on wire racks to cool. "Having Luc return is already a lot to take in, but having to deal with all the other-world implications is something else altogether."

Evie opened the fridge to grab the fresh veggies she'd bought to make veggie trays. She wasn't sure why she was bothering; Lily only ate cauliflower, and she'd never seen Kevin or Shelby eat a vegetable at all. But hope springs eternal, and it wasn't a veggie tray without carrots and celery and snow peas.

"Argh! Where's the cauliflower?" Evie opened the fridge doors even wider and looked around.

"Oops," Hope said. "I didn't realize you were saving it. I finished it off last night."

"You ate an entire head of cauliflower?" Evie asked. "That is…a lot."

"I was hungry, and cauliflower is amazing."

Evie shook her head. "It's fine. I'll run to the store and grab some. I wish I'd bought two, though." Her breath hitched a bit, like she'd *almost* gotten winded. The sudden drop in energy was something she'd been meaning to talk to her doctor about. Every once in a while, she'd had a stutter, a moment when her heart and respiration skipped a beat. She was sure it was nothing, but not as sure as she would've been twenty years ago.

But now, paired with the words she'd just spoken, she wondered if it was something else. She opened the fridge again. Right there, front and center, was a huge head of cauliflower—bigger than anything she'd ever bought at the local grocery store.

"Never mind!" she called. "Guess I bought two after all." She pulled the wish-veg out and wondered if there were any ill effects from eating magic food. Although, that ship had probably sailed a few months ago when she'd eaten a platter of wish nachos when Lily was spending the night at Shelby's house.

Evie plunked the cauliflower down on the cutting board and picked up her knife.

"That wasn't in there before," Hope said. "I would've seen it."

"Lots of stuff gets shoved to the back," Evie countered.

"You are the worst liar. Always have been." James put the finishing touch on the twelfth swan and stood up to examine the rogue vegetable.

"Fine. I made it appear with magic, then," Evie said.

"What kind of magic is that?" Hope asked. She'd moved from cakes to large, round pizza pan lined with what looked almost like a pale pizza dough.

"Are you making fruit pizza?" Evie asked. "Now you're being ridiculous. There is no reason whatsoever to have three desserts."

The time on the second oven dinged, and Hope smiled unrepentantly as she opened it and pulled out two baking sheets with large chocolate chip cookies on them. "Four desserts. But you didn't answer the question."

"I don't have any answers, but the man who might should be here any minute."

The doorbell rang.

"Speak of the devil," Evie sighed.

"I'll get the door," James said. "You've got your hands full, and holding a knife is a good look for you when Luc enters the kitchen."

"Thanks, Dad," Evie said.

James winked and left the room.

"Where's Lily?" Evie asked.

"Playing with her invisible dog in the backyard," Hope said. "She'll have to have a talk with her about how to manifest properly if she doesn't want to scare anyone."

Evie stared at her mother for a moment, then let it go. Some things were just too much, even in this time of everything being too much.

🌱 🌿 🌾

JAMES WAS PUSHING the canoe out alongside the dock, and Hope was grabbing lifejackets from the garage and dusting them off. Lily was running back and forth between her grandparents, trying to hurry things along.

"Is this what it's like all the time?" Luc asked. He'd been tasked with peeling carrots and monitoring the oven, which had the bonus effect of completely distracting him from castigating Evie for taking Lily to look at the hellmouth.

"How do you mean?" Evie asked, resolutely keeping her eyes on her pile of veggies and not looking at Luc. Like not at all.

Luc waved the vegetable peeler around, encompassing the entire kitchen. "This. Stuff baking in the oven, doing kitchen work, watching your kid have fun outside."

"No. Not always. Although there's a lot more kitchen stuff than I'd ever imagined when I was younger. And a lot more watching her, trying to freeze the moments where everything feels perfect so I can look back on them whenever I'm sad or lonely."

"I've missed so much," Luc said. "I wish…"

"Don't you start making wishes," Evie interrupted. "Who knows where we'll end up."

"Nothing untoward will happen," Luc said. "I can control the powers of hell."

"Control would be nice," Evie muttered. "Although I guess the cauliflower saved me a trip."

"It'll come with time and practice. I can teach you. Teach all of you."

"All of us what?" Evie pointed her knife at Luc. "No more 'I don't want to be wrong' crap. Tell me what you know. Or at least what you suspect."

Luc looked down at the sink and peeled two carrots before

speaking again. "When Lily did her demon summoning ritual or her letter to Santa or whatever it was, she asked for her dad, right?"

A sinkhole—smaller cousin of the one outside of town—was forming in Evie's stomach. "Yes..."

"So, Hell recognized her power and delivered her dad. What else did she ask for?"

"She wanted me to see Sprinkles—"

"Who?" Luc tilted his head.

"Her dog. Turns out that she'd been misgendered. Her full name is Princess Surma, of the Cerberina Surmas, but she prefers to be called Sprinkles. Apparently it's more dignified."

"Sprinkles is the dignified choice?"

"That's what I've been told. It's entirely possible dignified is one of those words Lily doesn't fully understand yet. She has a pretty amazing vocabulary, but she misses the mark occasionally."

"If Sprinkles is her name, then that's what we'll call her. Hell-hounds are usually pretty good at conveying their true names to their owners."

Evie crossed her fingers under the table that the conversation had been derailed enough to keep Luc from asking for the third item on Lily's wish list.

"Did Lily ask for anything else?"

"Nothing important," Evie replied. She focused all her attention on the celery sticks in front of her.

"Ah, so there was something else. You might not regard it as important, but I really should know. Lily's powers are nascent and uncontrollable. Kinda like how a baby rattlesnake can kill more easily than an adult. Not because it's more venomous, but because it doesn't have the control and releases all the venom in one go."

"She asked for me to be happy," Evie mumbled, running her words together.

"How could you say that's unimportant?" Luc demanded. "By my calculations, that was the most important thing she asked for. Where was it on her list?"

"Third of three."

"Best for last. Tell me that's not how she orders all things."

Evie couldn't. She grabbed the peeled carrots from Luc to finish the veggie tray. The timer dinged, and while Luc was preoccupied with cookies, Evie grabbed her coffee and made her escape.

EVIE STOOD at the end of the dock watching her parents canoe Lily around the lake. The girl was squealing in delight. She wasn't often allowed on the lake. There was a swimming beach on the other side, but the lake had hidden depths, patches of icy water caused by glacial runoff that could shock the breath from a swimmer, and seaweed that seemed to have a mind of its own, wrapping around legs and snaring them before pulling them under.

Almost every summer, someone died. Usually tourists who ignored the caution signs and left the swimming area to prove that they were better/cooler/stronger than the town's residents who respected the lake and didn't tempt fate. The year before Lily was born, three teenagers, in the middle of an afternoon of surreptitious drinking, had dared each other to swim across the lake and back. Someone else on the beach had called 911—there was a rescue boat for a reason—but it'd been too late. The other people on the beach had had to watch as the boys disappeared. One minute they were there. The next gone.

They dredged the lake—they always did—but didn't find the bodies. The lake never gave anyone back.

Evie didn't swim in the lake at all. It creeped her out to swim in a mass grave. She went out in the canoe with Lily from time to time, but rarely and only when Lily had begged while Evie was having a moment of weakness.

Luc walked up and joined her on the dock, brushing her arm as he did so. Something stirred deep in her abdomen, shaking loose desires she'd long since suppressed. Her right arm was hot, and that heat spread throughout her body, eliminating the goosebumps that'd been trying to overtake her body with a little help from the breeze kicking from the lake.

"Wanna go skinny dipping later?" Luc asked.

That eliminated every ounce of desire that'd been bubbling up. "Not for a million dollars and a normal life," she said, revulsion dripping from her voice. She shuddered.

He leaned in so close she could feel his breath on her ear when he spoke. "I'd keep you safe."

"Not the point. There is nothing you could say that would induce me to hop into a watery grave."

Luc straightened.

Evie dared a glance at him. His brow furrowed, and his gaze moved from her to the lake. "Watery grave?" He crossed his arms and stepped forward to the end of the dock. He glanced back at her over his left shoulder. "Are you talking about those boys who died that summer?"

"And every summer," Evie said. "For as long as I can remember. For as long as Mom and Dad can remember."

"How many?" he demanded.

Evie stared at him. He'd straightened his stance, and his entire body was almost vibrating.

"How many?"

"I don't know," Evie admitted. "But one or two every summer for at least sixty years. Three was an anomaly. There's a reason locals seldom set foot in the lake and never swim past the barriers."

"Somewhere between sixty and one hundred twenty deaths, minimum? And no one thinks it's weird?" Luc raised his eyebrows and frowned at her.

"It's not weird." Evie floundered for an explanation. "It just...is. The lake is dangerous, and tourists are stupid. The last time a local drowned was before I was born."

Luc turned his attention back to Eden Lake.

"I guess it's a little shocking if you didn't grow up here."

"Only in summer?" The tension hadn't yet left Luc's body, and his head moved slightly from side to side as he scanned the area of the large glacial lake.

"Who'd swim any other time?" Evie asked. "It's frozen from October to early March, and wicked cold until late June. Some out-of-town folks tried to get the town to agree to host a mid-September extreme triathlon; the swim would be laps around the lake, but there was no way we'd risk it. One or two a year is enough. Don't want the lake to get greedy."

Luc spun all the way around and stared. "Greedy? Are you saying the lake is sentient?"

Evie laughed. "Of course not, Luc. But sometimes people anthropomorphize things. Lily does it all the time when her laptop doesn't do precisely what she wants when she wants it to. It's almost always user error. Just like with the lost swimmers."

Luc exhaled, shrugged his shoulders up around his ears, then rolled them back. His brow unfurrowed as he tilted his head from side to side. Another deep breath, and then Evie watched the tension cascade off him like a stress waterfall.

"I wish I could do that," she muttered, then closed her eyes and gritted her teeth. "Ugh. I have got to eliminate the 'W' word from my vocabulary. Although this time, it is an actual legit wish." She opened her eyes and grinned wryly at Luc. Her phone alarm went off, reminding her to pick Lily's cake up from the bakery, not that it was needed at this point. Viv's text warning her about Luc was still on the notification screen. Evie opened her messages to read the full message and let Viv know she'd failed to heed her advice. *Be careful. I have a really bad feeling. Stay away from Lake Eden today.*

Evie whipped around and stared out at her parents and her daughter. Lily looked back at Evie and Luc standing on the dock and waved. Then she stood up and yelled, "Sprinkles!"

Evie looked behind her but didn't see anything. She turned back around just in time to see Lily wobble and tip over the side of the boat.

"Lily!" she screamed.

Lily bobbed in the water, her life jacket keeping her buoyant.

James reached out to his granddaughter to catch her hand even before Evie finished her scream. Lily grabbed at it but missed. Then she disappeared under the water and Evie's heart stopped. A second later, Lily's lifejacket floated to the surface, but there was no sign of her daughter.

Evie watched in horror as her dad kicked off his shoes and dove into the water. Evie followed suit, removing her shoes and jacket and running to the edge of the dock. Before she could dive in, she heard thundering footsteps behind her. Something rushed by, nearly bowling her over.

A huge splash soaked her and created concentric rings that flowed outward. Luc grabbed her, wrapping his arms around her, and prevented her from jumping in.

"Let me go!" she screamed. "Lily!" Evie scanned the lake, but the only thing visible was the canoe with her mother staring in horror at the place where James and Lily had gone under.

"Do something," Evie raged, straining against Luc's grasp. "Do something or let me go so I can."

"Wait. Watch." Luc's voice was calm and even.

"Don't you show up here pretending you want to play house and then make me watch our child die," Evie screamed. "You might not have been here for the first ten years of her life, but don't act like the heartless demon you say you are."

"Evie, look. Lily is going to be fine. Your dad, too. Watch."

This time, Evie couldn't ignore the command in his voice. She stopped fighting him and looked—really looked—at the lake.

Whatever had made the splash was moving so quickly it created a wake and was nearly to the canoe. The movement stopped long enough for Evie to start panicking again, then Lily's head broke the surface. Hope reached down and hauled her granddaughter into the canoe. Another splash, another breathless moment, and then James appeared. Hope couldn't get him in the boat.

"Luc, can you help?" Evie asked, unable to take her eyes off her family.

"I'm not needed," he said.

James started towards shore, looking for all the world like he was levitating a couple inches above the water. When he was close enough to the dock, Evie and Luc hauled him up. Moments later, the canoe started speeding to shore, seemingly under its own power. Evie leaned over to take the rope her mother tossed her and secured the boat to the dock. Hope lifted the unconscious Lily up and Evie grabbed her, cradling the child who was almost as big as her in her arms.

"Is she…" Evie couldn't finish the sentence.

Hope climbed out of the canoe. "She's still breathing, although how, I don't know." Evie recognized Hope's flat, calm voice—her mother's typical emergency response. As soon as everyone was safe and well, Hope would disappear to fall apart in private.

"James is ok, too," Luc confirmed. "Just unconscious."

"I'll call 911," Hope said. "They'll need emergency attention."

There was a noise on shore, but nothing was there. Wet footsteps appeared on the dock, moving silently closer. Lily stared at the space above the footsteps that halted next to Lily.

"Sprinkles?" The ridiculous feeling she had talking to an invisible dog was perfectly balanced with the knowledge that Lily's "imaginary" friend had just saved two lives. A soft chuffing near her right hand startled her, and she jumped back a bit. Warm breath heated her hand, and she felt it suddenly forced upwards by a large, hard, furry head. Evie scratched hesitantly. The smell of wet dog wafted upwards, and she wrinkled her nose in defense.

She looked down at her hand, willing herself to see the impossible. *Wishing* she could see what Lily saw. A vague theory she'd heard when she was younger—that adults couldn't see the magic because they grew up and stopped believing—floated through her mind. It was hard to ignore the evidence in front of her, even if she couldn't see it with her own eyes.

The air shimmered, then went from translucent to opaque in the blink of an eye. One of Sprinkles's heads was underneath Evie's hand, the second was giving an enthusiastic tongue bath to Lily, bringing color and life back into her daughter's corpse-like body, and the third was giving the same treatment to James.

Lily's eyes opened and her nose wrinkled, making her look like a miniature replica of her mother for a moment. "Ew. Sprinkles. You have very bad breath."

Evie collapsed in relief, the tears she'd been holding back racking her body. When she finally stopped crying, Lily was on her knees patting her mother on the shoulder, Luc was helping James sit up, and Hope and Sprinkles were nowhere to be seen.

CHAPTER TWELVE

April tenth dawned clear and bright. There was enough chill in the air to warrant a fleece sweater to begin party setup, but even this early, there was the promise of a warm afternoon.

Evie wiped down the large outdoor table and covered it with a black tablecloth with tiny, pink polka dots adorning it. She shook her head looking at it, a smile creeping across her lips. She tried not to think about the events of the day before. She still had to fight down panic at the memory of her Lily slipping below the surface of the water.

"Everything's fine," she said to herself as she anchored the tablecloth with the skull-shaped tablecloth clamps Lily had found on Amazon. "It's okay." She took a deep breath, closed her eyes, and concentrated on the realness of her feet touching the earth. She wasn't going to let yesterday's fear ruin today.

Evie opened her eyes again and stared at the lake. Although she'd always felt a great deal of cautious respect for the body of water she'd grown up next to, she'd never really attributed to it the malevolent hunger she'd felt yesterday, no matter what she'd said to Luc about anthropomorphism. Today, it was still, not even a ripple marring the smooth as glass surface.

Evie marched down to the water, kicked off her shoes, and waded in until the water touched the hemline of her calf-length skirt.

She stared out towards the middle of the lake, deceptively placid and hiding whatever evil she could feel lurking beneath the surface.

"Don't ever touch my family again," she said. "I don't know what you are or what you want, but if ever try to take my daughter again, I will find out and I will end you."

The formerly still water churned. Waves broke against her legs, soaking the bottom of her skirt. She felt something reach her. It didn't grab her—it felt more like...tasting. Measuring. Evaluating.

The waves stopped as suddenly as they'd started, and the lake returned to its former placidity.

Evie stayed in the water for another minute for emphasis, then turned and walked back up to the house. She didn't know what she'd done, but it felt like something significant had happened. A deal had been struck, and Lily would be safe. With equal certainty, though, she knew there would be a price to pay. Not today. But whatever presence was in the lake would collect eventually, and sooner than she'd like.

The kitchen, which had been peaceful and empty just thirty minutes before, was now bustling—a cacophony of noise and activity assaulting Evie's ears. James was frying bacon and flipping pancakes, Lily was snitching bacon from the growing pile whenever James wasn't looking and blaming the dog, and Hope was frosting one of the cakes.

"That's a lot of bacon, Dad," Evie said, grabbing a strip and popping it in her mouth while her father threatened her with the tongs Lily had dubbed "bacon pliers" when she was six.

"Shelby and Bev called to say they're on their way over, and my guess is Kevin will show up, too. Your young man said he'd come early to finish setting up as well. That's eight people just for breakfast."

"That's two-thirds of the party guests," Evie said. "Might as well call Viv, too. Guess it's an all-day party."

Lily looked smug. "I told you so, Mom. I said, let's have an all-day party. Should've listened to me. I'm ten now."

Evie smiled at her daughter. "You are. Happy birthday, monster. I love you so much."

Tears threatened to choke her again, and she smiled through the sudden blur in her vision. To disguise the panic, only partially alleviated by whatever deal she'd made with the lake, she held her arms wide. "I hope you're not too old for mom hugs."

Lily ran forward and nearly knocked Evie over. "Never too old for mom hugs," she said, squeezing her mother tightly. Then she whispered, so quietly that Evie doubted anyone else could hear, "The lake is scared, Mom. Something's happening, and it's getting ready."

"Ready for what?" Evie asked, rocking back on her heels and looking into her daughter's eyes.

"What?" Lily asked, wrinkling her nose. "Ready for my party, of course." She snagged another piece of bacon and ran outside, whistling for Sprinkles.

🌱 🌿 🌾

EVERYONE WHO'D BEEN INVITED, with the exception of Viv's mom, who was never anything but unfashionably late, had shown up by ten—in time to devour the endless supply of pancakes and bacon James was producing.

The adults had helped clean up and get the table ready for the birthday feast while the kids and Sprinkles—whose three heads were intermittently visible, at least to Evie—disappeared into the woods, presumably to share secrets and commune with the old gods, or whatever it was kids these days did when out of earshot of grown-ups.

By mid-afternoon, everything was set up, including all two cakes, the fruit pizza, and the snack trays.

Evie had bustled around, not staying still long enough for anyone to strike up a conversation with her, and assiduously avoiding Luc. She was angry—so angry—still. Even though he'd been right and everything had turned out okay, she was furious that he'd stopped her and had made zero effort to rescue either Lily or her dad. He couldn't have known Sprinkles would get there in time, that the dog would be able to save them both.

She might have to let him into Lily's life—particularly if he made a legal claim—but she didn't have to let him into her heart. No matter how hot he was. Or how he was doing the dishes—which was the single sexiest thing a man could do in a room full of people. Or how he'd agreed to play the part of Sprinkles in Lily's dramatic reenactment of her near drowning. And the way Luc looked at Evie, like he was wishing away everyone else and her clothes on the ground... It was heady to be desired.

A towel flicked Evie's elbow, and she jerked back into herself.

"Stop staring at your eye candy and start getting the burger accoutrements ready," Bev said.

"He's not mine. And he's not eye candy."

Bev tipped her head to one side and joined Evie in admiring Luc's backside. "Yeah, that man isn't candy, he's the whole Devil's Food cake."

Evie flinched.

Bev rolled her eyes. "Still dealing with the whole 'my baby daddy has bat wings' thing?"

"Of course I'm still dealing with it," Evie said under her breath. "He has wings. And is a demon. It's not like I'm trying to get over the fact that he irons his socks or has a yellow cartoon bird tattooed on his hip or..." Evie gave up on trying to come up with additional examples of bad but overlookable habits.

"So, you've seen his naked hips lately?" Bev asked, lips pursed.

Evie huffed out a breath. "No. I haven't. But..."

"So he could, then. You don't know what kind of things he's gone through in the last ten years. After all, you're sporting a tramp stamp now."

"Whatever, Bev." Evie tore her eyes from Luc and turned to face her best friend. "You know what I mean, though, right?"

"I do. His 'thing,' and we all have 'things,' isn't the kind of weird we expect. His weird is weird."

"Somehow that all made sense." Evie grabbed the basket of elaborately folded cloth napkins.

"At least if it turns out his family is insufferable, they all live really far away, right?" Bev asked, grabbing a stack of plates.

"I guess... But I don't think he'll stay. He's absolutely a Disneyland Dad type." When Bev looked at her quizzically, Evie added, "You know, fun dad. Shows up for one weekend a month or a couple weeks in the summer with gifts and no bedtimes and junk food, then leaves before he has to see deal with the fallout of an overtired kid resentful of vegetables."

"I don't think he's that kind of guy. Would Disneyland Dad drag your friends out of a pit if they needed help?" Bev set the plates on the table.

Viv came over with a basket of silverware. "I've finally been released from servitude to your mother," she said. "What'd I miss?"

"Evie is worried that Luc will be a weekend fun dad and not a good dad," Bev said.

"Not worried. Certain. And, to your point, Bev, that kind of person would absolutely go out of his way to help my friends if he thought it would weaken my resolve. I think it's called love bombing."

Viv paused and walked around the table to where Evie was aggressively slamming linen swans on the table and put her arm around her friend. "He's not Jeremy. Don't let what Jer did to you destroy every last chance of happiness. I'm not going to push you into Luc's arms, but don't let fear be the reason you don't take a chance. I know you can't stop thinking about what happened in the past, but you can't let Jer hang out in your head cockblocking every relationship you try to get in."

"I don't think that's the right term for this situation," Bev said. "I believe she's running clitorference on herself. There are valid reasons to keep Luc at arm's length but equating him to Jer is not one of them."

Evie and Viv stared at Bev, eyes wide and heads tilted to the left with identical expressions of shock and confusion.

"Beverly Hill," Hope said, hand over her mouth. "What kind of language is that?"

"Adult language. Because we are all adults. Don't pretend you're shocked. We used to spy on your book clubs, and I know you could make a sailor blush," Bev retorted.

Hope laughed and set down the veggie tray she'd brought out. "Fair enough. I'll leave you ladies to it, then."

The three women watched Hope walk away, then turned back to the subject at hand.

"I refuse to use that kind of language," Viv said primly, a broad wink negating her sudden attack of prudishness. "But the point stands. Don't get in your own way."

Evie straightened out the napkin swans she'd smooshed during her fowl temper. "Fine. I'll think about it."

"Don't think too long," Bev warned. "No matter what you decide, you need to talk to him and figure out how to navigate co-parenting."

"And if you want more, tell him. Take a chance. Put yourself out there. I know confident Evie is in there somewhere. Remember how you felt the summer you met Luc, and channel that self-esteem," Viv said, then shook imaginary pompoms. "Gooooooo Evie!"

Evie sighed. "I just wish—"

"No!" Bev and Viv yelled in unison.

"Fine. It'd be nice, though, to have an uncomplicated relationship."

"Would it, though?" Viv asked, finishing laying out the silverware. "When have any of us had that?"

"We laugh because otherwise we'd cry," Bev said. "Three women, all in their forties, and all of us single."

"Viv's not single," Evie said.

"I am now," Viv said, not making eye contact with either of her friends.

"What?" Bev exclaimed. "What happened to Scottie? How could you keep this from me?"

Viv said, shrugging nonchalantly, "She wanted to 'take things to the next level' and get a place together. No way am I tying myself to one person for the rest of my life. I'm really more of a tapas person. I prefer a lot of small bites rather than the commitment of a Claimjumper over-the-top serving. Just as much food, but a lot more variety."

"You've gone from wanting to leave early for a date with Scottie to breaking up because she's shopping for monogrammed towels inside of three days?" Evie asked, narrowing her eyes at her friend.

"You know women," Viv said, waving her hand dismissively. "Always moving too fast."

"Did you end things because she was texting too much?" Bev asked.

"No. Of course not. That would be ridiculous." Viv glared at her friend. "She just wouldn't stop calling. I don't think three dates in four weeks warrants daily phone calls."

Children erupted from the woods like a forest tsunami.

"Is it time?" Lily yelled. "Is he here?"

Evie shot a sharp look at Viv. "Don't think these children will get you out of this discussion. We will be revisiting your commitment issues." She turned her attention to her daughter. "Is who here, monster?"

"Papa Abe! He promised he'd come to the party."

"Who is Papa Abe?" A sick feeling twisted Evie's stomach. Had Lily been spending time with strange men? How had she failed so completely as a mother?

Luc walked over to Lily and crouched in front of her. "Does Papa Abe have horns growing out of his head?"

Lily nodded enthusiastically. "He promised he'd come when he gave me Sprinkles as an early birthday present."

"Who's Papa Abe?" Evie demanded.

"My father," Luc said. "This is going to be a disaster."

CHAPTER THIRTEEN

E vie poured herself a glass of lemonade—her wish had apparently been interpreted as a never-ending supply of fresh, delicious lemonade would always be available—and watched the organized chaos in the backyard. The kids were running back and forth between the deck and the woods. Usually, they'd be skirting the edges of their adults' sanity by pretending to jump off the end of the dock, but Lily's close call yesterday had scared them off—at least for today.

"Evelyn Addams?" a tentative voice asked.

Evie turned around and stared at the diminutive woman with tan skin, black curly hair, and a prominent nose. She opened her mouth to answer but blanked on a name. "Call me Evie," she said to buy time to come up with a name.

"Aurielle Jones," the woman said, holding out her hand. "Kevin's… mother. Please call me Elle."

Evie filed the woman's hesitance at naming herself Kevin's mom to examine later. She shook Elle's hand. This was the first time she'd ever seen the woman outside of the school their kids had attended since kindergarten.

"Do you want me to go?" Elle asked, worrying at her lip. "It's only Kevin said I could come."

Evie's instincts—honed from twenty years of bartending—kicked in. "No! Of course not. Please stay. I'm sorry if I was rude... I just wasn't expecting you. Come, sit down, and let me get you a drink. The kids are running around down near the lake right now, and there's food everywhere." Evie smiled brightly and cut herself off before the babbling got out of hand.

"I'd like that," Elle said. "Thank you. And did you say the kids were near the lake?" Elle let Evie escort her to the drinks table and accepted a large lemonade.

"They are, but they're being safe. They know better than to set foot in the lake," Evie hastened to reassure Kevin's mother.

"I'm not worried." Elle shrugged and looked out over the lake. "There's no one safer to have near the lake than Kevin."

Evie tilted her head and regarded the shorter woman. "Kevin has always been good about lake safety..." Something about Elle's wording didn't make sense.

Before Elle could reply, though, her father walked up brandishing a large meat fork. He was on grill-duty and was wearing a giant chef's hat and white apron and looking way too cheerful about everything. Not much ever ruffled James's feathers—decades of life balancing between his free-spirited wife and more cautious daughter had smoothed any edges he might've had.

"Hi! I'm James, the birthday girl's grandfather. You're Kevin's mom, right?" He grinned at the women.

After a beat, Elle responded, "Yes. I am. Pleased to meet you."

"I'd love to meat you!" James beamed. "Burger? Hotdog? Veggie burger? Let me hook you up with the good stuff."

Elle let herself be steered away by James, and after making sure that her guest was okay, Evie resumed her scan of the party.

Hope, Bev, Viv, and Gwen were sitting at the far end of the table sharing a bottle of Cairdeas chardonnay. Viv had briefly dated one of the winemakers there, and once they'd parted—on the best of terms, as Viv ended most of her relationships—Charlie had kept Viv in chardonnay and syrah and hosted the women for their annual girls' wine weekends, often joining them for gossip and a glass of wine or three.

Viv and her mother were sitting as far apart as possible, but no one looked about to strangle anyone else, so all was good.

And Luc... Where was Luc?

Evie scanned the backyard but didn't see her daughter's father. She narrowed her eyes. Her feelings might be all over the place still, but that didn't mean she didn't want to keep an eye on him. Especially after the "Papa Abe" bombshell Lily dropped.

Finally, she sighted him. He was down by the lake, pacing in the shadow of the big pine trees that leaned over the water, and gesticulating wildly. Evie walked towards him. She was still angry with him and was looking forward to giving him a piece of her mind for ignoring their daughter at her tenth birthday party. Sure, he hadn't known about his daughter until a few days ago, but he chose to show up, and now he was choosing to be absent. Evie's anger grew with each step, and she clenched her fists. When she realized what she was doing, she forced herself to relax. She might be furious, but she would never let it control her.

As she got closer, she could hear his side of the conversation, and he did not sound happy. She slowed down, telling herself it was less eavesdropping and more giving him space and time to wrap up his conversation before she interrupted him to tell him off.

"There is nothing you could say that would excuse not telling me. I missed ten years. Eleven, if you count the months Evie was pregnant. Years I could've been here, supporting them. And now you want to waltz into their lives with extravagant gifts and even bigger promises, and for what?"

A pause stretched out long enough for Evie to start moving again.

"Are you insane?" Luc said. He was no longer yelling. Instead, his voice had dropped to a deadly quiet, sending chills over Evie's body.

She froze in place.

"You cannot do that. I don't care what precedent is. You lost any leverage over Evie's and Lily's lives when you ignored their existence for the last decade. Do not screw this up for me, Father." Luc punched a finger at the phone, presumably ending the call, then hurled it at a stand of young pine trees. It shattered against the bark, pieces of glass and plastic scattering around.

Evie's lips thinned. A man with a temper like that was never a good sign, even without the littering. They start with destroying their own possessions, move on to yours, and then to you. She'd been right to keep her distance. She turned to head back to the house when a movement out of the corner of her eye caught her attention. She watched, jaw dropping, as the shattered smartphone flew back into Luc's hand, repairing itself as it approached.

Luc's shoulders lowered, and he rolled them a couple times while Evie watched. She knew. She *knew*. But even after the wings and the weird tattoos and the hellmouth and Sprinkles, it still felt like a dream. Not quite a nightmare, but not necessarily something she wanted to continue, either.

Luc turned around before Evie could make up her mind whether or not she wanted to confront him or flee and pretend she hadn't heard a thing.

"Evie." His voice was flat.

She winced.

"I'm sorry," he said, raking his hand through his hair. "How much did you hear?"

"Just the end before you threw your magic phone," Evie admitted. "That was your dad?"

"Yeah. Apparently he's been keeping an eye on Lily this entire time. He knew about her and didn't tell me. Ten years of her life I'll never get back."

"Did he say why? Or how? Has he been watching us?" Evie shuddered.

"I don't know." Frustration grated through Luc's voice, and he dropped his head in his hands and massaged his temples. "He's going to—"

Movement at the edge of the trees caught Evie's eye. A figure stepped further back into the shadows as Evie looked up. "There's someone back there," she said, slicing off whatever Luc had been about to say. Before she could tentatively identify the lurker as Brandy, a scream rent the air.

Evie sprinted up the incline towards the house, Luc hot on her heels. Adrenaline coursed through her body, joining up with the adrenaline left over from yesterday and pushing her faster.

She skidded to a stop, red-faced and gasping, in front of the deck. The conversations stopped and everyone turned to stare at Evie and Luc, who jogged up behind her, unfairly breathing evenly and not sweating at all.

"I heard a scream?" The tentativeness in her voice turned her statement into a question.

"Sorry, Mama," Lily said. "That was me. I didn't mean to scare you."

"She was doing a very realistic dramatic reenactment of the events of yesterday. This time she was playing the part of the worried mother while Shelby slipped below the waves," Bev explained.

"That's what I sounded like?" Evie put her hands on her hips and stared at her daughter.

Lily grinned. "Probably. I was under the water and couldn't hear you…only the monster." She clapped her hands and smoke flew up into the air. A figure emerged from the blue-gray smoke, looking like a mixture between the Loch Ness monster and a Kraken. A flash of light from the edge of the lawn made Evie look away from Lily's monster. There was definitely someone there. Gwen jumped up and looked around wildly, pointed at Evie and said, "I knew she was one of them," then headed towards the house without another word.

No one else reacted with anything but wonder. Apparently illusions were well within the wheelhouse of everyone's expectations for a half-demon child with a well-developed sense of showmanship and a love of being the center of attention.

Evie stared at her daughter, who was smugly regarding her creation. A movement under the table caught Evie's attention, and a black nose poked out into Lily's waiting hand, snarfing up the chocolate chip cookies she'd been holding. Finally, something she could handle.

"Lily!" she said. "You can't give dogs chocolate, it's like poison for them!"

Lily paled and dropped under the table. "Sprinkles! No! Give them back!"

Viv and Bev stood up and craned their necks.

"Is that…" Bev's voice trailed off. "I think I see something there."

"I see it. I mean her," Viv said. "That's a giant three-headed dog. I knew she existed but seeing her in the flesh is something I wasn't prepared for."

"It's okay, Lily," Elle said, ignoring Evie's distress, Bev and Viv's curious stares, and the smoke monster floating above the table. "Hellhounds have very strong digestive systems. There's not much that could poison Sprinkles." She smiled encouragingly, then nodded at Evie. "Thank you for having me. If it's okay, I'll see if Mrs. Kane needs a ride home. I need to get back to Brand."

"It was good to see you," Evie said. "We'd love to have you over for dinner sometime less chaotic."

Elle laughed, then turned and headed towards the house.

Lily climbed out from under the table and looked at her mother, then stuck her tongue out and blew a long, slobbery raspberry.

❀ ❀ ❀

IN THE MIDST of the activity, Evie's anger at Luc had faded away. She looked around to ask him what he'd been about to say about his father, but he'd disappeared again. She dropped into the empty chair between Viv and Bev that Hope had recently vacated and laid her head on Bev's shoulder.

"This is a lot," she said. "I thought we'd have to talk about periods and makeup and sex and drugs, not smoke illusions and lake monsters and demon summoning rituals." She shook her head. "I'm sorry. I'm being so self-centered lately. I haven't even asked after you. How do you feel, Viv? Back to yourself? Still branded?"

"It doesn't look like a brand anymore," Viv said. "It's more like a tattoo now—kinda matches some of the other ones I have. And the shape is changing—rapidly. I can feel it moving. It's not painful, but it is creepy...like spiders crawling in my skin." She shuddered.

"Mine, too," Bev said. "Although it's still a mess of lines. Viv's is a lot clearer. Kinda looks like a headless DJ."

"Headless DJ. That sounds...powerful." Evie snorted, trying to hold back laughter.

"Hey, it's hard enough to be a good DJ with a head," Viv pointed out. "Imagine the difficulty when you can't even see what you're doing."

"No one said it was a *good* DJ." Bev grinned.

"Whatever. At least it doesn't look like someone spilled their tinker toys on my back." Viv shot her middle finger up and waved it towards her friends.

"Is that Bev or me?" Evie asked.

"Yes." Viv nodded decisively. "Both."

"I love you both so much," Evie said. "And as much as I'm enjoying my baby girl turning ten—you know, a lot and not at all at the same time—I am looking forward to this week being over and everything returning to normal. Well, not normal, but at least less hectic and with two hundred percent fewer big reveals."

Viv nodded. "Right. That is absolutely a thing that is going to happen."

"I'm sure the hellmouth will disappear, as will Sprinkles, our tattoos, your daughter's ability to create *smoke monsters*, and your Genie in a Bottle magic." Bev side eyed Evie. "I know you're riding high on your wish powers, but I'm not sure wishful thinking falls under that. Besides, do you really want normal if it means your Tall, Dark, and Handsome disappears, leaving Lily without a father and you without someone to blame your hot flashes on?"

Evie sighed. "I don't know. It's not like I don't want Lily to be fatherless—especially now that they've met—but life was sure easier a week ago before I saw my daughter's imaginary friend save her and my dad from Lake Eden."

"The good news is, it can't get much weirder than this," Bev said.

Viv and Evie stared at their friend, slowly shaking their heads.

Bev clapped a hand over her mouth as soon as the words were out. "I can't believe I said that," she whispered.

"What's happening now is all your fault, Bev," Viv said. "Duck!" She pushed her friends' heads down under the table just in time to avoid the fireball that whizzed over them and landed in the middle of the table.

The fire elongated until it was about six feet tall and almost two feet at the...shoulders? Evie squinted against the heat and light. It was definitely human-shaped. Arms separated from the fiery torso, and space appeared from the bottom of the flames. In seconds, the fire had transformed from vaguely humanoid to a fiery person, and as Evie watched, into a man with brick red skin wearing a royal blue suit and matching tie and a black silk shirt. Ebony horns sprouted from his head, curving delicately inward, and from the bottom of his pants legs, cloven hooves appeared. He spun around, exactly like a model on a catwalk, and a tail followed his spin.

"I hope I'm not late," he said, his voice deep and gravelly.

"Papa Abe!" Lily said, arms held up wide. "You made it!"

"Of course I made it, Jelly Bean! I wouldn't have missed your big day for all the souls in hell." He leapt lightly down from the table, picked Lily up, and spun her around.

"I wish I had a drink right now," Evie said. A glass of wine appeared in front of her. "No. Not wine. I wish I had a dry martini with a twist. Better make it a double." She tilted the glass in her hand up to her mouth and took a long, slow drink.

CHAPTER FOURTEEN

"I have totally lost control," Evie said to no one in particular as she stood on the porch watching the chaos. Papa Abe, who she still hadn't officially met, had shifted into something a little more ordinary looking after his big entrance. Instead of snazzy Satan, he was now merely a well-dressed and way-too-attractive man. The height and width of his chest stayed the same, but his skin darkened to mahogany and he lost the horn, hooves, and tail. The flamboyant suit, however, stayed put. He was now trotting around the lawn in the late afternoon sun, giving the children shoulder rides.

Bev was hanging out with Abe, wrangling the kids who were waiting their turn for the pony rides, and James and Hope had settled down with a bottle of wine to watch the chaos.

Luc, once again, was nowhere to be seen.

Evie heard a car coming up the driveway and checked her watch. She wasn't expecting anyone and thought Elle wasn't coming back. She walked around the house to where she could see the driveway. A classic Impala was coming up the drive.

Evie closed her eyes, took a deep breath, and wished as hard as she could that Dean and Sam were here to take care of her demon problem.

When she heard the engine turn off and the car doors open, she peeked through her fingers, not sure what she was hoping to see. Instead of sexy fictional brothers, a man and woman were walking up the drive. They had the same mahogany skin as Luc and Abe, and the same sultry walks. Evie recognized them immediately—from her dreams and from the blurry photos Viv had taken in Ambrosia the day Luc had arrived back in town.

The woman had long, jet black hair, brown skin a little lighter than Luc's, and was wearing yellow pants and a matching blazer buttoned at the waist—and no shirt underneath. She was breathtaking. The man was equally beautiful—his features a harder version of the woman's—although he didn't have the smolder she had. His outfit was less flamboyant but just as sexy; he wore tight, dark jeans, a tight t-shirt the same yellow as the woman's suit, and a black leather jacket.

"Hi," the woman said. "I'm Sam, this is Mat."

Evie giggled nervously. "Not Dean, then?"

The people in front of her tilted their heads and wrinkled their noses in the exact same way, and their resemblance went from merely superficial to striking.

"Sorry," Evie said. "It's been a weird night and the characters in my favorite show drive a car like yours, but their names are Sam and Dean, not Sam and Mark."

"Mat," the man said, a touch of impatience coloring his voice. His nearly black eyes regarded Evie with an intensity that almost made her take a step back. Only her knowledge that this was Luc's younger brother and therefore unlikely—she hoped—to hurt her made her stand her ground.

"Mat, be polite." The woman turned to Evie and smiled. It was more predatory than comforting, and Evie's stomach clenched with nerves. "I imagine things have been weird for you, but my father arriving must have been the cherry on the sundae. He is such a show-man, especially when he's trying to bowl people over with his power and charisma. He's really quite nice once you get to know him."

"No he isn't," Mat objected. "You just say that because you're his favorite. He's literally the devil."

Sam rolled her eyes. "Ignore him. He's the middle child and has all the hang-ups you'd expect. I'm the baby, so I'm spoiled yet delightful."

"We're twins," Mat said to Evie, who hadn't managed to string together cohesive thoughts, much less get a word in edgewise. "She's only six weeks younger."

"You mean six minutes?" Evie asked.

"Labor is faster for humans," Sam said. "And that's not the point. Is Luc here? We need to talk to him."

"Luc is your brother," Evie said. "I'm so sorry. I feel like my brain is spinning in a million different directions at once, and I have no idea what's happening or why or when it will stop. Luc is here—somewhere—and your…father…is giving piggyback rides to the kids."

"Awww. He adores children and is always bitching at us to have a litter or two, just so he has someone besides me to spoil," Sam said. "Now, let's go find Luc."

"No need to look for me," Luc said, stepping out of the shadows. "Why are you here? Why is *he* here?"

"We tried to stop him," Mat said, "but you know how he is." He waved his hand dismissively and looked past Luc towards the noise of the ongoing party. "Besides, I'm here because you wanted me to question the small child, right?"

"No," Luc said, glaring at his brother. "I merely said that the boy child needed to be questioned. I did not recruit you to be the questioner. You have no idea how to talk to children."

"And you do?" Mat scoffed, buffing his fingernails against his t-shirt. "You just met your first child this week."

"Did you know?" Luc asked. "Did you know about Lily?"

"Not immediately," Sam hedged. She looked down at the ground, not meeting Luc's eyes. "But probably sooner than you did. I tried so hard to convince the mother to name her Lilith, but I guess I was only partially successful. Unless Lily is short for Lilith?" She looked hopeful.

"No. It's Liliana," Evie snapped. Then a memory caught up, and her jaw dropped. "Are you the nail tech who did my pregnancy pedicures? You looked way less hot then."

"You recognize me!" Sam beamed. "Let's go to the party. I can't wait to meet my niece and the rest of her family."

Luc took a deep breath, and the air around them shimmered, then heated up. "Why?" he asked, the quiet voice in sharp contrast to the literal steam rising from his head. "Why keep it a secret?"

Evie swallowed her anger and let Luc do the talking—this time. He knew his sibs better than she did and would be able to tell if they were being straight with him or not. She was not, however, letting go of future opportunities to send her child's newfound relatives back to hell with extreme prejudice.

"The better question, big brother, is why didn't you know?" Mat pursed his lips and smirked, then held out an elbow to his twin.

Sam and Mat walked around the house, following the sound of the party, and disappeared around the corner.

"I'm sorry," Luc said to Evie. "For all of it. For my family showing up. For my dad being who he is. For the marks of power that have come to rest on you and your friends. For Sprinkles and the lake. I'm sorry for Lily and for that summer. I shouldn't have stayed. It wasn't fair to you."

Evie shook her head. "It wasn't fair. You should've either told me who you were or left me alone. A one-night stand is one thing, but you stayed all summer. My whole life has been turned upside down because of one summer—and you can be as sorry as you want, but it doesn't change anything. I want to ask you to leave, but I can't. Not now. Maybe not ever." She bit her lip to keep it from quivering. Everything was excuses and half-truths and everyone knowing more about the daughter she'd raised on her own for the last ten years.

Maybe Luc hadn't known, but he'd never been curious enough to find out. Evie squared her shoulders. She knew that wasn't fair to Luc, but right now, she didn't care.

"I'm going back to the party. Maybe you should talk to your sister and see what else they've been hiding from you." Evie turned her back on Luc and walked away, exhaling a shaky breath as she did so.

🌱 🌿 🌾

AFTER CHECKING that Lily was okay—or at least as okay as possible when playing with her demon grandfather—Evie pulled one of the Adirondack chairs into the shadow of the porch where she could see everything that was going on, but no one could see her unless they knew where to look.

Mat and Sam had settled in right away. Mat was hanging out with Abe, Bev, and the kids and appeared to be having a very serious conversation with Kevin.

Sam had homed in on Viv as soon as she'd returned, and if this was a bar instead of a ten-year-old's birthday party, they'd be out the door and halfway to happy town by now. As it was, they were skirting the lines of decorum, and Evie was tempted to ask them to get a room, or at least throw a sheet over them.

Evie took a breath. Nothing had changed in the thirty minutes since she'd hid in the corner, but at least the panic had receded. She checked her watch. It was cake time. Or cakes, more accurately. Not that anyone needed anymore sweets, but birthday cake was an absolute necessity. She'd been informed that without cake and candles and singing, the birthday might not take, and they'd have to try again and again until it settled. Under the threat of daily birthday parties until she got it right, Evie had caved.

She walked into the kitchen, put the candles in the cake—ten candles in a circle around the outside and a giant wax ten in the middle—and grabbed a pack of matches from the drawer. She walked to the door and groaned in frustration. It'd blown shut behind her. Normally, not a big deal, but today an annoyance that threatened to drive her to tears.

"I'll get it," Luc said, opening the door.

"Where have you been?" she asked, wincing at the bitter accusation in her voice. "Sorry, I don't mean…"

"It's okay. And I've been hiding from my family. It's bad enough my dad showed up, but the chaos twins?" He shook his head and ushered Evie down the stairs and out onto the patio. "Want me to light the candles?"

"The matches are in my front pocket," Evie said.

She'd meant that to be a no—the matches were too inconvenient for him to grab—but when he slipped his hand into her pocket, and the heat of his palm pressed against the top of her thigh, she gasped, fire igniting every nerve ending. For a moment, she forgot what they were here to do and all she could think of was all the other places she wanted to feel that heat. Her gaze met his, and the naked desire in his eyes made her breath hitch in her throat. She licked her lips and watched him follow the motion of her tongue with his eyes.

"Luc," she breathed.

Someone clearing their throat brought her back to herself.

"Your hand is still in my pocket," she whispered.

Luc shook himself. "Sorry. Well, not sorry. But you know."

"Light the candles. We can talk later." Logic and arousal fought for dominance. She tried to call up her earlier anger and frustration, but the only thing coming up were the memories of their summer together and the responses he knew how to pull from her body. Arousal was edging into the lead... At least in her pants.

"May I have everyone's attention!" Luc called. "We need the guest of honor to fulfill her time-honored task of making wishes and letting us serenade her!"

Lily squealed in excitement and ran up to Evie and Luc. Her father lit the candles, and Hope led the group in a rousing chorus of Happy Birthday.

"Make a wish, Liliana," Evie said.

"Do wishes really come true, Mama?" Lily asked. "It feels like they might."

"I think they do, baby girl. If you wish hard enough."

Lily closed her eyes, took a deep breath, and blew out the candles.

CHAPTER FIFTEEN

E vie was at one end of the table, temporarily alone. Bev and Luc had volunteered to take the perishables inside and get the food put away. Or, rather, Bev had volunteered herself and voluntold Luc.

Hope and James were fussing at the fire pit with Mat and the kids watching. Apparently, they'd promised Lily s'mores, and after two pieces of cake, countless cookies, some fruit pizza, and two bites of cheeseburger, she'd decided that s'mores were an absolute necessity. Evie was not looking forward to the sugar crash the next day, but a tenth birthday was a once in a lifetime event.

Viv and Sam were taking a walk along the lakeside and out of view of the rest of the party. Evie knew Viv hadn't left yet, because she was torn between supporting Evie and buying Sam a drink at Evie's bar. There wasn't much supporting left to do—just the post party cleanup and wrangling the sleepover kids into Lily's bedroom and hoping they came down from the sugar high and fell asleep before midnight, and Evie was planning on leaving the latter to Hope and James, since they were the ones who stuffed the children with more sugar than should be possible.

Evie took another drink of her lemonade and wished she had

something warmer to drink. Her hands curled around the mug that took the place of her glass and watched the sun slip below the horizon. The night air reminded everyone that it was still early April in the mountains.

As she sipped her peppermint tea, she felt a pang of impending loss. The last ten years had simultaneously crawled and flown past her. There were days she wanted to pull Lily onto her lap and squish her down until she was five years old again, when she was small enough to carry and thought her mama was the most wonderful and best person in the world. Most of the time, however, she loved watching Lily as she grew into the woman she'd become. Adventurous, bright and happy, kind beyond measure, and curious about everything.

"We should talk."

Evie looked at the chair to her right. Papa Abe was sitting next to her. No longer in his flamboyant blue suit, he'd changed into jeans and a pink shirt with narrow horizontal white stripes.

"We should at least be introduced," Evie said. "And then you need to tell me how to change clothes with the snap of your fingers, because that's a handy skill to increase efficiency and lighten suitcases."

"You deflect anxiety with humor. Interesting." Abe steepled his fingers and looked at her.

His features had become indistinct in the gathering darkness, but Evie had the impression his vision wasn't impacted at all.

"Why are you here? What do you want? And why did you keep Lily's existence a secret from Luc, especially since your other children knew?" Evie's anger that she'd put aside earlier rose to the surface again. She didn't know him—and, at the moment, didn't care that he was a king of hell—but he had manipulated Luc, manipulated Lily, and changed the course of Evie's life.

"So many questions when, as you so rightly pointed out, we haven't even been properly introduced." Firelight flickered behind him, and for a moment Evie could've sworn the horns he'd sported earlier had made another appearance.

Evie forced a grin and gritted her teeth. "Of course. I'm Evelyn Addams, Evie to my friends and family. You can call me Evelyn."

"Lovely to meet you, Evelyn. I am Abaddon, Dark Angel of Destruction, and King of Hell. You can call me Abe."

Evie swallowed past the lump in her throat. She'd known Luc was a demon, but his father showing up and dropping his titles in a casual introduction rammed everything home. Nausea and determination made her sway slightly before she reclaimed her control. She steeled herself and pulled up to her full height. She would not let this *demon* write the narrative. She took a deep breath and attempted to imagine him as the more palatable King of Hell from her favorite show. It wasn't working, but it did help her slow her heart rate to a manageable level. "Are you here to make deals and claim our souls?" she asked.

"No! Of course not. For one thing, I have minions to do the dirty work. And for another, your souls already belong to me. You are marked, are you not?" He smiled at her, and it was a terrifyingly cheery grin that evoked fear and comfort at the same time. "Your friends, too, bear my symbols. And of course, the darling Lily has been mine from the moment she took her first breath."

"So, if we're already yours, why are you here?"

"For my grandchild's birthday, of course. Ten is when the human children of angelic creatures often come into their power, and to have her turn ten on the tenth day of the tenth month—that is a milestone not to be missed."

"It's April," Evie said, cataloguing the rest of his statement to be dealt with in a moment.

"Time runs differently where I'm from. We celebrate the new year when the sun in your northern hemisphere has reached its zenith and begins its slow descent back into darkness. I was unsure of my darling Liliana until her hound and the book came to her, signifying both her aptitude and ability. She is ready."

"Ready for what?" The sinking feeling was back, this time accompanied by the fire of protectiveness, stronger than any fear this demon could evoke.

"To begin her education so she can eventually take her place at my side among the princes of hell."

"I think not," Evie said. "I think it's time you left. You are not welcome here, and you will stay away from my daughter." Evie's fists clenched, and she pictured herself landing a smooth, powerful uppercut to Abe's jaw, sending him back to Hell with a bruised face and dampened ego.

"Or what?" Abe laughed. "I already have her..." He turned around, and his voice transformed from harsh and conniving to jovial as he called out, "Liliana! I have one more present for you!"

Lily left the fire and ran towards them. Her face was sticky and smeared with chocolate, and she glowed with happiness. "What is it?" she clapped her hands.

Abe handed her a thick envelope with her full name engraved on it. Lily tore it open and removed a heavy card with an embossed gold border.

Evie tried to read what was on it, but the reflection of the firelight on the gold lettering made it impossible.

"Papa Abe!" Lily squealed, throwing her arms around the King of Hell. "Thank you thank you thank you!" She tossed the card at her mother. "I have to go tell Shelby and Kevin and Sprinkles!"

Abe smiled at Evie over Lily's head, then wrapped his arms around her and held her tight for a moment. "You are welcome, child. Remember, I would move Hell and Earth for you and your happiness. Now go—share your news with your friends and maternal grandparents. I will make the arrangements with your mother."

Lily ran off, and Evie picked up the card her daughter had thrown her way. It was an invitation and invocation.

Princess Liliana Faith Addams Morningstar
is invited
in perpetuity and without limit
to passage between her earthly abode and
her grandfather's court, at will
To RSVP, speak these words

zacam g ialprg

"What is this?" Evie demanded. Her desire to commit violence was taking a worrying homicidal edge, but she let that carry her along. Her hands trembled, wobbling the parchment, and it took all her willpower to still them and deny Abe insight into the whirlpool of fear and anger overtaking her.

Abe looked more smug than anyone had a right to look. "An invitation, my dear. Now, there is nothing you can do to keep her from me, from learning what she needs to know."

Evie looked at the invitation again. "Morningstar?"

"That is her father's last name, is it not?"

"No..." Evie drew out the o's uncertainly. "Oh. Oh my god. Morgenstern. Luc Morgenstern is—"

"Lucifer Morningstar, my dear. I'm surprised you hadn't figured that out. I'm even more surprised he hasn't yet shared that information with you. Interesting... Makes a person wonder what other secrets he holds."

Evie stood up, unable to stay still any longer.

Abe laughed. "It was lovely to make your acquaintance, Evelyn Addams. I'll leave now, but I will be back." A red flash of his eyes froze her in place. "By the by, destroying that invitation will not nullify it. The incantation is now burned into her soul—for lack of a better word—and she will never forget it." He winked at her and disappeared.

"Uh oh," Mat said from behind Evie, making her jump. "Looks like Lucy's got some explaining to do."

Evie turned every ounce of the fear and anger at Abe and his whole stinking family she'd been holding back on Mat. "Get out. Get out of my house. Get out of our lives. And, so help me, if I ever see you on my property again, chaos demon or not, you will live to regret every one of the hundreds of years you have left."

EVERY LAST DISH was washed and put away, and the party and house were cleaned up until no sign of the day-long party remained. Even the giggles and snorts and loud remonstrations to "be quiet, they'll hear us" had given way to silence, except for the sleepy chuffs of a three-headed dog.

Evie had sent her parents to bed an hour ago and was assiduously ignoring texts from Bev. The world was quiet, and after the cacophony and confusion of the last couple days, it was exactly what she needed. Throughout the colder months, Evie cozied up in front of the fireplace after Lily went to bed, either reading or watching her not-so-guilty pleasures on tv, but as soon as she could tolerate the evening air, she moved outside. In the last ten years, she'd spent countless nights on the wide porch looking out over the lake. She had a chest full of blankets just inside the door, a small battery-operated light for the evenings it got dark early and she wanted to read, and a small bar cabinet with glasses and a Champagne bucket for the nights she was having a drink and her friends stopped by.

Tonight, though, it was just her. Even the frogs had stopped singing for the evening. The full moon shone brightly, reflecting on the lake and creating almost enough light to read by. Evie poured herself a small glass of Port, tucked her legs up under the blanket, and watched the stars compete for attention with the moon.

Midway through her glass of Port, she realized something.

As over-the-top ridiculous as everything had been the last few days, she could deal with almost all of it. She had demon magic coursing through her veins because she'd carried a tiny half-demon for almost ten months—she should've known there was something up when Lily hung on more than two weeks after the due date—and solidified the magic with her tattoo. Viv and Bev had been marked because they fell in the hellmouth. The hellmouth had shown up because Lily summoned a demon—her father—who'd shown up in town with no clue as to why or how he'd gotten there. And Lily'd been able to do the summoning because her demon powers had woken enough to call a hell hound. The occult book that had traveled to Lily through Kevin had obviously come from Papa Abe—ugh, she didn't want to call him that—as well, although that provenance was a little unclear. She wasn't sure how the lake monster fit in, or if it was a part of this narrative at all, but magic monsters at least had mythological precedent.

Things that she'd never been able to decipher—or that she'd actively avoided even attempting to decipher—were falling into place, and although she wasn't sure she could ever admit it out loud, she felt lighter. It was a relief to realize that everything she hadn't understood was because she didn't have the knowledge to interpret. It wasn't all bad—the wish fulfillment was coming in handy and knowing Lily had a fiercely loyal hellhound to protect her eased a lot of the worry Evie carried around.

What was not easily filed away was Abe's insistence that Lily go with him. The invitation said the passage was between here and hell, but Evie was afraid that once Lily was in hell, being treated like a princess and learning all sorts of soul-sucking magic, or whatever they teach you in demon boarding school, she wouldn't want to return.

She'd visit, of course. But the times between visits would stretch out, almost imperceptibly at first, but eventually it'd be weeks, then months... Soon, Evie would be the boring summer vacation spot, living by the lake you could never swim in and in a town that had fewer than five thousand residents, most of them too old to be of much interest to a child and a princess.

"I wish..." Evie paused and thought very carefully about how she wanted to word things before starting again, sending her words towards the lake. "I wish I knew what was going to happen. I know that's not possible, but I wish I could have an explanation with no lies, no half-truths, no prevarications or obfuscations. I wish Lucifer Morningstar would show up and be straight with me, for once."

Her phone buzzed with an incoming call. Evie grabbed the phone, ready to give Luc a piece of her mind. Viv's number was on the caller ID instead.

"Is everything okay?" Evie asked by way of greeting.

"I had a simply delightful evening," Viv said. "Alas, it ended much too soon. But that's not why I'm calling. When Sam and I were walking by the lake, we ran into Brandy—not literally, unfortunately. She said she was mushroom hunting, but with all the other Brandy-sightings in the last week, it felt weird and worth mentioning. Also, I keep having these compulsions to tell people things, and I don't understand where they're coming from, but they're important. I need you to listen. You ignored my advice about the lake—"

"I didn't ignore it, I didn't see the message until after…"

"Fine. That's why I'm calling instead of texting this time. You need to look down instead of up tonight. Oh, and wear your warmest pajamas to bed."

"You called to give me sleepwear advice?" Evie's nose wrinkled in confusion. "Are you drunk?"

"No. Well yes, but just a little. I don't understand. I'm getting nothing except for this overwhelming need to tell people things that make no sense except in hindsight. This doesn't feel as urgent as the lake thing, but it felt important enough to call."

"Okay… I will wear my winter flannel pajamas and try not to stargaze too much. And I'll keep an eye out for Brandy. I saw her lurking a couple times during the party, but something always caught my attention before I could investigate further. Thanks for the reminder."

"You're welcome. Now, I've got to go before Luc shows up and you get all giggly."

Viv hung up before Evie could respond in any way to the last pronouncement. She shrugged. It'd been a long time since she'd had such good fodder to tease her friend with, and she was going to make it all count tomorrow.

CHAPTER SIXTEEN

I t was well past midnight when Evie gave up on her wish coming true and decided to go to bed, wish unanswered, at least for the night. Crunching gravel broke the silence and increased her heart rate, and the screen door behind her banging open elicited a scream, quickly smothered.

A long, wet, smelly tongue licked her arm from wrist to neck, a motion repeated two more times. The faint shimmer became more pronounced when Evie stared at it reprovingly. "That's really not necessary, Sprinkles."

The dog woofed, then sprawled out in front of the door to the house, effectively blocking her entrance.

Realizing she was trapped between a giant hell hound and whoever—or whatever—was coming up the drive, Evie panicked for a moment. The moment ended quickly, but not soon enough to plan and make an escape. She opened her mouth to scream for help, knowing that she'd wake her mother and probably Shelby.

"Please, don't," Luc said from the shadows beyond her porch light. "If you want me to leave, I will, but since you were awake, I thought we might talk."

"How did you know I was awake?" Evie demanded. "And why didn't you call first like a normal person."

"I think it's become more than apparent that I am, in no way, a normal *person*." Luc's gaze pierced her through the darkness. "And I knew you were awake because you wished for me to show up, and you wished with my name and not the alias I've always used. That latter informs me you talked with my father. I suppose it's possible it was Mat who filled you in—he does enjoy creating chaos wherever he goes—but it's far more likely you had a chat with Papa Abe."

Evie crossed her arms and took a backwards step; her calves brushed against Sprinkles's fur, and she was rewarded with another hot, wet lick for her troubles. She didn't know why she was so convinced Sprinkles would protect her against another creature from hell—protect her charge's mother against her father—but she knew that, at least for now, the dog had her literal and figurative back.

"You don't need to be afraid of me," Luc said, crossing his arms in a mirror of Evie's stance. "I would never hurt you. Even if I disliked you, which I do not, you would be safe from me."

"But is Lily safe from you? Safe from your father?" Evie asked, not relaxing even one bit.

Luc opened his mouth to answer, then snapped it shut. "May I come onto the porch?"

Evie nodded sharply, then moved her shoulders back and down and uncrossed her arms. She walked stiffly to the chair she'd been occupying moments before and sat, wrapping the blanket around herself, although she no longer felt the chill of the night air; anger and adrenaline were heating her now.

Luc pulled the other chair farther away from Evie, then angled it towards her and sat down. "She is safe from me," he said. "I wouldn't harm a hair on Lily's head for anything in the world, and I would never try to take her away from you or turn her against you. She may be, by blood, at least, part of my world, but she was born here. She is of Eden Valley, first. Of you. Of this world."

"Why'd you say the town before me?" Evie asked. She knew this wasn't the most important question to ask, but she was suddenly curious.

Luc shrugged. "I don't know why I didn't notice that summer I spent here, but there's something about this town. It's…alive. It's not part of either of our worlds—it sits apart, separate. Tell me something, of everyone you knew when you were ten, how many of them moved away voluntarily?"

Evie leaned back, glad to be distracted for the moment while she figured out what to say next. She counted in her head. "Lots," she said. "At least forty or fifty people."

"And how many of those forty or fifty people were *from* Eden Valley?"

Evie thought a moment. "That can't be right," she said aloud. "My parents, that's two. Viv. Bev's parents and sister, but they all died almost ten years ago. A few of my parents' friends—maybe a half dozen, or so—retired outside of the Valley."

"Do those who leave ever come back?"

"Well, yeah. To visit the families and friends who stayed."

"And to die?" Luc prodded. "Where did Bev's family die? Have any of your parents' friends died yet?"

Evie opened her mouth to refute his assumption, but then closed it again. He was right. Bev's family had died on the mountain roads west of town, taking the scenic route to Seattle. And of the two of her parents' friends who had died, both had died suddenly when visiting family in Eden Valley.

"Why?" Evie asked. "How?"

"I don't know. I think it's the lake, though. I'll keep digging, figure it out."

Evie drew a breath. "That's interesting and a little scary, but it's not why I wanted to talk to you." She drew the invitation Abe had given Lily and handed it over. "This is."

Luc scanned the paper, his brows coming together in a dark vee that contrasted the tight line of his lips. "Did he hand this directly to Lily, or did he ask you to pass it on?"

"He gave it to her. He said that summoning would be etched on her soul and that nothing could remove it. Did you have a hand in this? Did you know?" Evie heard the rising tone of her voice as she started to verge into anger and the tears that usually accompanied it and took a deep breath to tamp it back down.

"I swear to you he didn't tell me what he was planning." Luc leaned forward, eyes wide, as if willing Evie to believe him.

"But?" Evie prompted.

Luc ran his fingers through his hair. "But, I'm not surprised. I was worried he'd do something like this when he showed up at the party."

"Well, I wasn't!" Evie growled under her breath. The fury that had been simmering all evening—all week—bubbled up, and those traitorous tears she'd swallowed pricked at the corners of her eyes. "You should've warned me. You should've been up front with everything. I understand why you weren't when we met. It was a summer fling, and I don't know if I would've believed you. But when you came back, you shouldn't have doled out truths in bits and pieces."

"I didn't want to overwhelm you," Luc said. "It's a lot. It's more than a lot. It's enough to break some people's minds. You were already overwhelmed with your new gifts, and Lily's party, and the glowing symbol that matched my tattoo. I..." He trailed off and knotted his fingers in his lap.

Evie felt a flash of compassion she quickly squashed. Sure, he'd been summoned here for reasons he couldn't have suspected then found out that he had a daughter. That'd be enough to make most men run. But his actions after he got here were inexcusable.

"I'm angry with you," she said. She clenched her jaw and rolled her shoulders back, exhaling loudly through her nose. "I don't know how to move forward with this. Our daughter, *my* daughter, can skip off to hell whenever she wants, and I have zero control over when she goes or when—*if*—she comes back. I am angry and terrified. Tell me there's something I can do."

Luc looked at his hands for far too long before returning his gaze to Evie's face. "I don't know," he said slowly. "But are you sure this isn't a good thing?"

"How on earth could this be a good thing?" Evie spat. "Tell me how giving my ten-year-old a ticket to skip out whenever she wants to visit *hell* is a good thing."

"I know it doesn't look like a gift for both of you on the surface, but she will need training. She needs to learn how to help Sprinkles manifest in a socially acceptable form and how to control her powers so she doesn't accidentally blow up her school when she's angry. If she doesn't have a handle on things before she goes through puberty, those volatile emotions combined with her hell powers could wreak havoc. If you'll just think about it rationally…"

"There is nothing to think about!" Evie exploded. "I was not consulted. I was not informed ahead of time. It's been less than a week since you showed up here dropping hints about who you were and refusing to share your speculations on what was going on. You didn't even tell me your real name. I had to find out from your freaking father."

"I don't think you can stop her going," Luc said. "But you can set out some ground rules about when and why."

"And what do I do when she breaks the rules? She might be a pretty good kid, but she's still a kid. She tests boundaries all the time. She's definitely more of a 'beg forgiveness rather than ask permission' kind of person. I don't understand why you didn't tell me, Luc. What's the point in keeping secrets?" Evie slumped and wrapped her arms around herself, exhausted from maintaining her anger and staving off hopelessness and premature defeat.

"I didn't want to speculate, to scare you and your friends unless it was necessary."

"Well, it didn't work, because right now I'm pretty scared. Every five minutes there's a new revelation. As soon as I adjust to one thing, there's another on top of it, and it turns out that you could've warned me about a lot of this." Evie paced back and forth on the porch staying close to the shimmer in the corner of her eye that was Sprinkles.

Luc opened his mouth, but Evie kept talking. "Even now, you're holding back. You haven't told Bev or Viv what you think might be going on with their hell brands. You haven't told us why the marks started out looking like your tattoo but changed. Or how they changed. There is so much you're holding back. The only thing you've volunteered that I didn't know a week ago is…" She trailed off. "I can't think of anything." Sprinkles woofed softly and in three-part harmony.

Luc's chin dropped towards his chest. "I don't know what to say. I've screwed up everything, haven't I?"

"Yeah, you have." Evie turned her back on Luc and started towards the door.

"What can I do to make it up to you?"

Luc's voice was so despairing she almost turned back around. Almost.

"Fix it and leave us alone."

Evie walked through the door and closed it behind her. The click of the latch echoed in the total stillness of night, mimicking the too loud pounding of her heart in her ears.

CHAPTER SEVENTEEN

Evie changed into her warmest pajamas—black fleece pants dotted with wine glasses and a long-sleeved, scoop neck red fleece top—brushed her teeth, and went to bed. After tossing and turning for almost an hour, she got up and walked to the large picture window in her bedroom. During the day, she had a view of Eden Lake that was almost perfectly framed by the Cascades. Now, however, the lake was barely visible. The reflected moonlight made it look inky and almost sinister.

She settled into the glider in front of the window she'd gotten when Lily was born and propped her feet up on the Ottoman. They'd spent a lot of sleepless nights rocking and looking out over the lake, and this was still Evie's go to spot when she couldn't fall asleep. More than once, she'd woken to Lily curled up asleep in it, too.

Evie snagged her super soft blanket from the back of the chair and wrapped it around herself. Eden Valley didn't throw up a lot of light pollution and the Addams house was far enough around the lakeshore to be out of visible range from the town, anyway, making star gazing easy. Evie peered up at the sky and, after finding as many constellations as she could recognize, started counting stars, hoping they'd work at least as well as sheep as a soporific.

Even star counting didn't bring sleep any closer. Evie put her feet back on the floor, leaned her forearms on the windowsill, and rested her chin on her arms. Everything looked so peaceful out there—the opposite of how she felt. She knew that once she relaxed and found calm acceptance, she'd be able to deal with the situation as well as she'd managed everything else that'd come up. She did really well rolling with the punches until the punches started coming too fast to dodge. She knew Lily needed more instruction than Evie would ever be able to give her, but relinquishing control like that, allowing her to spend time with the grandfather she'd never known, the grandfather who was a King in Hell... It wasn't like sending her to Hawaii for a week's vacation with Evie's parents.

Evie inhaled deeply through her nose then exhaled forcefully through her mouth. She needed to figure out a way to release this tension if she was going to get any sleep—and be functional at all tomorrow. Later today, she corrected herself.

An image of one way to release tension rose unbidden in her mind, and despite the complete absence of anyone around to see her or read her thoughts on her face, she blushed. It'd been a while since she'd tried that kind of tension reliever, and even longer since she'd wanted to go back for a second helping. Being a single mom in a small town brought even fewer opportunities to date—or clear out the cobwebs— than being a recent divorcee had eleven years ago. She'd never wanted to admit it—not even to herself—but she'd spent the last decade waiting for Luc to walk through the door and sweep her off her feet the way he had the night they'd met at the Lucky Devil.

Her anger was cooling now, although not enough to text and apologize. Luc had been wrong and had screwed up a lot of things—some that might have catastrophic and far-reaching consequences for Lily —but she didn't think it was out of malice.

Tomorrow she'd reach out and hear him out, learn what steps he was planning to take to make things right and how he was going to protect his daughter. They'd probably have some legal things to talk about, too—custody, visitation, child support...

She remembered the other half of Viv's advice and pulled her eyes from the stars to the ground. The inky lake pulled her gaze in. Something moved by the lake, catching her eye. She squinted but couldn't make out anything other than a dark shape, generally human shaped, moving up and down the dock. Evie stood up and padded downstairs. She slipped on a pair of shoes she kept by the back door and went out to see what Luc was doing.

"Luc!" she called when she got closer. "Why are you still here? Is everything okay?"

Luc spun around and slipped a bit on the wet dock before catching his balance.

"Sorry. I didn't mean to startle you," Evie said apologetically.

"Why are you still awake?" Luc demanded. He walked towards her until she could make out his features.

"Couldn't sleep," she answered. "But I live here, and you don't. So I think you'll be the one answering the questions or I'll call the police and report a prowler."

"No you won't," Luc said. "Unless you've changed in the last ten years, calling the police is your absolute last resort."

Evie glared. He was right, but she hated to be called on it.

"If you knew it was me, why'd you come down? Looking to continue our argument?" Luc crossed his arms and leaned back, looking down his nose at the shorter woman.

"Honestly? I have no idea. I couldn't fall asleep. Everything that's happened—everything I don't know making everything I do know worse—gives me this panicky overwhelmed feeling. I don't know what's going on, and I hate the more than anything. I like having plans. Knowing what's likely to happen in the near future. I want to feel secure and comfortable. I don't want to worry about my child any more than usual."

"What's usual?" Luc asked.

Evie started listing on her fingers. "Sudden illness, accidental death, school shooting, car accidents, drowning in—and apparently being consumed by—the lake. I could go on."

"All the time?"

"Almost. It's better now than it was, although sudden illness is being quickly overtaken by school shooting, and this week's events have moved 'eaten by lake monster' up the list. I've had a lot of therapy to be as chill as I seem. I don't ever want Lily—or anyone—see how hard this is for me. My marriage broke me in ways I still can't articulate." Evie grimaced. Something about Luc made her overshare every time she started talking.

"I bet me leaving you alone to raise our daughter for ten years didn't help," Luc said.

Evie shook her head and smiled, but even she knew it wasn't reaching her eyes. "I don't hover. I'm not a helicopter mom. I try to let her make her own mistakes and fall when she overextends, but I'm always in the background ready to pick her up when she needs me."

"I should've been here. I should've helped share this burden. I'm sorry you've had to do this alone for so long."

"I haven't been alone," Evie said. "Far from it. Just because I don't have a man in my life, because I never found a stepfather for Lily, doesn't mean I've been alone. For the first few years, I lived with my parents, and even after they left, I've always had Bev and Viv. After Shelby came to live with Bev, we pretty much raised our kids together. I've had some of the best support systems I could've hoped for. But that doesn't make me worry any less."

"I feel like everything I say is wrong," Luc said. "I wish I knew what I was doing. I've never been a father. I've barely even been a partner, and my previous wife was not the uh...maternal type. Or the type of person who was a good partner—at least for me. I'm older than you are by quite a bit, but in years only. I've spent less time in this world than you have. Less even than Lily."

"Will you tell me about your life, Luc? You know so much about mine. I was never one to hold anything back, and I probably told you more than you ever wanted to know that summer. But you never said much about yourself other than you were engaged, in an arranged marriage situation, and didn't want to disappoint your father. I didn't even know you had siblings until this week."

"It's long and not very interesting," Luc warned. "I don't have any special insights on fallen angels or fights between heaven and hell. I don't even know for sure that there is a heaven."

"I want to ask how there can be a hell without a heaven, but I'm not sure the universe needs balance as much as I do. Regardless, if you're willing to talk, I'd love to listen." She held out her hand, and after a moment, Luc took it and allowed Evie to lead him back to the porch. "Would you like tea?" she asked.

"Not if it's any trouble," he answered.

"I wish I had two cups of peppermint tea," Evie said. "No muss, no fuss."

The tea appeared on the small table between their chairs. Evie hauled out the blankets from the small chest and handed one to Luc before settling under hers and picking up her tea.

Luc took a sip of his tea and looked at Evie. "I've never done this before. I'm not really sure where to start."

"Julie Andrews would say to start at the very beginning. However, since we're not singing in the Alps, why don't you start wherever inspiration strikes."

🌱 🍃 🌿

THE EASTERN SKY was almost imperceptibly lighter by the time Luc finished talking. He rubbed a hand over his eyes. "I'm sorry. I didn't mean to talk so long... No one has ever sat and listened before."

"I think it's wild you're named after your grandfather, but you don't know anything about his origins," Evie said. "It's like a living Biblical history class."

"Am I just as evil as advertised?" Luc nudged Evie with a toe and grinned at her.

Evie pursed her lips and considered. "Less evil, but as beautiful as I always imagined the original Lucifer to be."

"You think I'm beautiful?"

"Have you looked in a mirror?" Evie asked. "You're by far the most gorgeous man I've ever met. I know I'm conventionally white-lady attractive—and in my early thirties, fresh off a divorce, I was definitely at peak hotness, but you... You're on a different level."

Luc reached out and grabbed Evie's hands, then pulled her up as he stood. "You are beautiful still, and wonderful in so many other ways. I am so lucky to have met you, and even though I haven't been around, I am glad Lily called me up, accidentally as it was, so I could meet her and see you again. I don't know where we're going and what you'll want me to do, if anything, but I would do anything to stay here, to get to know our daughter, get to know you again. If you still want me to leave—"

Evie took a step forward, let go of his hands, and stopped his words with a kiss. At first, Luc froze under her lips, but it didn't take long before his mouth moved with hers, gently at first, but then with greater passion. Evie wrapped her arms around his neck, and he placed his hands on her hips.

By the time they broke apart, they were breathing heavily.

"I didn't mean to do that," Evie admitted.

"I'm glad you did," Luc said, one corner of his mouth quirking upwards. "If you'd like, you can do it again."

"I shouldn't. The sun will be up soon, I haven't slept at all, and I'll have three hungry kids needing breakfast before I shoo them out of the house."

"If you're not going to sleep anyway..." Luc slid one hand from the curve of her hip around to her low back, then down. He squeezed gently and pulled her close again. "Might as well make it worth your while."

This time, Luc initiated the kiss. As before, it started slow and sweet, but soon their tongues intertwined, and Evie forgot everything she'd told herself about keeping him at arm's length. She slid her hands under his t-shirt and up, splaying her palms across his chest.

Luc broke off their kiss, and Evie moaned in disappointment until she felt his lips again. He bit gently on her ear, then placed a kiss high on her neck, just below the ear. He trailed kisses down the side of her neck, over her collar bone, and across to the hollow of her throat.

Evie tipped her head back to give him more access and gasped when his hands moved from her ass, underneath the fleece top of her pajamas, and around to cup her breasts, lifting them up and brushing his thumbs over her nipples, erect with cold and arousal.

"You're not wearing a bra."

"I'm in my pajamas," she pointed out.

He groaned. "I should stop touching you. I should step back, take my hands with me, and thank you for the tea."

"Why?" Evie asked, surprising herself.

"I don't want to take advantage of you, to move things too fast." He didn't move his hands or step away. Instead, he brought his thumbs and forefingers together and pinched lightly. "Tell me to go," he said.

"I can't," Evie gasped. "I need you..."

"Where?" Luc asked. "Your room?"

"No," Evie said. "I don't want to risk anyone waking up. I don't mind people knowing what I get up to in my own bed, but I really don't want to answer any questions right now."

Luc pinched again, and Evie bit off a moan.

"Evil," she said. "I guess the rumors *were* true." She broke out of his grasp and grabbed the blanket she'd had on before. "Let's grab all these blankets. I know just the place."

"I don't have any condoms," Luc said.

"I'm in my forties, and I have an IUD," Evie said. "And I'm disease free. I can get you a note from my doctor if you want. Or I could wish a condom into existence."

Luc laughed softly. "It's up to you. I, too, am free from any sexually transmitted diseases, although I don't have a note to prove it."

"Your word is good enough for me. You might not always tell the whole truth, but you never lie, either."

Evie led him down towards the woods and along a barely visible path. They passed the witch's cottage that was now Lily's playhouse. Using the light of her phone, Evie scanned the path ahead of her.

"Here it is," she said softly. They stepped out into a clearing. "I know you can't really see it, but it's like a little piece of paradise here. I don't know if anyone knows it's here but me, Bev, and Viv." She laid down a couple blankets over the dewy grass, then kicked off her shoes and sank into a cross-legged position.

Luc sat beside her and toed off his shoes as well.

"I feel incredibly awkward," Evie admitted.

"Did the walk make you have second thoughts?" Luc asked.

"Not second thoughts so much as an attack of nerves compounded by ill-timed shyness."

"Nothing has to happen here just because we made the trek and carried blankets. We can head back or lay down and watch the stars fade. Whatever you want."

Evie leaned in and brushed her lips across his. "Thank you."

"For giving you a way out? You're welcome." Luc grinned at her as he cupped her face in his hand. He ran his thumb over her lips.

Evie's breath hitched, and she threw caution to the wind. She hooked one arm around his neck and pulled him down with her.

"I've never known how to take it slow with you, Luc. And I don't want to tonight, either." Evie sat up on her elbow and pulled off her shirt, then pushed off her fleece pajama pants.

"Are you sure?" Luc asked, eyes firmly on hers. His right hand was less circumspect; it landed on her bare hip and traversed her silky skin up her torso, pausing under her breast.

"I'm sure, Luc. I might be mad again later, but now, all I want is you. Make me forget everything else but you."

"As you wish," he said. He pressed her down onto the blanket and, after shimmying out of his own clothes, warmed her with his body and his breath.

Evie gasped as the first ray of light broke across the eastern horizon, then let her eyes drift closed as she gave in to pleasure.

CHAPTER EIGHTEEN

E vie woke to the sound of her cell phone ringing. She groaned as she cracked her eyes and was immediately blinded by the early morning sun. She grabbed her phone and checked the time. She'd been asleep less than an hour. She rolled over to see if Luc was sleeping and found a note instead.

I am so sorry I couldn't wake with you—maybe next time. Unfortunately, I've gotten a rather rude summons from my father, and I'm trying to head off any further unpleasantness for you, Lily, and your friends. I'll be in touch as soon as I can. Thank you for this morning. —Luc

Evie glared at the note. She wasn't sure if she was irritated with the contents, with waking up alone, or how stiff her body felt after a couple hours on the ground in the chilly early spring air and less than an hour of sleep. She stood, groaning as every ache and pain made itself known.

"I am much too old for trysts in the woods," she said to herself. "Should've just risked the bed and nosy family."

She shook out the blankets, then looked around. It'd been too dark last night to appreciate the beauty of her secret clearing, but in the early morning light, it was enchanting. Early wildflowers bloomed everywhere in the spring-green grass but where the blanket had crushed them. The burbling of a natural spring interrupted her observations and reminded Evie that the bathroom was really far away, and she'd had a lot of tea last night. She draped the blankets over her arm and headed back to the house, hoping she wouldn't see anyone until she'd had a chance to throw these in the wash and change her clothes.

"Hello, dear," Hope said brightly as Evie approached the house.

"Mom, what are you doing up? It's like two in the morning in Hawaii!"

"Four, actually," Hope corrected. "But we're not in Hawaii, and seven is a perfectly reasonable time to be up. There's coffee waiting in the kitchen."

"Thank you," Evie said gratefully.

Hope smiled at her and took a sip from her oversized mug. "By the way, dear. You seem to have some twigs in your hair and your pajama top is inside out and backwards."

Of course it is. Evie closed her eyes and forced a smile. "Early morning hike?"

"Braless and with a pile of blankets?" Hope shook her head. "I don't know why you try, dear. You've never been able to pull one over on me—not when you were sneaking around with that snake you married, not when you were trying to keep your fling with Luc a secret, and not now... You might be an early riser, but this strains the bounds of credulity."

"Nothing is more delightful than you listing all the times I tried and failed to keep you out of my sex life," Evie sniped.

Hope laughed. "It is delightful, isn't it? Now go, throw your dirty laundry in the wash and get a cup of coffee on your way to the shower. I'll keep an ear out for the kids and get them fed with something appropriately sweet and devoid of all nutritional value."

"Thanks, Mom," Evie said, leaning in and giving her mother a one-armed hug. "I'm so glad you're here. I've missed you and dad so much."

Hope kissed her daughter on the cheek. "I'm glad we could be here, too. Especially for such an exciting week."

Evie groaned and walked away. "See you in a bit."

AFTER HER SHOWER, Evie peeked into Lily's room. She hadn't heard a peep from them since she'd gotten home, and eight was late for Lily to sleep on a regular day, much less the day after her birthday sleepover day.

Her room was empty—at least Evie thought it was. It was possible there were three children under the piles of papers, clothes, bedding, and Legos. Lily's room always resembled a disaster zone, no matter how much time Evie spent helping her clean it up, but today it looked like ground zero of a three-way between a tornado, an earthquake, and a tsunami.

She shook her head. They must have snuck out before Hope got up. Evie was going to be pretty disappointed if her daughter managed to achieve what Evie never had—pulling one over on Hope.

Hope was plating a ham and cheese scramble, a side of breakfast potatoes, and a slice of toast when Evie walked back into the kitchen. "Sit. Eat. Call your friends."

"Have you seen Lily?" Evie asked.

"They snuck out of the house right after you got in the shower," Hope said. "I managed to get them back here long enough to offload the banana chocolate-chip muffins I made. They were headed to the witch's house. Sprinkles was with them."

"I should go after them," Evie said.

"No. You shouldn't." Hope refilled Evie's coffee cup and poured herself one, too, then handed the cream to her daughter.

"Mom. You don't know what Abe gave her…"

"An invitation? A passport?"

"How?"

Hope sighed. "Something about this town attracts a lot of interesting characters. When I was about twenty, another prince showed up. Abe might pretend he's the king of everything, but in reality, as far as I understand things, there are fourteen principalities—seven each in hell and heaven. They are said to represent the deadly sins and heavenly virtues. The rulers, once princes, have elevated themselves to kings and queens, and each schemes to unite the thirteen other principalities under their rule.

"Abe is the King of Pride. But the last Prince who visited was of Asmodeus's line—a Prince of Lust. My best friend in the world at the time, Grace Kane, was entranced by him. We all were, of course, but she more than the others. Quinn was beautiful—more so even than your Luc. Everywhere he went, lust followed. He fell hard for Grace, though, and never spared more than a glance for anyone else. She got pregnant—it was the summer after we graduated—and when Quinn found out, he was beyond ecstatic. That summer before the baby was born it seemed like everything was perfect." Hope trailed off and stared into her coffee.

"I've never heard you talk about Grace," Evelyn said.

"I gave you her name, Evelyn Grace. And you're right. I don't talk about her because of what happened next. The baby was born—and she named her Lilith after Quinn's mother. One day, the child disappeared. Grace was frantic—of course she was. She came to me and showed me what had been left in Lily's bed. An invitation. If Grace wanted to be reunited with her child, she could say the words and be transported to hell, but it was a one-way ticket, and she'd never be allowed to return."

"Lily?" Evie asked. "Why didn't you say something?"

"What was there to say? You were going to name your child Katherine, but when it was time to make it official, you changed your mind." Hope shrugged. "Would've you listened if I told you the nickname derived from your daughter's name was the same as that from my dead best friend's kidnapped daughter?"

"I don't know," Evie admitted. "I'd like to believe I would've listened, but in the end, it wouldn't have made a difference, would've it?"

"Probably not. I hoped for years that since Luc left before he knew about Lily that you might avoid the same fate as Grace."

"What happened to her? Did she ever get her baby back?"

Hope sighed heavily. "I don't know... We spent weeks looking. The FBI were called in; they searched every square inch of these woods and dredged the lake. Again. There was no sign of her, and no sign of Quinn. Eventually, it was determined Quinn had kidnapped his daughter and run away with her, evidence born out by the invitation that'd been left for Grace.

"After three months and no leads, Grace came to say goodbye. She had the invitation—the one-way ticket—clenched in her hand. I thought she was leaving town, leaving behind the memories of her daughter and loss. But it was a permanent goodbye. After one last hug, she turned and ran as fast as she could off the end of the dock. She jumped. I remember screaming her name and running after her. Before I even got to shore, she'd disappeared, and the water was undisturbed. I waded in and felt something whip around my ankle, but before I could go any deeper, your father hauled me back and held me. I don't know if she drowned or if the lake is some kind of portal to hell. It doesn't really matter. She was gone, and I've never seen her again." Hope wiped her eyes and took a long drink of her coffee.

"Why didn't you ever tell me? Even if you'd left out the supernatural elements, Grace was your best friend, and she died in that lake." Something clicked in Evie's head and her eyes widened. "Wait. Grace Kane? Is she related to Viv?"

Hope nodded. "She was Gwen's younger sister. Guenevere always distrusted me after that, although I thought she'd put it aside after returning to Eden Valley. I was the last one to see Grace alive, besides James, of course, but as my boyfriend, he was equally suspect. No trace of her was ever found, and I think Gwen always thought there was more to the story than I shared. She was right, of course. I didn't tell anyone about the ticket to hell or how the lake looked undisturbed moments after Grace had jumped in. But after that, it felt...wrong to talk about her."

"How'd you know Quinn was a demon?" Evie asked.

"He told Grace after Lily was born with an unusual birthmark that perfectly matched Quinn's back tattoo, and Grace told me. There were no secrets between us, at least not until the end."

"That is a lot, Mom. I'm sorry you had to live through that."

Hope smiled, but it didn't reflect in her eyes. "I left Eden Valley after that. I tried to leave it all behind. I went to college. I spent a couple years hitchhiking across Europe. And then, when I was almost twenty-six, I ran in to your father at a tiny, backwater bar in Budapest. We hadn't seen each other in six years, but it was like no time had passed. I took him back to my hotel room that night, and the next day he found his fiancée and broke things off with her. We shacked up in a tiny apartment in Prague for a year—until I found out I was pregnant. We came back to Eden Valley, got married, and then you were born seven months later."

"Mother!" Evie gasped. "That is not the story you told me."

Hope shrugged. "It is, more or less."

"Less. Definitely less. You skipped over Dad being engaged when you reunited and being pregnant with me when you got married."

"Didn't you ever do the math?" Hope asked.

"You told me I came sooner than expected," Evie said.

"I told you that you were born earlier than anyone else expected," Hope said. "Your father and I were the only ones who knew—although there was speculation, of course."

"Huh." Evie rubbed her forehead. "I get why this story is important, but it makes it even harder to understand why you didn't warn me about Luc from the beginning, and why you didn't tell me sooner. How weren't you afraid this would happen to us?"

"Lily was never alone that first year," Hope said. "Every moment you weren't with her, your father and I took turns watching over her. When she turned five and nothing had happened, we relaxed. Grace's child disappeared when she learned how to walk, and we thought she was safe, that you were safe. We just wanted to protect you."

Evie bowed her head. "That wasn't fair to me, but right now it's just one more thing to add to the pile of knowledge that's been dropped on me in the last week."

Hope stood, kissed the top of her daughter's head, and said, "Call your friends. I don't know what happened to them, but Viv needs to figure out what's important and what's not when it comes to her newly awakened precognition. Sure, it was nice to be warned that I'd need a dozen muffins this morning if I wanted the children to eat breakfast, but I'm not sure I needed a six-thirty am phone call. It was 3:30 in the morning in Hawaii."

"I thought you liked getting up early," Evie teased.

Hope smiled, and this time it was reflected in her eyes. "I'll go wrangle the children so we can begin the process of returning them to their rightful homes. Lily and I have a spa afternoon planned, so you'll be on your own."

"She agreed to go to a spa?"

Hope winked. "I told her she could choose black nail polish if that's what she wanted, and she was instantly on board."

Evie shook her head, laughed, and picked up her phone.

CHAPTER NINETEEN

Bev and Viv showed up just before lunchtime. Hope had eventually gotten all three kids back to the house with the promise of leftover cake with lunch, then had taken off, kids in tow, to the day spa in Chelan for mani/pedis and, if Evie knew her mother, a stop at Dairy Queen for blizzards, because they sure weren't sugared up enough.

Evie made a mental note to send all future dental bills to her parents, then poured lemonade for her friends.

"There's leftover everything for lunch," Evie said. "I think the kids have decimated the desserts in the last twenty-four hours—sorry, Bev, my mother's a menace—but there's plenty of cut fruit, veggies, and cheese if you like."

"I have never turned down a cheese plate, and I'm not about to start now," Bev said. "Is your dad here, or are we alone in the house?"

"He's at the diner having coffee and shooting the shit with whoever comes in."

"Ah, so just like every Sunday morning when he still lived here?" Viv said, laughing. "You could set your watch by James Addams's arrival at Sunny's Diner."

Evie busied herself getting the lunch fixings out of the fridge. "Inside or out?" she asked.

"Outside. It's already almost seventy again," Bev said. "You just know it's gonna get cold and rainy again soon enough. Let's enjoy fake spring as long as we can."

"I'll meet you out there," Evie said. "Just gotta switch out the laundry."

"She means 'wash her sex blankets,'" Viv whispered loudly.

Evie couldn't stop the blush from staining her cheeks. "I'm sure I don't know what you mean," she said primly. "And I don't know if I want to know how you came to that conclusion."

"You have grass stains on your knees and a hickey just below your collar line," Bev said. "It doesn't take a Watson to figure out that something—or *someone*—went down last night."

Evie tugged down the hemline of her skirt to hide her traitorous knees. The blanket hadn't protected them, and the shower hadn't washed the stains away. "I hate you both. You're terrible, terrible people," Evie said, then disappeared into the laundry room and took her sweet time moving the outdoor blankets from the washer to the dryer, giving her embarrassment time to recede before joining her friends outside.

"You were going to tell us, right?" Viv said. "It's only fair."

"Fair how?" Evie said. "And why don't you go first. We all saw you and Luc's sister all over each other before you left the party."

"We were not all over each other. At the party."

When Evie and Bev made scoffing noises, Viv added, "Holding hands is *not* all over each other."

"Depends on where you're holding them," Bev said, then took a drink of her lemonade as Evie snorted.

"We were not inappropriate in any way at a child's birthday party," Viv said.

"Fine," Evie conceded. "You were not outwardly inappropriate, but I was about five minutes away from suggesting the kids use the heat you and Sam were putting out to toast their marshmallows instead of the fire."

Evie replayed the conversation in her mind. "I don't think so. Maybe if we search 'Grace Kane' obituary? And there must have been some mention of the abduction somewhere, right?"

"Ugh, how did people exist without the internet?" Viv complained. "It is so hard to find anything from that long ago." She scrolled through the newspaper archives, bemoaning the complete lack of a decent search function, before admitting defeat. "There's nothing here that I can find. Why isn't there an obituary?"

"What about one of those ancestry sites?" Bev asked. "The people who are hardcore into genealogy have posted all sorts of stuff—obscure records and obituaries and everything."

"Sure," Viv said. "I have an account. It might take me a minute to log in—I don't think I've looked at it in five years."

"If we knew she was dead, we could call my cousin Russell," Bev said. "You remember him, right?"

"Weird Russell?" Evie asked. "The guy who had a skull in his locker and wore black eyeliner and listened to Scandinavian folk metal? You mentioned him when we were reminiscing about our scandalous 'what I want to be when I grow up' essays."

"That's the one," Bev said. "He always claimed to be able to talk to the dead. I thought he was buying too much into his wannabe vampire persona, but now I wonder…"

"Where is he?" Evie asked. "He only went to school here a couple years, then dropped out and took off."

"He's living in some artsy town on the coast north of Astoria," Bev said, shrugging. "I can't remember the name of it. I just happened to see his name as a suggested friend on Facebook the other day, so I browsed his profile. He looks fairly respectable now; he's a bar manager."

"While you're searching for long-lost aunts, I'll see if my dad remembers," Evie said, pulling out her phone.

"Ask him if it's true your mom was two-timing him with the sheriff," Viv suggested.

"Not a chance," Evie said. "There are no answers to that question that I want to hear."

While Viv searched and Evie waited to hear back from her dad, Bev pulled out her phone and started typing.

"What are you doing?" Evie asked, peering over her shoulder.

"Eden Valley cemetery records," Bev said. "They might not have had a body, but I bet there was a funeral and a headstone."

"Good thinking," Viv said. "I'm getting nowhere with this ancestry site. Apparently, my relatives are the least nosy of all time. There's nothing in here about Grace at all. It's like she never existed."

"Nothing listed in the cemetery records for a Grace Kane," Bev reported. "It's all up to your dad, now."

Evie's phone buzzed.

"I'd almost forgotten about that... I think it was in 1972. That baby had just started walking, and your mom had just finished her second year of community college and was getting ready to head east to NYU for college."

"Thanks, Dad. Can you ask around at the diner and see if anyone else remembers the date?"

Evie read her dad's text out loud and then stared at the screen while the three dots indicating someone was typing flashed on and off the screen.

"I'll look through the headlines from May to August 1972," Viv said. "That's only sixteen issues."

After ten minutes with no reply from her dad, Evie texted again. *"Anything?"*

"What are you talking about?" James replied.

"Grace Kane's death?"

"Oh, I'd almost forgotten about that," James said. *"I think it was in 1972. Your mother had just finished her AA and was heading east to college."*

"Is your dad having a stroke?" Viv asked. "Should we call 911?"

"This is weird," Evie said. "It reminds of when..." She stopped talking and called her mom. When Hope answered, Evie greeted her with, "When was dad's last PET scan?"

"Two weeks ago, why?" Hope asked.

The noise of the salon was in the background, and Evie clearly heard Lily complaining about not being able to bring Sprinkles in for a pedicure.

"I texted him and asked him a question. He answered, but was going to get a little more information and get back to me. When he didn't, I nudged him. He responded almost exactly the way he had when I asked the first time."

"Were you asking about Grace?" Hope sounded unruffled—as always.

"Yes. How did you know? Did Gwen call you to complain?"

"She didn't, but I bet she wasn't happy to have Grace's memory dredge up. Most people remember when prompted, but it's hard to keep hold of it," Hope said.

"We just wanted some details—dates, timeframes... And I didn't want to bother you on your spa date with the monster."

"It's no bother. Lily managed to talk me into springing for spa days for all three of the children, so they're entertaining each other, leaving me to really relax into it. Lilith disappeared three days after her first birthday—April 13, 1972—and there were probably a few stories covering the FBI search, but not as many as you'd think, especially for a small town and a slow news cycle. Grace disappeared June 20, 1972, and you won't find a mention of her apparent suicide other than a small note somewhere in the Gazette issue following her death. There wasn't an obituary. I remember, and I suspect Gwen does, too. But everyone else...forgot. And any news stories at the time never made it to internet archiving as far as I've been able to tell."

"Who was the sheriff in 1972, Hope?" Bev asked.

"Greg Union," Hope said. "I thought Gwen had let that go years ago. She was so convinced I was trying to steal him away from her. He was twenty years older than me, had a pot belly and a receding hairline, reeked of cigarettes, and was a cop. She got him in the end, though, and never forgave me for my imagined sins. He stuck around exactly as long as it took to see his daughter born... And, I hope you know that story, Viv, because otherwise your mama is going to come after me with a machete."

"Uh yeah. Of course," Viv said.

"Thanks Mom!" Evie said. "Later!" She hung up and looked at Viv.

"Between the demons and the never-ending stream of revelations, I think we might be living in the end times."

"Did we learn anything new, or are we floundering in even more muck than before?" Bev asked. "And what if history repeats itself with Evie and Lily? I don't know how to prevent it, but we should make sure they're never alone—at least for a while."

"Lily just turned ten, not one, and Luc would never orchestrate a middle-of-the-night kidnapping. I think we're pretty safe. She might click her heels three times and take an unauthorized day trip, but at least I know she won't leave without saying goodbye... She'll give me that much, at least."

"What are you talking about?" Bev demanded.

Evie explained about the ticket to hell and laid out her fears.

"She won't run off without your permission," Viv said. "That girl loves her mama too much."

"I don't know," Bev countered slowly. "She might if she was mad or frustrated... Imagine a half-demon Lily mid-puberty."

Evie clapped her hands. "There is nothing we can do about it now. I'm going to talk to Lily about it next week after my parents head out and life is returning to some semblance of a routine. If I start to feel like jumping in the lake, I promise to call before it gets that far."

"Pinky swear?" Viv asked, holding out her hand.

Evie linked her little finger with Viv's, and Bev wrapped hers around them both.

"Pinky swear," Evie replied.

"Now that we've settled that," Viv said. "Can I spend the night tonight, Bev? I am not in the mood to go home. I'll just lose my temper. I need some time to cool off before I leave tomorrow."

"You're still leaving?" Evie asked. She tried to keep the disappointment out of her voice but failed miserably.

"I was only ever staying through Monday," Viv said. "I can't be here longer than five days."

"Why not?" Bev asked. "I never really noticed that you always stay five or fewer. Always, since that summer you came back to help with Lily."

"I almost didn't leave after that summer," Viv said. "And it's harder and harder to leave here—leave you, and your kids, and this stupid town—but as long as I don't spend more than a hundred hours here, I can still walk away."

"What about your back and your compulsions and my demon baby-daddy?" Evie asked.

"And her demon baby-daddy's demon sister?" Bev added.

"Sam was taking off last night with her dad and brother. I can't imagine a world where I'll see her again. I'll try to get back next weekend if you still need me. And I'm hoping the compulsions and the new back art will fade away once I'm not here."

Evie bit back the hurt she felt; Viv was no more abandoning her than her parents would be when they went home. "Of course. I'm sorry I freaked out."

"Hey, lady. It's okay. It's been a freakout kind of week. I'll be back, if not next weekend, the weekend after. I just need the space to figure out how to deal with my mom."

"Of course," Bev said. "Beyond just the things you learned about your aunt and your dad today, there's the whole issue of her complete homophobic bullshit she's been pulling lately. She needs to stop saying the quiet stuff out loud and get right with Jesus or I'll sic Lucifer on her."

Viv laughed. "She's never going to change. She's a bitter old woman, and while I understand a bit more why, it doesn't excuse anything. I don't know why I keep trying. One of these days, I'll stop. As soon as the guilt does."

"If I'm not going to see you again this trip, you'd better give me a hug, abomination." Evie stood and opened her arms.

"I may be an abomination, but at least I wasn't having extramarital sex with one last night," Viv smirked.

"Yeah, and how disappointed were you?" Evie said, throwing her arms around her friend and squeezing tightly.

"Only a little," Viv said. "I don't do one-night stands."

"Since when?" Bev asked.

"Since I turned forty," Viv said primly. "I turned over a new, chaste leaf."

"I love you, Genevieve Kane," Evie said. "Even though you're a terrible liar."

"Love you, too, Evelyn Grace." Viv closed her laptop and shoved it back in her bag. "I hear a car in the drive," she said. "The kids are back, so we can grab Shelby and head home."

Bev hugged Evie. "I'll come over after work tomorrow. Unless you have an evening shift?"

"I'll be here. I told my crew they had to cover for me through Monday night, but that I'd pay time and a half if they did," Evie said.

"See you tomorrow, then. Kiss kiss!" Bev blew air kisses at Evie.

The women walked towards the driveway, and Evie tried to muster up some excitement so she could present a happier face to her family.

Viv turned around just before they disappeared from view. "Before you go to bed tonight, check on Lily. Give her a kiss from me."

"Is this one of your compulsions?" Evie asked.

"Yes. No. I don't know." Viv rubbed her breastbone and blew out a breath, then nodded and said decisively, "Yes. You need to check on her and give her a kiss before you go to sleep. Trust me."

"Okay," Evie said. "I can absolutely do that."

"Thank you." Viv stopped rubbing her breastbone and waved. "See you next week."

CHAPTER TWENTY

E vie shuffled into the shower and tried to wash the sleep away. She'd had another mostly sleepless night, and this time it didn't end with a roll in the hay—or grass, as it were. Once she'd toweled off and dressed—a jersey maxi dress with purple and black color blocks—she grabbed her phone to text Viv goodbye before knocking on Lily's door to wake her for school.

"Wake up, sleepy!" Evie called. When there was no answer, she opened the door a crack. "Good morning, sunshine! Time to get ready for school."

The stench of sulphur floated out of the room, and Evie remembered Viv's instruction the afternoon before. The instruction she'd completed forgotten about. She'd kissed Lily when they'd finished their bedtime meditation ritual, but she hadn't checked in again.

Evie flung the door open. The room was not only empty, it was cleaned out. The floor was visible, the bed made, and there wasn't a single visible Lego anywhere. Evie felt a scream rising in her chest as the blood drained from her face.

She dropped her phone and sank to her knees on the rug next to her daughter's bed. Evie pulled her knees in tight to her chest, wrapped her arms around her legs, and rocked back and forth. Tears dripped down her cheeks, but she stayed silent.

She didn't know how long she'd been there when she felt a hand on her back. Evie turned around and threw herself into her dad's arms. "She's gone. Daddy. I don't know what to do. She's gone."

The dam broke and Evie started sobbing, big, gulping cries of heartbreak and terror.

Hope walked into the room but didn't say anything until Evie's sobs had quieted. She handed her daughter a glass of water and said, "We know where she is, Evelyn. That's a start. I called the school to let them know Lily would be absent for a few days. I also called Bev and let her know what was happening. She's going to drop Shelby off at school and will be right over. We will find her. I promise."

"Have you called Luc?" James asked.

"No. He left town early yesterday, and I haven't heard from him."

"You need to reach out to him," Hope said. "Either he knew this was going to happen and left you to find out like this and deal with it alone, in which case I'm going to research how to kill a demon, or he has no idea that his daughter is missing and is the best person to find her."

"You're right. Sorry. I didn't even think." Evie scrubbed the tears from her face and grabbed her phone from where it'd fallen.

"I don't know why you're apologizing for falling apart," James said. "I'm only barely holding it together myself, and I didn't even give birth to the little monster."

The fist squeezing her heart relaxed long enough for her to chuckle.

"Come downstairs with us and call Luc. I'll make you some coffee and French toast. You have to eat if you're going to get through today."

"Should we call the police?" Evie asked.

Her parents exchanged a glance. "If you want to, dear," Hope said. "But since we already have a pretty good idea where she is, I'm not sure it'll do any good."

EVIE STARED AT HER PHONE, waiting for Luc to pick up. It was the tenth time she'd tried to reach him and the tenth time she'd gotten his voice mail. None of her texts had been read, either.

"I wish he would get his stupid butt here," she said, then waited. It'd worked every other time she'd wished for him, although there had been a bit of a lag.

She stood up, grabbed her coffee, and began pacing. It'd been forty-five minutes since she'd found Lily gone, and she hadn't done anything but fall apart. She was no closer to getting her daughter back.

"I will kill that fucking demon," she said.

Her phone rang. Unknown number. Usually she'd let those go to voice mail—she didn't need to learn anything about her car's warranty or the outstanding arrest warrants in Florida if she didn't hand over her social security number and bank account information.

But today, she wasn't ignoring anything.

"Hello?" She sounded breathless, and she knew it.

"Evie, it's Luc. What's going on?"

"Where are you calling from?"

"Sam's phone. Mine had an...unfortunate accident."

"How'd you know to call, then?" She hated the suspicion in her voice, but nothing was right today, not even a return phone call she'd been hoping would come.

"I felt you wishing for me. Is everything okay? You don't sound right."

Evie broke into tears again. She could hear Luc trying to talk to her but couldn't understand him through the torrent of her sobs. She felt the phone being pulled from her grasp and vaguely heard her mother's voice.

"He'll be here as soon as he can," Hope said, handing Evie her phone back. "He sounded shocked and angry, but we all know that doesn't mean anything."

"How long?" Evie asked, wiping her eyes on her sleeve.

"Twenty minutes," Hope replied.

"He's always twenty minutes away," Evie said. "It's weird." She gripped her coffee cup and closed her eyes.

Every time she'd wished for Luc, he'd shown up. In fact, almost everything she'd wanted had come to her lately. She couldn't believe she'd overlooked the most obvious solution.

She closed her eyes, concentrated on Lily—her honey-brown eyes, lit up with mischief, her long, shining hair that never stayed in a ponytail, the slightly crooked teeth that Evie thought were adorable and potentially expensive in the future and Lily thought ruined her smile, and the sheer joy and exuberance with which her daughter barreled through life.

Once she had a clear idea of who Lily was—who Liliana Faith Morningstar Addams was—Evie inhaled deeply and said aloud, "I wish my daughter was with me, in this kitchen, in this house, in Eden Valley. I wish she would appear in front of me now." She was tempted to add a bonus wish that Abe would get boils on his balls, but refrained, not wanting to taint the more serious wish. She could always give him magical ingrown butt hairs later.

Evie opened her eyes expectantly. No Lily. But that was okay. It took Luc twenty minutes to get anywhere, and he was an adult. She was prepared to wait upwards of an hour for Lily before giving up in despair. Hope and James stayed at the edge of her awareness. They didn't invade her space, but made her feel loved and supported from a distance. That had always been the best part of her parents—they always seemed to know the correct distance she needed.

Gravel crunched in the driveway. Evie's head shot up, and she was on her feet and out the front door in a flash. A silver Audi screeched to a halt in front of the house, and Luc was out of the car almost before the engine cut.

Evie and Luc met halfway between car and house, and she collapsed in his arms. He stroked her hair, murmuring comforting nothings, and Evie felt herself hope—truly hope—for the first time since she'd realized her daughter was gone. Until the odor that clung to Luc's clothes registered.

She pushed back from him. "You smell like sulphur. Were you there? Did you have a hand in this? You were trying to convince me to let her go, that she needed training. Was the sex just a way to get me to relax so you could breach my defenses?"

Luc held up his hands and took a step back. "I never would've allowed this to happen if I'd known. Believing she needs training is one thing. Secreting her out in the dark of night without your permission or knowledge is underhanded, sinister, and frankly, a little evil."

"But the smell..." Evie trailed off, uncertain. Luc looked sincere, but everyone knows Lucifer is the Lord of Lies.

"He gets bad hell-BO when he's angry," Sam said, getting out of the car.

Luc stepped forward again and pulled Evie into his arms. "I am so sorry. We will find her, and I will make that bastard pay."

"Maybe she went willingly... The ticket?" Even the suggestion that Lily had left on her own without saying goodbye made Evie crumple against Luc.

"You know Lily sleeps like the dead," Hope reminded her from where she stood in the doorway. "I checked on her before I went to bed, and she was out. Besides, if she had left of her own volition, would've she stopped to make her bed and clean her room first?"

The relief that Hope's practicality brought was instantaneous, although it did nothing to alleviate the churning in Evie's stomach.

Sam leaned against the car and examined her nails. "You'll never get him to admit he was wrong," she said. "But you might be able to jolly him into a more reasonable custody schedule."

Evie's jaw dropped in disbelief, and she rounded on Sam. "There is no such thing as a reasonable custody schedule when it comes to some random guy who showed up two days ago to play grandpa and then kidnapped my child. There is only one person who might have the smallest claim on Lily's time—although even then, he might be hard-pressed to convince a judge that his parenting time required long, sudden trips to hell."

"I hear what you're saying," Sam said. "And, for the record, I agree with you. But Dad has never felt constrained by earthly laws or conventions."

"Or ethical considerations and decency," Luc muttered.

"I'm just trying to be realistic," Sam said. "I want you to get your daughter back."

"Why?" Evie asked. "You don't know me or Lily. Why do you care?"

Sam flashed a smile, and Evie almost sighed with the beauty of it. "Lucifer is an amazing brother. He's always been there for me, protected me when I needed it, and pushed me to be my own person. I owe him so much more than you could ever understand, and I would do anything, kill anyone, if it made him happy. I love him. And he loves you. Therefore, I want you to be happy by extension."

"That, and she wants to get in Viv's pants and thinks being nice to you will shorten the odds of that happening," Luc added.

Sam flipped him off without turning her attention away from Evie. "Right now, we are both cut off from hell. It's a deeply uncomfortable feeling, and one I've never felt before. I don't know how the old bastard did it, but neither Luc nor I can return. We'll have to find another way."

Evie crumpled under the weight of knowing her one plan for getting Lily back had just gone up in smoke.

"We will get our daughter back, Evie," Luc said. "I promise."

"I wished for her to come back, but she hasn't yet," Evie said.

"If we're shut out, she might be shut in," Sam said. "And it's possible your hell-given powers don't work across the boundary. There could be any number of things preventing her from being whisked to your side—and one of those things might be her own will. You might be able to wish inanimate objects into being, but you can't wish people to do things or be places they don't really want to be."

"But Luc..." Evie looked at him, then the words Sam had said moments ago hit her like a truck. Her jaw dropped.

"You got it," Sam said.

"I banished him once, though," Evie said.

"You surprised me," Luc admitted. "And all I could think was how much I wanted to do whatever you wanted me to do if it would make you happy."

"You guys are borderline gross already. I am not looking forward to the googly eyes you're going to make at each other once this whole kidnapping situation is sorted." Sam wrinkled her nose, but the hint of a grin peeking out countered her disgust.

The breath was knocked out of Evie again, and she swayed on her feet.

"Why don't we go inside and sit down?" Luc suggested. "Sam and I will continue trying to get through to our father or find a way down. You need to eat, stay hydrated, and rest. Neglecting yourself won't make her come back any faster."

Luc took Evie's hand and led her into the kitchen. "Sit. Please. Have some water." He looked at her parents. "Has she eaten? Is there anything I can get her?"

James gestured towards a plate of half-eaten French Toast. "It's her favorite breakfast, and she barely got through half, but she did try."

"That's a good start." Luc filled up two glasses, one with lemonade and one with water. "Drink these."

"What are you doing to get our granddaughter back?" Hope demanded. "This is two too many Lily-related disasters in four days. Before you came back, nothing like this had ever happened."

"It would've, though," Luc said. "This, I mean. Not the lake thing. My father has known about Lily since before she was born. He's been watching her for the last ten years, waiting for her to be ready."

"Why not just snatch her up like Quinn and Asmodeus did with my friend's daughter?"

Sam and Luc exchanged glances, then looked back at Hope. "I don't know what you're talking about," Luc admitted.

"Quinn does have a daughter, though," Sam said. "We didn't go to her ascension ceremony, but we were invited—of course. All the principalities were. I never really thought about where she might've come from—about who her mother was. I just assumed..."

"When demons have children together, it almost always results in a male child, a full demon." Luc flexed his fingers and continued, sounding more like a college professor delivering a lecture than a demon prince explaining the reproductive quirks of demonkind. "Most of the female demons are the result of a human and a demon. It's a nephilim-like situation. There are exceptions, of course. Sam here has two demon parents, as do I. The nephilim are highly coveted. Female demons are more powerful than the males—"

"Which is why it makes zero sense that six of the seven principalities are ruled by men," Sam said, flexing her fingers.

"—and are held in high regard. However, the chances of conception between a demon and a human are quite low. One of the reasons I didn't worry about anything on my last visit." Luc looked up, realized he was talking about impregnating Evie in front of her parents, and rushed on. "So, we should've realized that Quinn's daughter was a nephilim, not only because most girls born to demons are, but also because she was raised to the throne and made heir, supplanting Quinn altogether, which means she was far more powerful than him."

"Not that it means anything," Sam said. "We're almost universally immortal, so the chances of any of the heirs taking the throne are just about nil."

Evie let the sounds of Sam and Luc explaining demon husbandry drift over her until she didn't hear their words as much as the comfort of Luc's voice. She knew they were prattling on about things that didn't really matter to keep her mind occupied while they tried to reach their father, but Evie couldn't even bring herself to care anymore. It was a stupid problem. Everyone knew where her daughter was, but no one could bring her back.

She stood. "I want to sit outside," she said. "I need some fresh air."

"Of course." Luc stopped talking about the great demon uprising that'd resulted in his grandfather's deposition and grabbed her beverages, escorting her outside. Hope, James, and Sam followed. There was a small flurry as everyone arranged chairs and tables before resuming their conversations, but Evie paid no attention. Instead, she gazed out over the lake. She could see the place where Lily had gone under just a few days ago—the first time she'd thought she was going to lose her daughter.

Her eyes drifted closed, and her breathing slowed to match the rhythm of the waves lapping against the shore. When she concentrated, she thought she could almost hear the lake speaking to her.

I have her. She's safe. Come to me and hold her again.

Evie let go of any attempt to listen to the conversation around her and concentrated on the lake. It whispered to her, called to her.

Come to me, and through me to her. There are many worlds hidden in my depths, and your despair calls to me. Find what you are seeking. Come to me.

Images of Lily flashed into her head. Lily, bound in chains. Dirty. Abused. Tears streaking down her grime-stained cheeks.

Save her. Save yourself. Come.

Evie jumped to her feet and ran as fast as she could towards the lake. She just needed to get to the place where Lily had disappeared Friday, and then they'd be reunited. She could save her daughter and be whole again. She leapt, closing her eyes and bracing for the icy water to break around her body. But instead of hitting the unforgiving surface of Eden Lake, hard, warm arms closed around her and took her up instead of down. Luc's wings beat, almost deafening her with the sound as the lake fell away below her.

"Let me go!" she screamed, struggling against her captor. "Lily is down there. I have to go to her!"

"Shhh," Luc said, cradling her body against his. "She's not down there. I promise that if I thought you could get there through the lake, I would've dived in with you. Eden Lake is playing tricks again."

Luc set Evie down on the porch and turned her so her back was to the lake.

Hope was shaking, tears streaming down her face. Evie stared. She'd never seen her mother fall apart.

"It was just like Grace," she said. "I thought for a moment you were a ghost of a memory. Please, Evie. Don't make me watch you go, too."

CHAPTER TWENTY-ONE

"Bev's here," James announced.

They'd moved back inside and away from any windows overlooking the lake. Evie could still hear its call, but it was further away now, not as demanding.

The front door bounced open, and Bev and Viv burst into the room.

"Who would you like me to kill?" Viv growled.

"You came back?" Evie said.

"I never left," Viv corrected. "I started to, but something held me back, and I kept delaying and delaying. I'm here as long as you need me."

"But your five-day rule?"

Viv shrugged. "What's more important right now? My silly rule or my best friend and her kid?"

Evie felt tears welling up in her eyes again and blinked them back. "All I've done today is cry. Well, cry and try to launch myself into the lake."

"Luc grew wings and caught her before she even hit the water," James said. "He's pretty handy to have around in an emergency."

"There wouldn't be an emergency like this if he'd never come around in the first place," Bev said, glaring at Luc.

"Don't say that," Evie begged. "No matter what happens, I can never regret Lily. Even if…" A sharp pain in her chest interrupted her before she could give voice to her worst fear.

Bev looked at Evie, then down at her impeccably manicured nails. "This is probably nothing, and it seems weird to mention it at a time like this, but Brandy was at the school drop off this morning, and she asked me about Lily. It's probably nothing, but…"

"It might be nothing, but the Brandy-related coincidences are piling up," Evie said. "I don't know what her game is, but I can't play it right now. She has to wait her turn."

"What do we now?" Viv asked. "What *can* we do? If we're stuck here, and she's stuck there, how do we open a door and extract my niece? There has to be something. I can't just sit here." She started pacing back and forth, a tightly coiled spring waiting to snap.

"There might be a way in," Luc said. "But I don't know if it'll work the way we want it to."

"The hellmouth?" Viv asked. "Of course. But why wouldn't it work? That's how you got here, isn't it?"

"It is, and I can't get back that way or any other. But it is a portal to hell, and only those of us born there are barred from entering right now."

Hope started rising in Evie's chest. "Are you saying I can get through? I can go find Lily?"

"I'm not sure what I'm saying," Luc said. "It'd be impossible for you to find my father's court, to find Lily, if you didn't know where you were going. Everything down there is labyrinthine—corridors that don't go anywhere, hidden doors, staircases that toss you into the abyss. Without a guide…"

"But there's a chance." For the first time since Evie'd walked into Lily's room that morning, the cloud of overwhelming despair lifted partway.

"It's not really," Sam said. "Luc's right—it'd be highly unlikely you'd be able to find your daughter and get her out before you wandered into somewhere you shouldn't be and died. He probably shouldn't have even mentioned it." Sam glared at her other brother.

"I didn't want to hold back any speculation, any ideas at all. I'm laying everything out on the table. I can't see a way around this particular issue, but that doesn't mean there isn't one."

"Could she Theseus it?" Bev asked. "That was a dangerous labyrinth situation that turned out okay."

Sam pursed her lips. "If someone was waiting on the hell side of the door... But where would we get something long enough to work?"

"And hell isn't self-contained like a maze in Greek mythology," Luc pointed out. "There are almost infinite possibilities."

"So, this isn't practical," Hope said. She was taking everything in stride, and only the tightness around her eyes and the set of her jaw betrayed her emotions. "What would make it practical? Ignoring whether something is possible, what could we do to make this solution work?"

"A guide," Luc said promptly. "The only way to find your way safely is to have someone who knows where they're going."

"Does the portal come out in the same place every time?" Viv asked. "Because a map could work in that case."

"I don't know," Luc admitted. "I walked through it when Lily summoned me, but I don't know how I got *to* the door. She didn't really know what she was doing, and in her mind, the only way someone could move from wherever they were to here without using time-consuming travel was to walk through a door."

"Lily made the hellmouth?" Viv asked. "Wow. Better not let Buffy know."

Bev rolled her eyes at her friend. "Buffy doesn't care as long as vampires don't start crawling through, and since vampires are still fictional, we're fine."

Sam opened her mouth, but Luc elbowed her before she could say anything else. Evie saw James fix Sam with a piercing stare. Her mother might have accepted Sam as part of the extended family, but clearly her father still had serious reservations. He was being very careful to always keep himself between Sam and his wife and daughter.

"Sorry, sorry," Viv said. "I use humor to deflect each and every emotion, but especially fear and grief and helplessness. I don't want to be insensitive, Evie. I can't even imagine what you're going through right now."

Evie waved off Viv's apology. "It's fine. Usually, I'd be right there with you, and I appreciate your bits of levity. I need it all to distract me, or I'll jump in the lake for real."

"That was pretty real," James said. "Is it still whispering to you?"

"A bit," Evie admitted. "It's not as bad, now that I can't see it, but it's making promises that are difficult to ignore, showing me pictures of my daughter, broken and battered. Covered in filth and blood." Evie dropped her face into her hands and drew a shuddering breath.

Sam leaned in and said, "Evie, that's how you know that this isn't genuine. My father may have taken Lily without your consent—"

"Kidnapped her," Hope corrected Sam.

"—kidnapped Lily," Sam nodded in acknowledgement to Hope, "but he wouldn't abuse her. She'll be treated like the princess she is. She'll have a plush room, servants to do her bidding and fulfill her every whim, tutors, fine clothes, all her favorite foods to eat, and a throne by my father's side."

"We have to get her back before she becomes accustomed to that," Evie said from behind her hands. "I can't give her all that, partly because I am not the queen of anything, and partly because being a parent involves setting limits, serving vegetables, and denying many, many childhood whims."

"Our kids would have so many ponies if they got whatever they wanted," Bev agreed.

"Ponies and an entire menagerie of baby reptiles," Evie agreed. She turned her attention back to Luc. "Are you saying that in hell, she has a super charged wish granting ability? Like what I have, but extra?"

Luc nodded. "Something like that. Neither Sam nor I had that, but we couldn't be true heirs to the throne. Only girl children born of a demon and human can rise to that level. I will always be a prince, and Sam here is a princess—"

Sam bared her teeth at her brother and growled. "I told you never to call me that again. It sounds too…"

"Frilly?" Viv suggested.

"Exactly."

"Well, if it's all pink and frills, we'll have Lily back in no time," Hope said.

"That's just it… It'll be whatever she wants, whatever her vision of hell is. There are no outside forces to shape her opinions. At least not at first," Luc said.

"After she becomes accustomed to life as a Princess of Hell, and is reminded constantly that everything she has, everything she loves, would not be possible here, with you… That's when the restrictions will start. It'll be small things at first, barely noticeable and certainly not worth fighting over—especially if there's a new aquarium full of sharks in her bedroom to distract her." Sam smiled, but it didn't reach her eyes. "Father never does anything overtly cruel, but I wouldn't leave a child with him unsupervised… At least not until she's old enough to see through his games and stand on her own."

"So it's an abusive relationship," Evie said. "Love bombing and then cutting off choices and social ties."

"Basically," Sam said.

"I cannot let that happen. It was bad enough that I fell for it as an adult. I am not going to let Lily go through that as a child." She stood up and paced the length of the room, then stopped and pointed at Luc. "You are not doing enough. You are her father. She is in your home. I don't care what the cost, what the obstacles, you need to find her, bring her back, and fix this. Find a way, Luc."

"I wish I could!" Luc scrubbed his hand over his eyes. "I am trying to figure it out. I've never been locked out of my home before, never had to brainstorm how to get back in. My father has been a devious, scheming pain in the tail for as long as I've known him—kind of the nature of The Beast, you know?—but he's never banished me before."

"He's never exiled me from Hell, but he has barred me from the

Principality before," Sam admitted. "When I told him I wasn't going to go topside to seduce pretty men until I caught pregnant."

"What about what's her name?" Bev suggested. "Luc's ex-wife? She lives around her, doesn't she? And she spent some time there…"

"Her name is Angelica Masters, but her father moved after the wedding. He'd made his deal and gave up his first-born daughter to get what he wanted." Sam shrugged and crossed her arms in front of her body. "After the terms were met—after Angelica married Luc—our ability to find him disappeared. And without him, I don't think we'd be able to track down Luc's bride."

"I thought it was an arranged marriage?" Evie looked at Luc, revulsion dawning on her face.

"It was," Luc said. "Her father desired money and power, mine desired a human wife for me. They struck a deal, but instead of giving up his soul, Brockton Masters III gave up his daughter."

"And she didn't get a say in this? That's revolting." Nausea churned in Evie's stomach. What had she done? Who had she tied herself to?

"Of course she got a say," Sam said. "It was her father's deal, but without her consent, his soul would've been forfeit instead of his daughter. No living human can enter hell except of their own free will."

"What about Lily, then?" Evie demanded. Everything was spinning, and she was afraid she'd faint if she didn't keep yelling.

"Ponies and alligator babies and a cookie buffet," Bev said. "Plus, her ticket was round-trip. She probably thought she'd be back in time for school."

"But if she didn't use her ticket to get there… Will it work to come back?" James asked.

"No," Sam said. "She walked in willingly, but still under false pretenses. She'll be there until Papa releases her or she finds a way out on her own."

Luc slammed his hand on the end table next to him. "There has to be a way. Something I'm not thinking of. Sam, when he banished you, how did you get back?"

"You impregnated a human, and he needed someone to keep an eye on her. It was either me or Mat, and…"

Luc grimaced. "Yeah. Mat would've been a disaster."

"Don't get me wrong, I love my twin, but he…" Sam trailed off and half-shrugged, looking sheepish and a bit apologetic.

"Brings the chaos to your Chaos Twins moniker," Luc finished. "But if he's on the other side, he could pull you in, right? You two are connected in a totally different way."

"He's not, though. Father booted him, too. He just isn't here… In his words, 'Why would I want to hang out in that boring town. There was only one interesting person there, and he said he had to go to school.' I think he's in Spokane. Apparently, it's a den of iniquity and he's excited to spread a little corruption." Sam shrugged. "He won't help."

"I'm going to make some food," Hope said. "We can't brainstorm if we don't feed our brains. Sam, Luc, do you require food?"

"We don't require it," Sam said. "But I, for one, would like some. Food is the best thing about coming topside. Well, food and the hot chicks." She winked at Viv, who uncharacteristically blushed. "I'll help you, Mrs. Addams."

"As will I." James stood and followed Hope and Sam into the kitchen.

Bev put her arm around Evie and pulled her in. "We *will* figure this out."

Evie let Bev's confidence buoy her and give her the strength to hold herself together. At least for now.

CHAPTER TWENTY-TWO

E vie mechanically chewed the sandwich her mother had placed in front of her, washing down the sawdust bites with drinks of lemonade. Despair had settled in her gut, leaving little room for food. The bursts of hope that had accompanied every new idea that morning had evaporated. Her head felt heavy, and her brain was fuzzy, like she'd had too much to drink the night before.

There was nothing she could do. Nothing left for her. Her daughter was gone. She knew now why Grace had given in to the lake. Why she'd grasped at that last bit of tenuous hope. When there was nothing left here, why not try elsewhere? And those promises, those murmurs, they were seductive. Creeping in through her defenses, drowning out the conversations and speculations and half-baked plans around her.

She wasn't ready yet. There were things she needed to do before she searched for the door at the bottom of Eden Lake. But soon.

The promise given in response to the Lake's whispers made the call dim—at least for now. She could still hear it, still feel it. But it was easier to ignore now that she'd promised to listen later.

Evie stared at the remnants of ham and cheese on her plate. A noise outside caught her attention, and her head snapped up. She was on her feet and out the door before anyone else registered what was happening. She heard her mother shout, "Catch her!"

But Evie wasn't headed for the lake. She was running towards the woods. Loud barks greeted her, and Sprinkles took shape. She was bounding towards Evie, tongues flopping in the breeze, and looking more smug than any dog had the right to look.

"Sprinkles!" Evie shouted. "What are you doing here? Were you left behind?" Evie let the dog paw her as she jumped up, muddying Evie's dress in her attempt to lick Evie's face with all three tongues at the same time.

Evie dropped to her knees and did her best to wrap her arms around Sprinkles's three necks. Sprinkles snuffled into Evie's neck with her middle head and whined in three-part harmony.

"Oh, do you miss her too?" Evie asked, scratching behind one ear. "Guess I should've let you in the house, after all."

Luc sank to the ground next to Evie and the dog. "It might actually be better this way," he said. "If Sprinkles had been in Lily's room when my father took her, Sprinkles would've likely gone with. She is, after all, Lily's personal hellhound and a gift from my dad. They wouldn't have left her behind, and Sprinkles wouldn't have let herself be left. Now, though, she's here."

"How is that better?" Evie demanded, moving her scratching hand to another head.

"Sprinkles is a hell hound. Born and raised in hell. And she is fanatically loyal to our daughter. She'll walk through walls and swim through lakes of fire to get back to Lily, and I'll bet hell isn't warded against her."

The hope that had bloomed and died so many times in Evie's chest today started to germinate. She squashed it down. She didn't want to be disappointed again.

"How can we tell? Do we take her out to the sinkhole and drop her in?"

Sprinkles growled lightly, and Evie resumed the ear scratches.

"Well, not literally like that, but that's the general idea." Luc tapped his index finger against his chin and furrowed his brow as he considered. "Someone will have to go with her, or she'll get distracted and not come back."

"Obviously it will be me," Evie said.

Luc shook his head violently almost before she stopped speaking. "I don't like this. I don't want you to go in there by yourself."

"I won't be by myself." Evie stopped scratching and looked over at Luc. Sprinkles's middle head ducked under Evie's hand and bumped it up repeatedly until Evie restarted her doggy ministrations. "I'll have Sprinkles." She smiled at the dog while Sprinkles woofed with the two heads not getting any attention at the moment.

"You know that's not what I mean," Luc growled, running his fingers through his hair. His shoulders were gradually making their way up towards his ears as tension rolled through his body. "Sprinkles is a wonderful dog—one of the most intelligent hellhounds I've ever seen—but she's still a dog. You won't be able to communicate with her, or rather, she won't be able to verbally communicate with you."

"What else are we going to do, Luc?" Evie demanded. "Wait until your father determines she's spoiled enough and brings Lily back for a visit? Bide our time until he forgets and lets you and your sibs back in? How long do you think that will be? And will the Lily I know be subsumed by her demon side? I want my daughter back, and I'll be happy to get her back any way I can, but I don't want her to come back a different person."

"She's strong-willed, smart, not easily led, right?" Luc asked, leaning in and putting his hand on Evie's shoulder. "She'll stay herself."

"No. She won't. She might be all those things, but she's still an impressionable ten-year-old girl being given access to everything her instant gratification-loving heart desires. She might know deep in her heart that unlimited everything she's ever wanted isn't good for her, but it will be pretty hard to walk away from ponies and alligators and unlimited screen time and pizza and cookies."

"Even with all the ponies and pizza and ice cream water slides she might want, there are at least three reasons for her to want to come back," Luc said, pulling Evie back into the circle of his arms.

"Sprinkles's three heads?" Evie hazarded.

"No, you ridiculous woman. You." He slid his hand up from her shoulder and caressed her cheek with his thumb. "I've seen the bond between you, and she will not last long without you."

"And the other two?" Evie asked, not ready to comment yet on Luc's assertion that Lily would leave never-ending Disneyland any time soon because she missed her mother.

"Her friends. Think back to when you were her age. How long would've you stayed away from your friends, even with all the glitter unicorns and shiny dragons in the world at your beck and call?" Luc brushed her hair behind her ear and grazed the outside of her ear with his thumb.

Desire stirred, sluggishly, but it was there. Evie tried to shut it down. Now was neither the time nor the place.

"She loves those two almost as much as she loves you. If you throw in your parents, your friends, and her dog—she has a lot she's left behind, and that's worth more than any ponygators or cobracorns." Luc's tone turned wistful. "If I'd been here sooner, spent any time with her at all, she might come back for me, too."

Evie couldn't refute his statement without lying to Luc, so she did the next best thing. She lied to herself. "When she comes home, there will be time. We'll figure out a way to make it work. Maybe you can take every other weekend and a couple weeks in summer or something. You'll have time to get to know each other."

"I was hoping for a slightly different arrangement," Luc said.

"We can work it out later. I'm sure we can figure things out ourselves without getting any lawyers involved. Although I'm probably a fool to make a deal with the literal devil without a lawyer on my side."

Luc rose to his feet, pulling Evie up after him. "Let's go back to the house. I think you gave your parents heart attacks when you dashed out of the house. We can take Sprinkles back and see if we can come up with something that'll work that doesn't involve you going to hell and back."

Evie pulled away from him. "Why are you trying to stop me from saving my daughter? *Our* daughter. Is it because you know you'll have better access to her there than you would here? Is this how you become *part of her life*? By standing back while your father kidnaps her and then preventing me from going after her?"

"No. Evie, no. That's not why." Luc reached out a hand to her, but she stared at it until he dropped it.

"Then why, Luc? Why are you trying to keep me from going after her?"

"I didn't realize how much I missed you until I found you again, and right now the thought of letting you walk willingly into my father's court is terrifying. The only reason I can bear it at all is because the idea of leaving our daughter where neither of us can protect her is even worse.

"You don't have a soul," Evie said, fear and anger making her harsher than she meant to be.

Luc bowed his head. "You're right; I don't. But whatever it is I do have, whatever it is that makes me me, that bit is incomplete without you. I didn't realize how much I was missing until I saw you at Ambrosia last week. And I cannot walk away from you again."

"What are you trying to say, Luc?" Evie demanded.

"I'm trying to say I love you." Luc threw up his hands and started back towards the house.

"Wait," Evie said in a small voice. "You love me?"

Luc stopped and spun around to face her. "Of course I love you. I fell in love with you eleven years ago, and I haven't stopped loving you since. Leaving you behind in order to fulfill my father's contract was the worst decision I've ever made. And letting you go into hell alone would be worse. Please don't make me watch you walk away."

Evie stepped forward, then stopped mere inches away from him. "What else can we do, Luc? If you really love me, you can't ask me to abandon our daughter and hope she'll return of her own volition. If you know me at all, you know that's not possible."

"I don't like it, but you're right. We will find a way to make this work, and I will wait for you here, even if it takes eleven more years."

Luc reached forward and grabbed her hip, pulling her the rest of the way into his body.

"It better not take that long," Evie said. "It might be nice to miss the teen years, but I don't even want to deal with a twenty-one-year-old brat who's been spoiled beyond rotten for that long."

"It won't be that long. It can't be."

"Viv said she'd be back in time for dinner," Evie said.

"Has she been wrong yet?" Luc asked.

"Don't give me false hope," Evie said, leaning her forehead against his chest. "Don't fill my head with maybes and predictions that might not come true. I need to go into this prepared for the worst, so I don't fall apart when it happens."

"I'm not trying to give you false hope." Luc slid his arms around Evie's waist. "I don't know if Viv is right and Lily will be home for dinner tonight, but I do know that we will get her back. That you will get her back." He pushed back far enough so he could look her in the eye. "There is something about human mothers—maybe all human parents—fiercer than anything hell can throw at them. I know Lily will come home because *you* are going to be the one to bring her home. And God—if he even exists—help my father when you decide to bring him down."

"I wish I'd gotten something more useful than psychic shoplifting powers. I wish I had something I could use."

Luc pulled her close again. "You have something infinitely more powerful than anything I could've imagined." He pulled her into his arms and held her tight. "You have boundless, infinite, and unconditional love."

Evie felt tears form in the corners of her eyes again. She blinked them away, raised her head, and kissed Luc. The world spun away for that one perfect moment—she felt stars and galaxies collide around her as fire rose in her chest and threatened to consume her.

Evie broke the kiss first and backed up far enough to look at Luc without craning her neck. "Thank you. For coming back. For staying. For not making me go through this alone."

"If I have my way, you'll never have to go through anything alone again," Luc promised. "I meant what I said. I love you."

The words swelled on Evie's tongue, and she bit them back. She knew what she wanted to say, knew how she felt, but she didn't know how much of it was real and how much was adrenaline-fueled emotion that would fade when the crisis had faded.

Instead, she stood on tiptoe and brushed her lips against Luc's, softly and gently, then stood back and snapped her fingers for Sprinkles.

She took Luc's hand. "Let's go make a plan."

EVIE HAD LET Sprinkles into the house, and the dog was using her freedom to sniff every square inch of everything she could find. Since her noses were, by nature, pointed in different directions, this urge resulted in some inadvertently hilarious and definitively destructive miscommunications between her three heads.

"Sprinkles," Luc said. "Come. Sit."

The leftmost head glanced at Luc, then back at the trashcan she'd been exploring. She made a low, disappointed sound but started towards him. The other two heads, however, were not on board, and the feet didn't know which way to go.

Eventually, Luc and Sam convinced Sprinkles to sit in front of the fireplace, which James lit to keep the hell hound warm and calm, so she'd pay attention to the plan.

"This is all dependent on whether Sprinkles can get through the portal," Luc cautioned. "But if she can, she should be able to lead Evie to my father's court, find Lily, and—this is the trickiest part—back to the portal and home."

The doorbell rang. Evie jumped up and ran to the door. She knew Lily wouldn't ring the doorbell, but she couldn't shake the hope that was threatening to suffocate her. She flung open the door.

"Brandy." Evie's voice was flat, and if Brandy had an ounce of sense, she would've heard the threat in it.

"Hi," she said, contempt oozing out of her over-large and too-toothy smile. "I heard Lily ran away, and I wanted to see if I could help look for her."

Growling behind Evie made Brandy take a step backwards, but the oily smile was back on her face in a minute.

"No." Evie said. She closed the door, but Brandy's foot blocked it before it could latch.

"It's no trouble. After all, we're practically related." Her smile went from derision to malicious.

Evie felt Luc walk up behind her and Sprinkles pressed in on the other side.

"She said she didn't need help," Luc said. "Please leave, or Sprinkles will run you off the property."

Brandy laughed. "You're threatening me with an imaginary dog? Cute."

Sprinkles growled in three-part harmony, low and threatening, and pushed past Evie and into Brandy. She shrieked and looked down. Evie could see the hellhound, but apparently Brandy could not.

Evie placed her hand on the head closest to her, crouched down, and said, "You can scare her a little if you want, but don't hurt her."

One growl stopped long enough for a wet nose to snuffle into Evie's neck. Then the hound stepped out from under Evie's hand and bumped Brandy back another step.

The woman looked around wildly. "I don't know how you're doing that, but I'm going to call the police, and you'll be sorry!" She turned and ran down the driveway, followed by Sprinkles's raucous barks. The dog turned and trotted back into the house, and Evie slammed the door shut.

Luc put an arm around Evie and led her back to the living room. "Sprinkles chased that horrid woman away—at least for the moment. I'll deal with her later."

Evie sat down, took a deep breath, and said, "Okay. Navigating a labyrinth. Where are we with that?"

"If Eden Valley was home to the largest ball of twine, we could use that to bring you back," James said. "Alas, Darwin, Minnesota claims that honor." Evie saw Hope elbow her husband, and James winked at his daughter.

"Well, we don't have twine, but it'd probably burn up anyway," Evie said.

"Why would it burn up?" Sam asked.

"Aren't I going to be walking through a fiery pit with lava lakes and hell fire?"

"Oh. Oh no," Luc said. "I didn't mean literal lava lakes. Hell outside the principalities is...sterile. Clean, featureless, bright. Everything is white and seamless. That's what makes it so difficult to navigate. Everything looks the same—featureless."

"Is it self-cleaning?" Bev asked. "I mean, is it impervious to stains and dirt and blood, etc.?"

"No," Sam said. "One of the many fun activities planned for the wicked is cleaning the in-betweens. After nightfall, and in the dark, I might add, everything is scrubbed clean. Even if no one's been through and nothing's amiss, the cleaning crews show up and clean until not a single hair nor speck of dust remains. They are not allowed to leave the halls until noon the following day."

"Remind me not to be wicked," Viv said. "I hate cleaning."

"Not sure I want to remind you of that," Sam said. "Kinda think a wicked Viv might be fun."

Evie ignored the flirtation between Sam and Viv. "What are you thinking, Bev?" she asked.

"We might not have access to the world's largest ball of twine, but you do have access to the world's filthiest hellhound and a garage full of spray paint commandeered by our kids. You can leave a trail, and, unlike breadcrumbs, mud and paint won't blow away or be eaten by birds."

"I happen to know you have the largest sharpie collection this side of the Mississippi," James said. "We can make marks at set time intervals, so on the way back we know how much farther we have to go."

"What's this 'we' business, dad?" Evie asked. "You're not coming with me."

"Why not?" James demanded. "I'm not going to let you go alone."

"I'll tell you why not. Lily is gone. I am going after her. If you come too, and for some reason we don't make it back, that means Mom has lost her entire family in one day. I am not going to do that to her. Besides, you're still recovering from cancer treatments and don't have the stamina."

"That was cruel, Evelyn," her dad said.

"Not cruel. Realistic."

"She's right, James," Hope said. "Neither of us are as spry as we feel we ought to be. Stay with me. We will hold down the fort here with Sam and Luc and be ready with mac and cheese when Evie and Lily come back."

"You shouldn't go alone," James said, resignation in his voice.

"She won't be. Viv and I are coming," Bev said.

"But Shelby…" Evie protested. "You know what losing you would do to her."

"She won't be losing me because you are going to make sure that every single one of us makes it out of here alive." Bev nodded decisively in a gesture everyone who knew her well was familiar with. Her mind was made up and there was no changing things now. "I know you—if you go by yourself and things don't turn out the way you want, you will not make every effort to get back here. But if you feel responsible for me and Viv, for Shelby, you will move mountains to get home."

"She's right," Viv said. "Besides, if there are three of us, we can carry a lot more snacks."

"What about school? Shelby will freak out if you're not there to pick her up."

"I saw Elle at school drop off this morning. She asked if Shelby could come over after school to play with Kevin. Shel was thrilled by the invitation, so I said yes. I'm free and clear until after dinner, at least." Bev smiled at her friend, and there was more than a hint of smugness in the expression.

Evie knew when she was defeated. "Fine. You can come with, but if, at any point, we're in danger, you will drop everything and run."

"Of course, Evie," Bev said benignly and patted her friend's arm.

"Anything you say," Viv added in the same tone.

"We need markers, paint, and bottled water," Hope said. "Lily has several backpacks we can borrow so you can divide the supplies up evenly between you. Sprinkles should run around outside in the muddiest places she can find."

"And snacks," Viv said. "We will require snacks."

"It's noon-thirty now," James said. "That means the cleaning crews will be done. If we meet back here at one, we can caravan out to the sinkhole and see if it's a viable plan."

"I'll stay here," Hope said. "You won't need me there. I can give my best wishes to Evie before she heads out, and that way I can make sure the house is spotless and the food is ready for dinner."

Evie hugged her mom. "Thank you," she said.

"Just get out of here soon so I can pretend you all don't know I'm falling apart in private," she said.

"You don't have to wait to fall apart, Mom. We'll always put you back together."

"I know, baby girl, but today I will hold you together instead. You'll have your chance someday. Now go. Get the paint. Muddy up that dog. And go save my grand baby."

CHAPTER TWENTY-THREE

It was just after one when Evie stood above the sinkhole, still glowing with Luc's symbol, and stared in. Viv was visibly shaking, but insisted that she was going in regardless, and the only way past fear is through it.

Evie had given up trying to talk her friends out of coming with her and decided to be grateful she wasn't going alone. Luc walked up behind her and wrapped his arms around her waist.

"Are you sure?" he asked. "We can find another way."

"What other way?" Evie asked as she tipped her head back to rest on his chest. "If this doesn't work, we can talk about other ways. But for now, this is the only thing the collective minds of all of us came up with."

"Please come back, Evelyn Grace," Luc said.

Evie twisted around within the circle of his arms and kissed him. "I will."

Luc's wings shot out from his back and he launched them into the air, then drifted slowly down to the bottom of the pit. Sprinkles scrambled after them, getting more dirt on her dirt and covering herself with yellowish dust on top of that.

"I'll be back with Bev in a moment," Luc said.

Viv and Sam landed lightly beside Evie. They didn't exchange words, just a glance, and for a moment, it wasn't the fire beneath them heating things up.

Sam took off, her beautiful, purple-streaked wings spread wide. Luc was back seconds later with Bev, who looked a little pale. "I do not like flying," she said. "At least on an airplane, you can close the window and pretend you won't plunge to your death."

"I'm a lot safer than an airplane," Luc said. "I have a one hundred percent success rate of never accidentally plunging to the ground."

"Accidentally?"

Luc smiled at Bev, then turned his attention to Evie. "Be careful. Trust your instincts. I'll see you in a few hours." He kissed her lightly, then flew back up to the top.

"Ready?" Evie asked, looking at her friends.

"As I'll ever be," Viv said.

"Let's do this thing," Bev confirmed.

Each woman hoisted her backpack higher and grabbed one of the three leashes Sprinkles was trailing. The idea was that if Sprinkles got excited and tried to take off, she'd be forced into a more sedate pace—and that at least one leash would make it through any sudden hellhound lunges.

Evie thought it was just as likely that Sprinkles would take off and drag three disembodied arms after her, probably earning several treats from whoever saw her first.

"Okay, girl," Evie said, crossing her fingers that this would work. "Take us through!" Evie braced herself, not sure what to expect but certain that being pulled through a portal to hell by a three-headed dog wouldn't be pleasant. She felt something sucking at her, like a thousand leeches being pulled off at once, and then... Nothing.

🌱 🍃 🌿

EVIE OPENED her eyes and squinted against the bright light bouncing off the impossibly white walls. She felt...fine, other than a burning thirst and the odd fatigue she always felt when a spontaneous nap went on too long. She pushed herself into a seated position and looked around. Bev and Viv were laid out flat, but their eyes were fluttering open. Sprinkles was sitting a few feet away, unconstrained by any of the leashes, and cheerfully chasing her tail.

She glanced at the watch her mother had insisted she wear—an old one that ran on gears and didn't require batteries or wifi to work. "It's been almost an hour since we walked through," she announced. "We have to get going."

Bev and Viv made their way to their feet. Evie looked behind her. The portal on this side was nothing more than a white doorknob in the middle of a white wall. If she squinted, she could make out the shape of the door, but even that was quickly fading.

She grabbed one of the cans of spray paint from her backpack and drew Luc's symbol on the door in fluorescent pink, then followed that up with an arrow on the floor pointing directly at the door.

"Ready?" she asked the other women.

"Let's do this thing," Bev said.

"I wish we were safely hidden in the room that's been designated for Lily and had an easy way out," Evie said, then paused expectantly. Nothing happened. "Worth a shot," she said.

"Yeah it was," Viv agreed. "Looks like we'll have to do this the hard way."

Each woman picked up a leash, felt for the boundaries of the walls, and started walking away from the door.

"Ready to find Lily, Sprinkles?" Bev asked. "When we find her and get her home, there will be three meaty bones for you, one for each head. Does that sound good?"

All of Sprinkles's head barked enthusiastically, and she took off down the hallway, dragging the women behind her.

🐾 🐾 🐾

BEV AND VIV took turns spraying marks on the floor and walls while Evie kept time on her watch. At every stop, they each took a small sip from the water bottles they'd brought—it'd seemed excessive when they were packing, but even though Hell was cold and sterile instead of hot and volcanic, they were constantly parched. When Evie looked behind them for the tenth time in as many minutes, she saw their trail of fluorescent paint and muddy footprints.

They'd been walking for over an hour and Evie couldn't tell if they were getting somewhere... The only thing she felt sure of was that they weren't walking in circles. A snippet from a movie she'd loved as a child rose unbidden in her mind, and she tried not to panic at the thought that someone might be moving their marks as soon as they were out of sight keeping the women in a never-ending spiral to nowhere.

"Sprinkles, are we getting closer?" Evie asked.

Sprinkles woofed and wagged her tail.

"I guess that's a yes?" Viv said.

"In light of any other evidence, I'm calling it a yes," Evie said. Moving forward, doing something, *anything*, was keeping her anxiety in the background. As long as she felt like something was happening, like she was making something happen, she could imagine a happy outcome, or at least ignore the millions of awful potential futures playing out in her mind.

"Is anyone else's demon tattoo burning, or just mine?" Bev asked as they turned another nearly imperceptible corner to walk down another solid white corridor.

"Mine feels fine," Evie said.

Viv wiggled her shoulders experimentally. "I wouldn't say burning... More of the kinda painful itch of a new tattoo. I can feel something's there, which you don't usually get when it's just regular skin."

"That's not what it feels like for me. It's more like that time I gave into Jeremy Butthead's dare to stick my arm in the bonfire because it was 'just like fire walking, and no one ever gets hurt.'"

Evie shook her head. "He really was a butthead, wasn't he? I can't believe I went out with him after that. I can't believe I *married* him. What was I thinking?"

"You were thinking you wanted to get laid, and he was right there for the riding," Viv said. "And then your misplaced morality talked you into marrying him."

Sprinkles tugged them to the left, and after the corner was marked, Evie said, "I really went through a weird stage in my late teens, didn't I? I don't know where I picked up my notions about purity and sexual shame... You know my parents were never like that."

"It's that whole rebellion thing," Viv said. "Have you ever met a preacher's daughter? They are the wildest ones—as soon as they see a way to slip the leash. A couple years ago, I dated a preacher's daughter for a couple months, and the stories she'd tell... She eventually evened out somewhere between, but definitely closer to the fun end of the spectrum rather than the repressed."

"That's basically your story, too," Bev pointed out. "Only your dad wasn't a preacher."

"Until yesterday, I didn't even know my dad's name," Viv said, notes of bitterness flavoring her words. "But you're right... My mother carried enough shame for the both of us. The only difference is I didn't wait until I was out of the house and out from under her thumb. I was always a rebel."

"My rebellion was boring," Evie said. "And stupid, if it brought me to Jeremy."

"Right there with you, sister," Bev said. "When your parents are self-proclaimed free-spirit hippies who only settled down long enough to have a couple kids and get them almost all the way through school before taking off to hitchhike across the US, leaving their kids behind to finish high school... Well, you *might* decide to never leave town again. I like being settled and knowing where I'm going to sleep the next night. It is not boring to have stability and a job that has benefits and an actual house with indoor plumbing and enough bedrooms for everyone."

"Whoa, Bev!" Evie said. "I had no idea you felt like that. I mean, I knew you didn't want to emulate your parents' nomadic lifestyle the way Holly did, but you've never talked about it this way."

"And of course stability isn't boring," Viv said. "Your parents were fun at a party, but they weren't very good parents."

"I don't know why I said all those things just now," Bev said. "I honestly haven't thought about it like that in ages. When they died in that accident with Holly and Shelby, I went to a lot of therapy and thought I'd worked through it all. It's weird that it's coming up here and now. It just feels like... Like they're whispering in my ears, telling me how disappointed they are in how I turned out."

"I think you're the bees' knees," Viv said. "And your dead parents can suck it."

"Um wow," Evie said. "That was way harsh, Viv."

Bev laughed. "Thank you for that. Not sure why I suddenly needed validation in the middle of Evie's crisis, but I appreciated it."

"If you waited to have your crisis for the time you thought was most appropriate, we'd never know what was on your mind," Evie said. "For three women who claim to be best friends, I really feel like we've drifted away from each other's lives in the last few years."

"It's my fault," Viv said. "I know you guys can't travel as easily as I can, especially since James and Hope moved to Hawaii and aren't available to be on weekend grandkid duty anymore. So you can't come to me, and I refuse to come to you all more than one weekend a month for brunch. You probably know more about me from my Instagram than from me actually telling you."

"I love you both so much," Evie said. "And you're both wonderful people and the best friends I could've ever wished for. Life happens. We've all been busy. Raising a kid is no joke, but neither is having a successful design career and breaking hearts all over Seattle. It's a different energy, but not any less worthy than seeing your oops baby or adopted niece through to adulthood. No shame in our different paths."

Sprinkles took a hard right and started barking.

"Shhh... Sh, girl," Evie said, crouching next to the dog and scratching her right head behind the ears. "We're trying to sneak, remember? We can't get Lily back if we get caught."

Two of Sprinkles's heads stopped immediately. The third went on for another couple woofs before shutting it down.

"Good girl," Evie said. She reached out with both hands to spread the ear-scratch love around. "We must be close now."

Bev and Viv took the spray paint and marked the location. Bev gasped and dropped her paint can. The clanging of metal on the floor echoed even louder than the hellhound's barking.

"It burns," Bev hissed, arching her back and clawing at her shirt.

Viv pulled Bev's shirt up. "Holy shit," she said. "Evie, come look at this."

"What is it?" Bev asked, trying to turn her head all the way around to look at her shoulder blade.

"It changed," Evie said. "It looks kinda like a lazy C with a circle on the top end, a horizontal line about a third of the way down the C curve, and a T almost at the bottom, crossed with another short horizontal line. Like a capital and lowercase T together."

"Why is it changing?" Bev asked.

"I don't know. Mine changed, too, though. That was one of the things Luc was investigating for us but never got around to sharing. It's been a wild week."

"Well," Viv said pragmatically. "We're not getting any answers here. How long have we been walking, anyway?"

Evie glanced down at her watch. "Two and a half hours already—with the hour we lost crossing over, it's almost four-thirty. If we don't find her soon, it's gonna be a late dinner." The reality of the situation came rushing back in, and Evie tried not to choke on a sob.

"We are going to find her," Viv said. "I've never been so sure of anything."

"Sure like before? Or sure like you're trying to make me feel better?"

Viv dropped Bev's shirt gently. "Let's keep going."

"Okay, Sprinkles. Home stretch, right?" Bev said, picking up the hellhound's leash again. "Find our girl."

CHAPTER TWENTY-FOUR

Twenty minutes passed in silence other than the sounds of Sprinkles panting in excitement and Bev suppressing gasps of pain. They turned a corner—the latest in an interminable series of corners, paused to mark the corridor, and started to walk again.

Sprinkles stopped walking and started quivering. Three tongues lolled out of three mouths, and puddles of drool appeared almost imperceptibly against the backdrop of the shiny white floor. She took a couple small steps forward, looked back at the women, and woofed softly, pawing at the wall in front of her.

"Is this it?" Evie whispered.

Another soft woof and some light scratching looked like confirmation.

"How do we get in?" Bev asked. "I don't see a handle or a knob or any hinges…"

Viv started running her hands over the section of wall Sprinkles was pawing at. "There must be something… Luc and Sam would've said something if these doors only opened from the other side."

"Corridors would be pretty useless if you could never get out," Bev agreed. She winced, her face screwing up in pain, before smoothing out again.

Evie waited, worrying her lip with her teeth, as Viv performed a detailed examination of the wall.

"Aha," she whisper-shouted triumphantly. "Found a seam."

With the parameters of her search narrowed, it didn't take long for her to find the outline of the door. She borrowed one of Evie's markers and traced the seams.

"Boost me up," she commanded.

Evie and Bev each made a sling with their hands and held them out for her to step in.

"You'd better hurry," Evie warned. "We're not going to be any better at this than when we pretended to be cheerleaders when we were twelve."

Viv finished sketching the doorway and hopped down. When the starting and ending points of her line met, they glowed briefly then disappeared, leaving behind a visible door.

"Still no way to open it, though," Bev said.

"I got this," Viv said. "It's ingeniously designed. Hell must have some great artistic minds." She used the marker to lightly draw in the details of a door—elaborate, ornate, and massive. Bev and Evie were briefly called into service again to do some of the higher up details. When she was done, it looked all the world like a heavy door on a centuries old chateau... Wrought-iron hinges, a large iron door pull, and a sliding bolt lock.

"I wonder why there's a lock on this side?" Evie asked.

"I thought it might be handy when we're leaving," Viv said absently as she put the finishing touches on the door. Iron fancy work that evoked images of flames took shape across the door. When she was satisfied, she capped the marker and stepped back. Just like with the outline itself, the door she'd drawn glowed brightly for a moment then the marker lines disappeared and in their place was a perfect door.

"Ready?" Evie asked.

"Almost," Bev replied. She turned around, found the opposite wall, and spray-painted a four-foot high arrow pointing back the way they'd come. "Let's do it, then."

Evie grasped the door pull, braced herself, and pulled.

🥀 🦇 🌹

EVIE TOOK a step forward then stopped so abruptly that Viv and Bev crashed into her, pushing her forward. Sprinkles took care of the sudden traffic jam by barreling past all three women and pulling them forward.

Viv braced the door with her foot and held out her hand. "Find me something small to shove in here so we can find it again."

Evie tossed Viv an errant sock. "I don't know how she's lost a sock already," Evie grumbled. "She's had sock-repelling feet since the day she was born."

Viv let the door close slowly behind her, slipping the sock in between the latch at the last minute to keep it from shutting all the way and providing an unobtrusive visual to make the door's location.

"Is this… Is this her room?" Bev asked, awe coloring her voice.

Viv stepped further into the room and joined her friends. "Ten-year-old Viv just died and went to heaven. This is sparkle-goth paradise."

The walls of the room that had at least as much square footage as Evie's entire turn of the last century farmhouse had black walls, a hot pink ceiling, and a black rug with a glittery pink skull pattern. A king-sized bed was along the far wall—black sheets and comforter and a pink-lace trimmed black canopy overhead—there was an open wardrobe stuffed with clothes and shoes, and toys everywhere. An oversized dog bed—a miniature version of the large bed, was at the foot of Lily's bed, and an aquarium took up one entire wall.

"This is so much stuff," Evie said, her heart sinking. "I can't ever give her this much stuff."

"Don't be an ass," Bev said. "You can give her so much more than stuff. Why are you suddenly worried that Lily has turned into a materialistic monster?"

"You're right. I need to shake it off and figure out how to find her now that we're here."

Sprinkles bounded around the room, sniffed her dog bed and jumped up on Lily's bed, snuffling through the covers. She ran to the wardrobe, then back to the women, then to the wardrobe again. She barked commandingly.

"Are we supposed to get in there?" Bev asked.

Sprinkles ran back to the women and used her center head to bump Evie forward.

"I think we are," Viv said.

"I always wanted to go to Narnia," Evie said. "This feels like my best chance." She allowed herself to be herded into the wardrobe.

"If I learned anything form that book it's that we definitely don't want it to latch behind us," Viv said as the door swung closed. She caught it and held it open just a crack.

Sprinkles started barking in three-part cacophony.

Seconds later, the too-familiar sound of a door being violently opened made Evie wince.

"Sprinkles! You made it! Papa Abe said you'd find me."

The three-headed dog went into what sounded like paroxysms of delight. There was a squeal from Lily, excited panting, and the sound of something heavy galloping around the room.

"Papa Abe!" Lily shouted. "Sprinkles is here!"

Evie didn't hear a response, but Lily replied, "We're going to have some alone time while I show her everything in my room and jump on the bed."

The door slammed shut hard enough to make the wardrobe shudder.

"Sprinkles, wait until you see everything Papa Abe got for us. There are no rules here. We can do whatever we want. Eat whatever we want. And we only have to shower if we want to. Plus, Papa Abe says I can play Minecraft all day if I want to and I can stay up as late as I want.

Evie shoved her fist into her mouth to stifle a sob. She grabbed the wardrobe door, her mind going a mile a minute. How was she going to get Lily out of there when she had everything she'd ever wanted and more here?

"Can I tell you a secret, though, Sprinkles?"

There was a low woof in response.

Lily's voice dropped to a whisper. "I miss Mama. I know Papa Abe said she wanted me to be here for now so I could learn how to be a proper princess, but I didn't get to say goodbye. And Grandma and Grandpa came all the way from Hawaii for my birthday. And Kevin and Shelby are going to wonder why I wasn't in school. I don't want to leave. Not really. But I am a little scared. Not as much now that you're here."

Sprinkles woofed again, louder this time, and thumped over to the wardrobe.

"What are you doing, Sprinkles?" Lily asked. "Do you want to see if there are doggy outfits in there for you?"

Lily pulled open the door and screamed, jumping back several steps. She looked around, then leaned in. "Mama? Aunt Viv? Aunt Bev?"

"It's us, sweetheart," Evie said. "I came to take you home with me."

Lily worried at her lower lip. "I thought you wanted me to be here? Papa Abe said…"

"Did he say, or did he let you believe?" Viv asked.

"No, he said. He said, 'Do you really think your Mama would let me take you without her permission?'"

"Oh, baby girl," Evie said. "He asked you a question that you thought you knew the answer to. But he didn't say I gave permission. Do you see the difference?"

"He lied!" Lily gasped. "Not exactly, but he made me believe something that wasn't true!"

"I'd like you to come back with me," Evie said. "Once we're home, we can call Papa Abe and have a talk with him about visits and training and princessing and all those good things, but those are conversations that should happen with all of us together. You, me, Papa Abe, and Luc."

Lily pursed her lips. "With that many grownups talking, no one will care what I think."

Bev reached out and tapped Lily on the shoulder. "Lily, have you ever known your mom to discount your opinion unless it was a safety issue you didn't understand?"

"Well, no, but..."

Viv stepped forward. "And even when it is a safety thing, doesn't your mother always listen anyway and then explain her reasoning?"

"Yes... But..."

"Lily, I promise that you can be an equal part of any discussions about your time here and your training. Pinky swear." Evie held out her pinky, and Lily locked onto it with her own.

"You also have to swear on the River Styx," Lily said.

"I wouldn't dream of skipping that. I solemnly swear on the River Styx that I will not make any decisions about your future and your training and your visits to hell without you present and a full participant in the proceedings." Evie nodded, shook Lily's pinky, and then pulled her daughter in for a hug. "Are we set? Can we go home? Grandma's making mac and cheese."

"Should I say goodbye to Papa Abe?" Lily asked. "I don't want to be rude."

"Once we get home, we'll call him and invite him to dinner at our place so we can have our first discussion. Does that sound fair?"

Lily squeezed Evie tight. "I love you, Mama."

"Love you, too, Monster."

"Sprinkles!" Lily called. "Ready to go home?"

LILY GASPED as they walked through the door—that sock had come in really handy—and into the white corridor. "This is so weird! How did you know where you were going?"

"Sprinkles knew," Evie said. "She's an amazing dog."

Lily kissed each of Sprinkles's heads. "She is the best dog ever."

Lily straightened up and looked at her mother, absolute trust shining in her eyes. "Let's go."

"How long do you think we have before someone notices that you're missing?" Viv asked Lily, taking a moment to slam home the deadbolt she'd drawn onto the door.

"Sunset," Lily said. "That's when dinner is, although I don't know how to tell when sunset is. There aren't any windows or a sky or an outdoors or anything."

Evie glanced at her watch. "It took us almost three hours to find you, which means its after five o'clock in Eden Valley and three hours until sunset. But I don't know what time it is here."

Lily shrugged. "I'm not sure, but I think later than that. I'm hungry."

Bev slipped off her backpack and rummaged around for a moment before finding a chocolate granola bar for Lily.

"Thanks, Aunt Bev," Lily said around a mouthful of food.

"Manners," Evie said.

Lily looked at her mother, eyes wide. "Mama, after everything that happened today, don't you think it's a bit silly to worry about my manners?"

Evie shook her head at her daughter. "Glad to see you're still as sassy as ever."

Lily grinned unrepentantly, shoved the rest of the bar into her mouth, and crumpled up the wrapper, shoving it her pocket.

"Is it my imagination or is the corridor changing color?" Viv asked.

Evie looked around. The color was still uniform, but it was no longer blindingly white. "It's a kind of...peach."

"Like the western horizon when it's approaching sunset?" Viv pointed at the arrow on the floor pointing them in the correct direction.

"I hate to ask," Bev said as they started walking in the direction their arrow indicated. "But if the walls are reflecting a sunset, which not-so-incidentally means we're almost out of time, do you think it'll be a full-on spectacular one?"

"Why do you ask?" Evie picked up the pace and reached for Lily's hand.

"Well, the most spectacular sunsets I've seen are vivid oranges and pinks. You know, the colors of the paint we used to mark our path."

"Oh shit," Evie said. "Sprinkles, do you think you'll be able to find your way back out when you're not looking for Lily?"

Sprinkles whined and hung her heads.

"That's a no, then," Evie said. "We've got to hustle, then. Get as far as we can before the marks fade into the walls, then hunker down and wait for them to become visible again."

"Will they show up against black? Will we be able to see at all?" Bev asked. "And will we run into the souls of the damned who show up to clean?"

"I don't have a better plan, do you?" Evie snapped, then paused for a moment. "I'm sorry, Bev. I didn't mean to snap at you."

"It's fine, Evie. We're all on edge." Bev waved her hand, dismissing Evie's rudeness along with her apology. "I suggest we power-walk. I don't think it'll take us three hours to get out. We don't have to stop every few feet to mark our path and we don't have to wait for Sprinkles to determine the best course."

"How long does sunset last from beginning to spectacular?" Evie asked. "I've never paid attention."

"It depends on where this is imitating—if it is imitating anything," Viv said. "But if I were to guess, I'd say we have about ninety minutes until twilight. An hour of the sun slipping towards the horizon, a period of spectacular sunset, and then the post-sunset thirty to sixty minutes of gradually purpling sky."

"Wow," Bev said. "Way to drop some knowledge, Viv."

"I knew that photography minor would come in handy eventually," Viv said. "I mean for more than picking up photographers at gallery shows, that is."

"What does 'picking up' mean?" Lily asked. "Does it mean dating? Or sex?"

"Dating, Lily," Viv said firmly.

"Definitely dating," Evie agreed.

They picked up the pace again until Lily was jogging to keep up with the longer-legged women.

Evie obsessively checked her watch as the walls slowly deepened in color, the peach turning to light coral and then gradually brightening.

"How long has it been?" Bev asked.

"Thirty minutes," Evie replied. "What do our timestamps say?"

They paused at the next arrow to read the time elapsed marker that had been graffitied on the wall. "Two hours from the portal," Bev said.

"That means it's taking about half as long to go back," Viv said. "That's another hour."

"And that's about how long we have before dark?" Lily asked. "We can make it in time for dinner!"

"Pretty soon the marks will fade into the sunset," Viv said. "We'll have to pause and wait for the walls to change color again."

"It'll be a good opportunity to rest, have some water and a snack, and get ready for the final sprint back," Bev said.

She sounded cheerful and positive, but Evie heard the fear in her voice.

"Let's keep going now until we can't make out the arrows anymore," Evie said. "I have an idea of how to keep moving after that. It'll be slower, but any forward motion will be useful."

"Mama, why are you all afraid? If the sun sets while we're in here and we're not back in Eden Valley yet, Papa Abe will find us and invite us to dinner at his place and then we can all go home together. Why are we sneaking?"

Evie jogged along in silence for a moment with Lily's hand in hers. She didn't want to lie to her daughter, but neither did she want the whole truth to come out. Lily didn't deserve to be scared, too.

"You know how Papa Abe tricked you into coming with him by implying he'd already talked to me and gotten my permission? Well, I think Papa Abe is a trickster all around, and I'd feel better if our next conversation was at our home and not his."

"What does implying mean?"

"Suggest without saying," Evie said. "He asked a question that you answered with your truth, even though the real truth was different, right? That means he *implied* that I had agreed because he knew what you would answer before you answered."

"That was tricky," Lily said. She was starting to sound a little winded. "So he's kind of like Loki?"

"Kind of," Evie said. "And it's always best to talk to tricksters on your home turf. I'm more comfortable in my home when I'm not worrying about you and I know where I am."

Lily nodded. "That makes sense. You're worried he might trick you the way he tricked me, even though you're a grownup."

"I might be an adult, but I think Papa Abe has a lot more experience in making tricky deals than I do," Evie said.

The walls were deepening into bright orange, and the marks on the walls were nearly imperceptible now.

"Let's stop to catch our breath and have some water," Evie said. "Then we can keep going, although a lot more slowly."

"How?" Bev asked, handing out waters and more granola bars.

"One of us will follow the wall forward until they find the next mark, then the rest of us will catch up. As long as we don't lose sight of each other, we'll still be on the right path."

"I'll do it," Viv said, finishing her water and tossing the empty back into Bev's pack. "I'm the expendable one."

"What's expendable?"

"It means the one who isn't a mom," Viv said, meeting Evie's eyes. Her hard stare said she wouldn't back down.

"It means Aunt Viv is a big dummy," Evie said. "None of us are expendable."

"We'll take turns," Bev said. "That should prevent any weird delusions of heroics."

Their progress slowed almost to a crawl, but they kept going forward. The sky turned from orange to red to pink, then slowly started fading into a velvety lavender.

"We have about thirty minutes before it'll be too dark to see," Viv said. "And the last marker said we were seventy-five minutes from the portal."

"We should jog," Bev said. "We'll all hate our old bodies tomorrow, but I'd rather make it that far and switch to a diet of heating pads, ibuprofen, and icy hot than see what happens in the hallways when the cleaning crew shows up."

They picked up the pace and soon were at a slow jog.

"I can go faster," Lily said.

"Not sure I can," Evie replied. "It's been about eleven years since I was running thirty miles a week."

The walls went from lavender to a deeper purple, and the marks began to fade into the darkness.

"Twenty minutes," Viv read from the next marker. "Almost there."

They slowed from a jog to a fast walk to a near crawl.

"Should've packed my own backpack. I always have flashlights," Evie said, trying to keep the fear out of her voice as the passage purpled around them. "I feel like I'm in a void."

"I have matches," Lily offered. "Maybe we could use them to see the marks?"

"I don't want to know why you have matches, but I've never been so grateful that you broke a rule before," Evie said. "Hand them over."

Lily pulled a dozen matchbooks out of her pockets and gave them to her mother.

"Don't want to know," Evie muttered to herself. She struck a match and the light flared for a second before flickering down.

"I saw it!" Bev announced. "This way."

They linked hands and headed towards the mark Bev had seen. Twenty steps later, Evie lit another match.

"Five minutes," Viv announced. "We are so close."

The walls vibrated, and the sound of a large engine echoed through the corridor.

"What's that?" Lily asked. She grabbed her mother's hand tighter.

"Cleaning crew. We have to find the door."

"Light a couple matchbooks up," Viv said. "We have to be here by now."

Evie did as instructed. When they flared, Viv yelled triumphantly. "Found it!"

Bev was looking back the way they came, and the expression on her face was anything but triumphant. Sprinkles growled low in her throats, and the menace accompanying the noise made Evie's stomach churn.

"Open the door, Viv," Bev urged. "Hurry."

"I can't get it open." Viv rattled the doorknob, then kicked the door. "It's stuck."

"Let me try," Lily said, walking forward. "Please."

Viv backed out of the way to let Lily in. Evie lit another book of matches up and watched as Lily touched the doorknob. The seams of the door glowed brightly and appeared. Lily turned the knob and pulled it open.

"Run through!" she yelled. "Hurry!"

Viv and Bev raced through the door, followed by Sprinkles.

"Go Mama!" Lily said. "I have to hold it open."

"There is no way we're not walking through together," Evie said. "Grab my hand."

Evie stepped through the portal, Lily's hand held tightly in hers. When she was all the way through, she squeezed and pulled.

This time, the trip was slower. She felt trapped between doors and unseen hands pulled her backwards. Then she heard voices in front of her—Bev and Viv, her father, and... Luc.

Fresh air hit her face and chased away the sulphur she hadn't registered until it wasn't there. She pushed forward, using all the strength she could muster, and stepped through the door. For a second, she didn't feel Lily's hand in hers, and the adrenaline of sheer panic flooded her body. Then the pressure in her hand returned and Lily tumbled to the ground beside her.

The portal clanged shut, shaking the earth around them.

"You're safe. You made it." Luc pulled Evie and Lily into his arms. Evie bit back sobs. There'd be time for that later.

"Let's go home," Evie said. "I'd really like some of that mac and cheese."

CHAPTER TWENTY-FIVE

L ily was halfway through her mac and cheese when she started nodding off.

"Lily, let's get you to bed," Evie said.

"I don't want to. I'm ten, and ten-year-olds never go to bed before it's dark." Lily paused to consider her words, then added, "Unless they're sick. Then it's okay. But I'm not sick, so I'm staying up. Besides," she fluttered her eyelashes at her mother and widened her eyes, "I had a rough day, and I deserve some birthday cake."

Evie laughed, her first genuine laugh of the day that wasn't tinged with fear. "Did you have breakfast with Papa Abe?"

Lily's eyes shifted to the left. "Maybe."

"And what did you eat for breakfast?"

"Pancakesandbaconandsyrupandcake." Lily's words ran together as she continued to not make eye contact with anyone.

"And for lunch?"

"Not just cake. There were vegetables, too."

"Liliana, dear," Hope said gently, catching her granddaughter's eyes. "Was the vegetable carrot cake?"

Lily huffed and crossed her arms. "Fucking fine. But what if Papa Abe shows up? You promised I could be here when you talk to him."

"If he shows up to negotiate before dark, I'll come get you. Otherwise, I'll send him away and tell him to come back tomorrow." Evie looked at Luc, a question in her eyes.

"She'll be safe," Luc said. "As long as she doesn't agree to go with him, he can't take her."

"Did you hear that Lily?" Evie asked. "Under no circumstances are you to go anywhere with anyone unless I am standing right in front of you saying it's okay."

"What if I need to pee?"

Evie rolled her eyes. "If you need to pee, you have my express permission to leave your room and walk across the hallway to the bathroom, pee, wash your hands, and go straight back to your bedroom in this house only."

"What if—"

Evie held up a hand. "No more what ifs. Skedaddle yourself upstairs. I'm right behind you. You need to brush your teeth, brush your hair, find some pajamas, and hop your booty into bed."

Lily turned around and did an enthusiastic wiggle. "My booty wants to stay here and dance!"

Luc looked at Evie, eyes wide. "Is this...usual? Or the exuberance of today's adventure?"

"This is pretty typical," Evie said, grinning as Lily ran up the stairs. "Welcome to parenthood. Pro tip—if she asks any questions about moon phases, do not fall for it."

Lily reappeared in the dining room. "Did somebody say full moon?" She burned around, dropped her pants, and redid her booty shimmy.

"Upstairs now, monster!" Evie said, unsuccessfully holding back laughter.

Lily cackled and ran up the stairs. Evie followed more slowly. The events of the day she'd been carefully compartmentalizing burst forward, and her knees wobbled for a second. She grabbed the banister and bit back a sob. She couldn't fall apart yet. If she'd learned anything from her mother, it was that falling apart was a later activity.

It took place after everyone had gone to sleep and she was alone. You never let anyone else see you crack.

"Mooooooom!" Lily yelled. "Where are you? How am I supposed to brush my teeth if you're not standing behind me telling me I'm doing it wrong?"

Evie pasted a smile on her face and pushed it up into her eyes. She walked into the bathroom. Lily was holding her toothbrush perfectly still and was moving her face back and forth.

"You know, you could just turn it on. It's an electric toothbrush."

"Oh yeah! I forgot." She turned on her toothbrush and looked sideways at her mom. "You know, I bet I'd never have to brush my teeth if I'd stayed with Papa Abe."

"You would've looked real cute as a toothless demon princess," Evie said. "Less talking, more brushing."

Evie felt herself pushed forward, and the odor of sulphur filled the room. Abe's face appeared in the mirror. He looked almost completely human this time—no horns, and no flamboyant suit. The only thing marking him as other, besides the smoke curling up around his head, was the cloudy yellow of his pupils. He winked.

Evie spun around, breath catching in her throat.

"She's right, you know. There's no toothbrushing in hell. Instead, there are perfect teeth, perfect health. Everything is easy and you never have to do things you don't want to. Don't like vegetables? Doesn't matter. Don't want bedtimes? Fine...you're always well rested. It's a lot easier."

A wide grin split across Lily's face. "Papa Abe! Hi! My mom said you'd show up." A scowl like a thundercloud formed on her face. "You lied to me."

"Liliana, I would never lie to you. I cannot lie to you." The King of Hell put one hand over his heart and adopted a wounded expression.

"You lied by im...implying...that my mom said it was okay."

"That wasn't a lie, Liliana. I simply asked a question and let you draw your own conclusions. Is it my fault you assumed I would've asked your mom and she agreed?"

Lily narrowed her eyes. "You are a trickster. I don't think I like you anymore."

Abe didn't lose his jovial expression, but Evie saw his eyes harden. "Alas, my darling granddaughter. You are the only grandchild I have, and you have powers you need to learn to harness. You don't want to hurt your mom or your friends, do you?"

"Noooo. But—"

"That means you have to come with me so you can learn. Otherwise, an accident might happen, and BOOM!" Abe clapped his hands together, and it sounded like the crack of too-close thunder.

"Can you take her against her will?" Evie asked.

"I don't want to resort to force."

"That's not what I asked. Can you take her against her will? If she says no, can you make her go with you?"

"He can't," Luc said from behind his father. His eyebrows came together over his narrowed, furious eyes. "No living person, no matter how much demon they have in them, can be taken to hell against their will. It's argued that no one, living or dead, can enter hell against their will, but that the will is exercised in wickedness while alive. Our philosophers—most of whom were very wicked people while alive—have spent centuries on that question. But that doesn't matter. What does is that Lily doesn't have to go with him if she doesn't want to."

"Then you will consent and give her leave," Abe said. He spread his arms expansively, palms up, and a too-jolly smile on his face. "If you convince your child to return with me, I will welcome you and your sister with open arms. You will no longer be barred."

"This decision isn't mine to make," Luc said. "It's primarily Lily's, but Evie's opinion has much more weight than mine."

"You'd cede your paternal right to a human woman who didn't have the sense to know who you were when you took her to bed?"

"You know what?" Evie interrupted. "I am anxious to have this conversation. But, I would like to not have it in my bathroom. Lily, finish your teeth and brush your hair. Luc, will you escort your father downstairs? You may offer him some lemonade—there's plenty in the fridge. We will be down in a minute."

Abe looked for a moment like he was going to argue, but he nodded, his chin slicing through the air so sharply Evie half-expected a rift in space to appear. The demons headed downstairs. Evie closed the bathroom door behind her.

"You will need to be there, of course," Evie said. "No decisions will be made without your agreement. While you're brushing teeth and hair, think about what you want."

Lily brushed her teeth slowly, doing the best job Evie had ever seen her do. When she finally spit and rinsed and grabbed her hairbrush, she looked at her mom. "I don't want to go with him, but I need to. It's been really awesome to have magic powers, and I had plans at school for next time Mr. Kruse is our substitute, but the more I do, the harder it is to put it away when I'm done. Everything is bubbling up inside, and I'm afraid I'll explode. I didn't want to tell you. I don't want to be in trouble. But Papa Abe was right."

"I don't want you to go either," Evie said. "Maybe we can find a compromise."

"Do you mean I could stay with you most of the time and visit Papa Abe sometimes for lessons and cake?"

"That sounds reasonable to me. You have a father now, and a new aunt—Aunt Sam—and they'd be great people to take care of you while you're visiting."

"I don't know. I don't really know them. It might be weird."

"We can figure the details out later. For now, let's go and get this over with so you can get to bed and be awake enough for school tomorrow."

THIRTY MINUTES OF ARGUING—OR rather Evie arguing and Abe talking over her and twisting everything she said—and they were no closer to a resolution than they had been when they'd started. Evie glared at Abe. "I don't care what precedence you're talking about. The only thing I care about is what's best for my child. And if you don't stop talking over her, you can leave and come back when you're cooled down enough to have a mature conversation."

A noise to her left sounded suspiciously like someone choking back laughter, but Evie didn't take her eyes off her adversary.

"Evelyn... May I call you Evie?"

"Call me whatever you want. It won't change my stance. Now, shut up and let Lily talk. This is her life you're trying to negotiate with me, and she deserves to be heard."

"She's a child. Are you telling me you'd let her make such far-reaching decisions? Do you let her decide everything? If the answer is yes, you don't need to be here at all, do you? Lily and I can come to an agreement without you."

Evie found Luc's hand under the table and squeezed. She was about ready to throw something at Abe, and if she thought that would make him shut up for five minutes, she'd give in to that urge.

Luc squeezed back, then turned all his attention to Abe and addressed him with a cold, even voice. "Father. For once in your life, you need to stop talking. You will not get what you want by steamrollering the people whose assent you need. This is a negotiation, and if you won't negotiate, then we will have to ask you to leave."

Abe looked around the table. Evie was flanked by Luc and Lily; Hope and James were on Lily's left. Sam sat on Luc's other side, and Viv leaned against the wall behind them.

"Where's the other one?" he asked. "There were three of you, weren't there?"

"Don't change the subject," Evie said. Bev had left as soon as they'd gotten back to Evie's house, but now Evie was wondering if she should've invited her and Shelby to spend the night.

"Papa Abe," Lily said. "Can I just talk for a minute?"

"Of course, darling child!" Abe said, beaming at her. "You should've said something earlier!"

"I did. And you're doing it again. I was planning on telling you that I wanted to stay with you sometimes. Not always, but sometimes. I know I need to learn more things. But now I'm afraid. You tell big lies without lying, and I'm confused and worried."

Abe leaned back. "So you would consider coming back with me?"

"Not now, and not during school. But maybe on weekends sometimes when I don't have plans with my friends. And during school breaks and summer. But never in the middle of the night and never without saying goodbye to Mama."

Abe glanced over at Evie and Luc. "And you'll approve this?"

Evie nodded. "We can give it a trial run in a couple weeks. Lily has a three-day weekend, and if it works for her and you, we can spend a weekend in hell."

"We?" Abe said. "This is an invitation for Lily only."

Evie laughed. "No. I don't know you. I don't know anyone at your place. I do not trust you to be alone with my daughter for an entire weekend. Maybe we'll get there eventually, but for now, she and I are a package deal." She glanced at Luc and amended her statement. "The three of us are a package deal."

Abe looked back at Lily. "Is this your final offer?"

Lily nodded. "For now."

Abe held out his hand. "Shake on it?" he said to Lily.

"Absolutely not," Luc said. "There will be no sealing of deals today. This is a trial run only. We can formalize things later. But definitely not now."

"I am going to bed," Lily said. "And that means you need to leave, Papa Abe."

Abaddon stood up and bowed. Horns curved out of the crown of his head as he tilted it towards Evie. When he straightened, he was once again clad in his shiny blue suit.

"It's been a pleasure doing business with you. I look forward to our weekend, Lily."

"I don't know if I do," she said. "But I might forgive you. Eventually. If there's a black unicorn in my room when I get there."

Abe nodded. "That can be arranged."

Another clap of thunder announced his departure.

Evie took a deep breath. "I can't believe it's over. At least for now." She didn't let go of Luc's hand.

"That went about as well as we could've expected," Hope said. "Be off with you now and put that grandchild of ours to bed. Your father and I are going into town to drink the young-uns under the table, start a bar fight, and hopefully get arrested. Sam, Viv... Want to come along and chaperone?"

"Nothing would please me more," Viv said. "Don't worry, Evie, I'll look after them and get video when they start dancing on tables."

Sam looked between Hope and Viv. "Are they really going to get arrested?" she asked.

"If we're lucky," James said. "Otherwise we haven't blown off nearly enough steam. Don't wait up!"

Moments later, the house was empty except for Evie, Lily, and Luc.

"Bedtime for monsters," Evie said. "For real this time."

"Will you come read me a story?" Lily asked.

"Of course, baby. What do you want me to read?"

"Clan of the Cave Bear?" Lily asked.

Evie shook her head. "Not on your life, kiddo. How about The Hunger Games?"

Lily considered. "Okay, but when I'm eleven, I get to read whatever I want."

"We'll talk about it," Evie said, ruffling her daughter's hair. "Go put on pajamas. I'll be there with the book in a moment."

"Goodnight, Lily," Luc said. He'd been mostly quiet since they emerged through the hellmouth a couple hours ago, and Evie was starting to worry this had all been too much and he'd be back in hell waiting for the weekends and school breaks... Or that he wouldn't be waiting.

Lily pulled her lower lip between her teeth, then looked at Luc. "Do you want to come read the story, too?"

Evie glanced over at Luc. His face lit up as a smile spread across his face.

"I would really like that," he said. "If that's what you want and it's okay with your mom."

"Of course," Evie said. "Now scoot. We'll be up as soon as you're changed."

"I'm not going to call you dad," Lily said, fixing Luc with her steely gaze. "At least not yet. You have to earn that title."

"I wouldn't dream of pushing you in any way," Luc said, hand on his heart. "But I hope you don't mind if I call you my daughter."

"Fucking fine," Lily said. She smiled at her parents and ran up the stairs.

🌱 🌿 🌾

"You need a swing," Luc said as Evie handed him a glass of wine and settled into the chair next to him. "This would be more fun if we were snuggling."

"I'll look into it," Evie promised. She sighed. "We should talk."

"About what to expect on Lily's weekend with my father?" Luc took a sip of his wine. "This is really nice chardonnay."

"Well, yes. We will need to talk about that, but not yet. We need to talk about us."

"Us?" Luc quirked up an eyebrow.

"You. Me. Lily. How do you want to do this? Are you going to want to make things official?"

"I would very much love to make things official," Luc said.

Evie nodded. "Of course. The devil loves a contract. I'll call a lawyer in the morning and we can get started."

"A lawyer?" Luc asked. "Aren't things like this normally handled by a judge?"

"Lawyer first, then judge," Evie said. "Mind you, if this is the route we're going, you might get dinged for child support. Of course, if you don't have a job, I might have to pay you." She shook her head. "We'll figure that out with the lawyer. What kind of time are you thinking you'll want?"

"Evie, I think we're not on the same page here," Luc said, setting down his glass and taking Evie's from her. "Look at me."

Evie wrapped her arms around herself and didn't quite meet his eyes.

"What do you think I'm asking for here?" Luc asked.

"Parenting time. Signed, sealed, and made official by the State of Washington. I'm going to lose so much time to you and your father. But I don't want to deprive Lily of a relationship with her father."

"Evelyn Grace. I do not want to take Lily away from you. The only thing I want to make official is my relationship with you. I walked away from you before, and I am the luckiest man alive that I have a second chance to make things right. I want you to be my—"

Evie put her hand over his mouth. "No. Not yet. Not so fast. I want to take things slow—we've never done that. Maybe we'll hate each other after three months. No sweeping declarations. No plans for the future. Just... You'll spend time with Lily. You and I will date. And you'll look for a place to rent in the area until we decide one way or another."

Luc nodded, and Evie started to remove her hand. Luc caught her wrist and held her still, then planted a slow kiss in the middle of her palm. Evie didn't know why that set her on fire, but heat was spreading through her body, and she gasped.

"Does taking things slow mean I shouldn't do this?" Luc cupped the back of her neck in his hand and pulled her forward, lightly brushing his lips along her jawline.

"Or this?" he whispered before biting down on her collarbone and eliciting a sudden, sharp inhalation.

He moved his hands to the swell of her ribcage and brushed his thumbs over her breasts. "What about this?"

Evie threw her arms around his neck and kissed him. She tangled her fingers through his hair and poured every hope and fear and dream she'd had in the last eleven years into that kiss. From their first kiss until this moment, every touch and every fantasy took hold, and she didn't protest when Luc pulled her onto his lap and slid his hands under her shirt.

"I can definitely take things this slow," Luc murmured against her neck.

"Maybe we can slowly walk upstairs," Evie suggested. "And then go on a real date tomorrow."

"You have the best ideas," Luc said. He picked her up and cradled her in his arms.

"What are you doing?" she gasped.

"I'll go slower if you're in my arms," Luc said. He kissed her gently, then turned towards the house and carried her upstairs.

Evie sprawled in the middle of the bed and watched Luc take off his clothes. "I wish this—you and me—could last forever."

"I'll do everything in my power to make this wish come true."

Evie smiled at Luc as he crawled onto the bed and into her arms. She kissed him and ran her hands over the hard planes of his body. "Let's see how slow you can take things tonight."

He covered her with his body. "As you wish."

EPILOGUE
THREE MONTHS LATER

Evie and Luc sat on the newly installed porch swing and watched Lily, Kevin, and Shelby run around the yard with Sprinkles in an elaborate game that Evie hadn't figured out yet.

Sprinkles was usually a Bernese Mountain Dog now—still huge, but at least not mythical. But now she was relaxed, and all three heads were on display. It always took a couple days after Lily came back from visiting her grandfather for everyone to pull themselves together enough for polite society.

"Are you sure about this?" Luc asked, taking a drink of the lemonade that still hadn't disappeared. "We can wait."

"I'm sure," Evie said. "Besides, half your stuff is here already. It makes sense for you to move in."

"It's more than half," Luc admitted. "I don't have a lot. No furniture. No family heirlooms. Other than my stylish and extremely expensive wardrobe, all I'm bringing to this relationship is a couple houseplants and a terrible collection of awkward relatives."

"That's not all you bring," Evie said, leaning into him and brushing her lips against his. Luc's arm tightened around her, and the kiss quickly went from sweet to serious.

"Mama! Dad! Don't be gross."

"Yeah," Shelby said. "There are children present."

"Corrupting the youth is a serious problem," Kevin added. "We could call the police."

"Get lost, monsters," Evie yelled. "This is my porch and my porch swing, and I will smooch whomever I want."

"Whatever," Lily yelled. "We're going to the witch's clearing."

"Be back for dinner," Evie said. "And no calling your grandpa with the Ouija board! It doesn't matter how many times you ask; he is not bringing you all unicorns to ride to school."

"Ugh. You ruin everything," Lily said, then flashed her mother a grin and ran across the lawn towards her. She threw her arms around her mom and planted a sloppy, wet kiss on her cheek. "I love you Mama."

"I love you too, demon child. To the stars and back."

Lily hugged Luc. "I love you, too, Dad. From here to Uranus." She cackled madly and ran back to join her friends to lead them into the woods.

"Now that no one's watching, can we be gross again?" Luc asked. "I can grab some wine, and we can toast to our official cohabitation."

Evie picked up her lemonade and drew a picture in the condensation. "Actually, there's something I need to tell you first."

"Something along the lines of 'Oh Luc, let's skip wine and go straight to bed'?"

Evie took a deep breath then exhaled in one noisy burst. "I'm pregnant."

"What?" Luc stared at her, jaw dropping. "I thought…"

"So did I," Evie said. "I'm forty-three, and I was on birth control. This shouldn't have happened."

"Okay," Luc said. "What do you want to do? Whatever it is, I've got your back."

"Do you mean that? Really?" She looked at him from under her eyelashes.

"Of course. It's all you, hot stuff." He shot finger guns at her.

Evie grinned. "No more unsupervised television time for you. Things are getting ridiculous."

"I want to keep it," she said. "I always wanted a big family, lots of kids running around. I would've been happy with never adding to my family now that I have you, but I... I want this. It might be my last chance."

"Are you ready for another demon baby?" Luc asked, pulling her close and resting his chin on her head. "My father will be twice as overbearing."

"Are you sure you're okay with this?" Evie asked.

"Are you kidding?" Luc exclaimed. "I can't wait to be there for everything. Diapers, midnight feedings, toilet training, first steps, first words... The works. You did an amazing job with Lily, and I can't wait to watch you in action from the beginning."

Evie's shoulders relaxed. "I am so happy. I didn't want to wish you into compliance, but I did have my fingers crossed that this wouldn't be the straw that breaks our relationship."

"There isn't a straw big enough to push me away. I'm in this for as long as you'll have me."

"I know, but..."

"There are no buts," Luc said. He moved away from her and stood up, then knelt in front of her and took her hands in one of his. He reached into his pocket with the other. "Do you know what day it is?" he asked.

"June twentieth," she said. "What are you doing?"

"It's not only June twentieth. It's eleven years to the day since I walked into Devil's Point and saw you sipping a G&T. Eleven years since I lost my heart. I'm sorry it took me so long to do this, but I hope I'm not too late." He pulled a box out of his pocket and flipped it open to reveal a platinum band with an emerald surrounded by a ring of fire opals.

"Evelyn Grace Addams, will you marry me?"

Tears started streaming down Evie's face, and she slid off the swing and into his arms. "I can't believe you! Yes! Of course yes!" The rift in her heart that had formed eleven years ago finally closed.

Luc slipped the ring onto her finger and kissed her. "I love you, Evie."

"I love you, too. This life is better than anything I could've wished for." She wrapped her arms around his neck and pulled his lips down to hers.

Evie closed her eyes as a swell of passion washed over her. Just before she lost herself in Luc's arms, she heard Lily yell, "Moooooooommm! Daaaaaaaaddd! I need you!"

MATCH MADE IN HELL

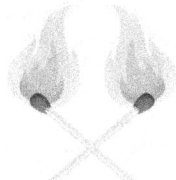

Evelyn Addams is fresh off a divorce and ready to kick up her heels. A fling with the sexy-as-hell Luc Morgenstern, in town for three months on a mysterious errand for his father, fits the bill perfectly.

Luc was supposed to be her rebound guy, nothing more than a second notch on her bedpost, but somewhere between the first night they met and the end of the summer, Evie did something she'd promised herself she wouldn't do. She caught feelings.

Just when she thinks she's worked up the courage to tell Luc how she feels and ask him to give their relationship a real chance, he drops a bombshell on her heart and fate follows suit. Will she overcome her fear and ask Luc to stay? Or will a match made in hell split them apart forever?

Match Made in Hell is an origin story novella in Eden Valley, a magical new paranormal women's fiction series from USA Today Bestselling Author Amy Cissell, author of the Eleanor Morgan novels and the Oracle Bay series.

Match Made in Hell has romantic elements, but it is not a romance.

Eden Valley
Book Two

Devil and the
Deep Blue Lake

USA TODAY BESTSELLING AUTHOR
AMY CISSELL

CONTENT WARNING

This preview contains depictions of alcohol abuse.

CHAPTER ONE

"Genevieve Kane, if you don't open this door right now, I will..." Evie's voice trailed off. She was probably trying to think of a suitable threat that might get Viv off the couch.

"She'll sic her demon fiancé on you," Bev said. "Or, if you're being particularly stubborn, her demon spawn. Both of them."

Viv sighed and pressed her hands to the bridge of her nose. Evie and Bev had been pounding on her condo door for the last fifteen minutes. If it went on much longer, someone would call the cops.

She knew what they wanted. Had known they were showing up. But her stupid flashes of knowledge seldom gave her enough warning to avoid uncomfortable situations, just enough to brace herself.

The knocking stopped.

"Viv?" Evie said, tentatively. "You know we love you, and ordinarily, neither of us would push you to see us if you really didn't want to, but we're worried."

"Please let us in," Bev said through the door. "Thirty minutes of conversation is all we're asking. If you want us to leave after, we'll go. No questions asked."

"And no repercussions," Evie said. "We'll be here for you when you need us, but right now we need to make sure you're okay."

Viv walked to the door but didn't open it. She dropped her chin to her chest and wrapped her arms around herself.

"I wish—" Evie's voice was interrupted by the hollow sound of a hand clapping over her mouth.

"Don't say that," Bev said.

"Shit. I didn't mean…"

Viv rolled her eyes and sighed loud enough for it to carry through the door. She unlocked and opened it. "Thirty minutes, and then you leave." She turned and walked back into her apartment, poured herself a glass of wine, and sat down in the overstuffed recliner.

Evie and Bev exchanged glances and settled onto the couch across from Viv.

Viv looked at her friends, fingers tapping on her knee. She looked at her smartwatch, then up at the women across from her. "Twenty-seven minutes."

Evie crossed her legs and leaned forward. "Viv, I know this year has been hard, and I know that Eden Valley is the last place you want to be. But you're shutting us out, too. Bev and I don't need you to come to us for our monthly brunch. We just need you."

Bev fixed Viv with a hard stare that Viv couldn't escape from. "You know I would move heaven and hell for you. Either of us would. But we can't help you if you won't let us in."

"I didn't even think that would be a literal situation ever, but here we are." Evie spread her arms to encompass the condo.

Evie and Bev leaned back, watching Viv expectantly. She took a large drink of the chardonnay she always had on hand thanks to an old lover who'd become a good friend. Her gaze dropped to the table separating her from her friends. It might be a narrow coffee table, but it felt like the gulf she'd put between them was widening the longer this went on. The visions that had been mere blips when they started in April of last year had picked up in frequency and intensity, if not usefulness, in the intervening fifteen months. They'd started in Eden Valley, and every time she went back, they'd ratcheted up another notch. Staying away was the only way she could protect herself, something her friends wouldn't understand. She took another sip. "Twenty-three minutes."

Evie sat up straight, folded her hands on her lap, and said, "We've been friends since we were in fourth grade. That's thirty-six years of history. In that time, we have seldom fought and, until a year ago, we've never gone more than a day without speaking. Bev and I have dropped so many balls with you, taken you and your trips back to Eden Valley for granted. I don't know how to make it up to you. Tell me what you need, and I'll do it. *We'll* do it. But I will not let this friendship die until you look me in the eye and tell me it's already buried. Can you do that?"

Cold spread through Viv's body, and a lump grew in her throat. She needed to tell Evie and Bev to go in a definitive enough way, so they never came back, otherwise they'd keep bothering her until she eventually broke down and gave in, making everything even worse. She didn't know how many more visits she could make and still come back to Seattle as a semi-functional human being. She'd broken up with so many people, hated it when the people she was dating got too pushy and asked for too much. She could use the same strategy here. She hardened herself, set her jaw, and looked Evie directly in the eye. "It's over. Our friendship ran its course at least a decade ago, but we were all too stubborn or too stupid to let it go. But now, I'm taking control of my life and telling you to leave. Delete my number. And don't come here again."

She almost winced at the look in Evie's eyes—she'd never seen her friend look that hurt and lost except when her daughter had been kidnapped by a King of Hell.

Evie dropped her eyes and cleared her throat. "Okay. If that's what you want. You can close the door, but I never will. Say the word and I will drop everything for you." She stood up.

Bev grabbed Evie's arm and yanked her back down. "By my calculation, we have almost fifteen minutes left. Evie's said her piece, and you've said yours, but now it's my turn."

Viv squirmed under Bev's steely gaze.

"Genevieve Kane, you are being an absolute idiot. Don't sit there and pretend this friendship was over a decade ago. We walked into hell together last year to save Evie's daughter, and I would, by all we hold sacred, walk right back into hell again to save your sorry ass. If you're going to end this, throw away everything the three of us have been through, then at least have the decency to be honest about it."

Viv's jaw dropped. She'd never heard Bev lose her temper like this. Not when her adopted daughter Shelby had destroyed her garden in a fit of PTSD-induced rage. Not when her parents had forgotten to show up for graduation leaving Bev the only person to walk off the stage with no family to meet, and not when Joanne Mills—now sheriff of Chelan County—had thrown Bev's backpack that contained her favorite jeans, two first edition books she'd saved up for months to buy from the local used bookshop, and her science fair project into the lake the last day of freshman year.

Bev was tapping her foot and waiting for a response. "You have approximately three minutes to tell us what the hell is going on before I let Evie wish it out of you."

"Her wishes on people only work if the subjects were already inclined to make those decisions," Viv muttered. Dammit. She hadn't meant to say anything.

"Oh, you want to tell us the truth," Bev said. "You just won't admit it." Her voice softened into the warmth more typical of Bev. "Viv, c'mon. If you can't trust us, who can you trust?"

"This isn't a path you have to walk alone," Evie said, laying down her best compassionate mom voice—the one Viv heard her use when Lily was in trouble and Evie was trying to coax her out of her defensive shell and back into the sunshiny girl she usually was.

She was resolute, though. Being alone was better than asking her friends to carry her baggage. Again. She opened her mouth to tell them that, then surprised everyone by bursting into tears.

🌱 🍃 🌺

Viv sipped a glass of wine on the rooftop bar Bev and Evie had dragged her to. She caught her reflection in the mirror behind the bar and winced. She looked like hell. No—she'd had a fling with a demon who'd been hotter than the hell she came from, and Sam looked infinitely better than Viv did right now.

After she'd started crying, Bev and Evie had fallen into "Mom-mode." Evie'd pushed Viv into the shower and talked her into getting dressed while Bev cleaned up the place and dumped the take-out containers and empty wine bottles that were littering the kitchen. Then, they'd dragged her to this bar, grabbed a table in the back with a clear line of sight to the bar and the entrance, and looked at her expectantly.

The weight of what they wanted her to say pushed her head between her shoulders until she was hunched over her wine.

Bev and Evie waited silently. Viv knew they were giving her time and not making her feel pushed aside by chattering to each other, but the silence was heavy and felt like judgment. She took a deep breath, flicked a long strand of jet-black hair behind her ear, and looked at her friends—her best friends.

"I'm sorry." As a start, it wasn't bad, but Viv knew it wasn't enough. She picked up the bar napkin and twisted it in her hands before shredding it into narrow strips. A flash hit her, the blinding headache close behind. She pushed back from the table just in time to avoid the tray of half-empty glasses that dropped onto the edge of the table and crashed to the ground where she'd been sitting an instant ago.

"I am so sorry!" the server said. "I can't believe that happened. I'll be right back to clean this mess up. Why don't you ladies move to that table." She gestured to the nearest table that had recently been vacated. "Don't take your drinks—they might have glass in them. I'll get you fresh glasses and a bottle. Obviously on the house."

Viv tried to breathe her heart rate into submission. She grabbed her purse, shook off the shards of glass and wiped it off with the rag offered to her by the small hoard of bar employees who'd descended to clean up the mess of broken glass and spilled alcohol.

The women settled at the new table and had been there less than a minute before their server was dropping off fresh waters and a bottle of wine with three glasses. "It's a good thing you moved when you did!" she said. "I'm so glad that tray didn't hit you."

"I'm just lucky, I guess," Viv said, forcing a smile. The stabbing pain behind her eyes was starting to dull down a bit, and her peripheral vision was slowly returning. She couldn't see well through the lights flashing in her eyes yet, but color was returning to her world, and she could see well enough to find the now-full glass of wine and down it like a college student in a tequila shot contest.

"Are you okay?" Evie asked. She poured a little more wine into Viv's glass, but it was not a full pour. Viv knew Evie was thinking about the empty bottles Bev had cleaned up earlier.

"Fine," Viv managed. She rubbed her temples and tried to bring the world back into focus. As long as she didn't get another flash, she'd be fine in about ten minutes. Wine numbed the pain that came with the flashes of insight, and wine kept them from happening. Wine and staying away from situations where she interacted with people and events that might need predicting.

"I'm going to the ladies' room," Viv said. "Be right back." She jumped up and ran away from the table before either friend could offer to come with her. Instead of using the restroom on the roof, she darted downstairs, bumping into the walls like a pinball ricocheting off the walls of a machine and activating too-bright lights.

She walked up to the bar. "Two shots of Jameson." She tossed a twenty down on the bar. The bartender brought her the whiskey and she took both shots, one after another, and slammed the glasses down on the bar.

"You're not driving anywhere, are you ma'am?" the bartender asked.

"Nope. I've got my designated busybodies upstairs," Viv said. She turned around to return to her wine and saw Bev behind her.

"I was coming to check on you," Bev said, disappointment and worry radiating from her. "To make sure you were okay."

Viv bit back every excuse she wanted to make and every angry thought that wanted to burst forth.

"Let's go back upstairs," Viv said. "I'll try to explain."

❦

Viv sat down, conscious that she'd spent most of the afternoon squirming under the gazes of her friends but not telling them anything. Instead, she'd cried, showed off the unpredictable and useless "gift" she'd gotten courtesy of the portal to hell that had opened in Eden Valley the year before to deposit Evie's long-lost love —and the father of her child—back in town, and done secret shots in the middle of the afternoon like a kid hiding from their parents. In other words, she was winning the friendship game.

When she'd gotten back to the table, the wine was gone, replaced with glasses of iced tea. A cheese and charcuterie tray showed up moments later.

"I don't want to push you," Evie said. "But this isn't like you. You're acting out of character, and you're trying to run away from us."

Viv felt resolve solidify in her chest. Evie was right. She had to tell someone. Carrying this alone was killing her. She took one more minute to push away the envy she felt—Evie's gift was useful and didn't cause killer headaches, and Bev hadn't gotten anything but the brand that marked her as hell's—and to make sure there weren't tears lurking in the corners of her eyes waiting for the dam to burst to flood what little dignity she had left.

"It's the damn flashes of intuition or knowledge or whatever you want to call them. I thought they'd go away if I left Eden Valley. Every time I came back to visit, it got worse. Things were clearer, no more vague urges. I know what's going to happen and how to change it. But I don't always know in time to do anything. And the headaches..." She trailed off, nausea twisting her stomach. She tried to remember the last time she'd put anything in her stomach that wasn't coffee or alcohol and came up fuzzy.

Viv made a cheese and cracker plate for herself and scarfed down a few bites, washing it all down with iced tea.

"I'm sure you've tried everything to get the headaches under control," Bev said. "So I won't offer suggestions unless you want me to."

Viv ticked off on her fingers. "OTC pain killers, meditation, acupuncture, yoga, Imitrex, Oxy. I've visited specialists, neurologists, naturopaths, reiki healers, and some shady guy in a back alley building who was probably doing illegal things in the other room but promised he was the second coming of Christ and had the ability to heal anything demon-related. The only thing that dulls the pain and keeps the flashes from showing up is alcohol."

Evie reached across the table and grabbed Viv's hand. "We one hundred percent believe you. But you have to know this isn't sustainable. It isn't healthy. How are you keeping up with work?"

"If I stay home and don't encounter anyone, it's not as bad," Viv said. "I get up early, get through everything I need to do for my clients, and then..." She trailed off. They'd already seen her home and her behavior today; she didn't want to admit that the wine or—if it was a particularly bad day—whiskey was now an almost daily habit.

"That explains why you don't want to come ho—back to Eden Valley," Bev said. "But it doesn't explain why you stopped taking our calls. You know we'd come to Seattle for brunch if that's what you needed."

"You think I wanted you to see me like this?" The anger was building again, and with it the headache that the whiskey had dulled. She yanked her hand back. "I know I'm a mess. I know this isn't sustainable. Not all of us were lucky enough to end up with a supernatural shoplifting ability, a hot guy, and a new baby. Not all of us got to avoid it altogether. That's why I didn't call. You can't understand what I'm going through, and I can't hide my resentment. I don't want your judgment *or* your help. I don't need an intervention. I don't need either of you."

Viv watched Evie's posture straighten and her face harden. Evie's eyes narrowed; her expression shuttered. Viv had been on the receiving end of the Addams stare before, but that'd been from Evie's mom Hope, and it'd been almost thirty years since she'd been subject to it.

"I didn't want to have to do this, but I see now there's no other way." Evie leaned forward and captured Viv's gaze. "We are taking you back to your condo. You are packing your bags. And you are coming home."

Viv wanted to argue, but with the weight of Evie's gaze on her, she couldn't fight back. Either something had happened to her will, or Evie's had gotten a lot, lot stronger.

Evie smiled, but it didn't quite reach her eyes. "It's amazing what two half-demon babies will do to a woman," she said. "I don't even have to wish out loud anymore." She threw several bills on the table and stood up.

Viv had no choice but to do the same, and the horrifying part was, she no longer wanted to resist.

CHAPTER TWO

Viv sat at Bev's dining room table, holding her face in her hands. Her head was pounding. It wasn't the "vision" headache. This was a hangover—something she'd gotten increasingly used to over the last year.

"Here, drink this," Bev said, shoving a glass of orange liquid in front of Viv's face.

"Sports drink?" Viv's nose wrinkled as she regarded the neon beverage.

"It'll help," Bev said. "And if it gets bad, let me know, and I'll take you to the hospital."

"If what gets bad?" Viv asked, downing the drink. It was replaced with another and a steaming mug.

"Drink the broth, too." Bev sat down across from Viv and watched her alternate between the two. "Withdrawal. I don't know how much you were drinking and for how long, but I will not risk you. If you start shaking or sweating, we are out the door and at the emergency clinic. If you think we should go now, let me know. Don't lie. Don't prevaricate."

"Where's Shelby?" Viv asked, ignoring the question for now and finishing her liquids. Her stomach growled, hunger and nausea warring for supremacy.

"She and Lily had a sleepover at Kevin's—those three kids are even more inseparable now than ever—and were headed to swimming lessons, then Evie's from there," Bev answered. "Do you think you could tolerate a smoothie? Or how about scrambled eggs?"

"Smoothie. And it's just a hangover. A really, really bad one, but only a hangover." The humiliation she felt at not only having put herself into this situation, but having others see, was as present as the headache drilling into her skull. Then Bev's words—and the casualness with which she said them—hit her. "Kevin's? Since when?"

Bev moved to the kitchen, and Viv followed. As Bev moved around the kitchen grabbing fruit and yogurt and juice, she said, "Since Hell. Kevin's mom Aurielle Brand—Elle—started going to school functions. She gave us her phone number and invited me and Evie to tea. I don't know what to make of it, but it's good. We've had brunch."

"She's your new brunch third?" Viv asked, failing to keep the bitter note of jealousy out of her voice.

"She's the fourth of five ladies who brunch," Bev said placidly. She turned on the blender.

"Five? There's five of you now?" Viv asked as soon as the blender stopped and the echoes of the noise no longer reverberated in her head.

"Yep. Evie, me, Elle, and Sam."

"That's four," Viv pointed out. "And why did you invite Sam? She's a demon."

"So are Lily and Alex," Bev said, pouring the thin smoothie into a tall glass and handing it to Viv. "So is Luc. Sam is Evie's almost sister-in-law. She comes by a couple times a month to visit her nieces, and we brunch. And the fifth is obviously you, dummy."

Viv closed her eyes and took a deep breath, trying to drown the irritation. She'd skipped the last—she counted on her fingers—five brunches. She hadn't been back to visit since just after Alex had been born—her tiny birthday twin—and only a couple times before that. Shit. She hadn't seen her honorary nieces more than two or three times in the last year and had missed Lily's eleventh birthday and Shelby's twelfth.

"I am awful," Viv said, taking a sip of the smoothie and willing her stomach to accept it without protest. "No wonder you replaced me."

Bev sat down across from Viv, handed her a cup of coffee heavily dosed with fresh cream, and took a drink of her own black coffee. "You're not replaced, but even if that were the case, it means it took two other people to take the place of one Genevieve Kane." She reached out and put her hand on Viv's forearm and squeezed until Viv looked up at her. "You're not replaceable, Viv. I'm sorry we didn't come check on you earlier. I knew something wasn't right, but I thought you were putting your broken heart back together and wanted to give you time and space. And I was too wrapped up in my own stuff. I failed you, and I'm sorry."

Viv blinked back tears. She'd never been much of a crier, but Bev always knew what buttons to push to pull her emotions to the forefront. "You didn't fail me, Bev. You and Evie are the best parts of my life, and I failed myself and you guys by fucking up this badly." She took another sip of the smoothie and let the cool liquid soothe her nausea.

Bev smiled at Viv. "We could play the self-recrimination Olympics, but I'm not sure that's the best use of our time. I have to go to work in a little bit. Will you be okay on your own?"

Humiliation threatened to burn away the cooling effects of the smoothie. "I'm not going to raid your liquor cabinet, if that's what you're asking," Viv said.

"It wasn't, but you wouldn't be able to anyway. This is currently a booze-free house. Not because of you, before you get defensive. It's been an interesting year for everyone." Bev grabbed her bag from the hook near the door and pulled out a keychain and handed it to Viv. "This key will open the medicine safe in the linen closet in case you need more aspirin, and if you need a knife or scissors or anything sharp, the smaller key will open the drawer next to the stove."

Viv took the keys and tried to make sense of the info Bev had just dumped on her. She opened her mouth to ask, but Bev shook her head. "Later, babe. Right now, it's all about you. How are you feeling?"

"Hungry. Nauseated. Headachy. But surprisingly not terrible," Viv replied.

"Finish your smoothie. Evie will be here in about fifteen minutes to hang out. If you think you're up for it in an hour or so, you can try some solid food." Bev grabbed a blazer she'd slung over the back of the chair. "I'm so sorry I have to leave. I've taken so much time off this year that I need to at least make an appearance in the office today. I'll be home before Shelby gets home, and you won't be alone."

Viv plastered a smile on her face and flapped her hands at Bev. "Go. I promise I'll be fine until my second baby-sitter gets here. I have your number, and I promise to call if I start to feel worse."

Bev hesitated, then flung her arms around Viv and kissed her on the top of her head. "I missed you, and I'm glad you're here, even if the reason sucks."

"I'm glad I'm here, too," Viv said. She stilled in Bev's arms and tested the unexpected feeling for the compulsion Evie had created the day before and was surprised to realize every word was genuine.

❦

As soon as Bev walked out the door and Viv heard her car drive away, Viv found a portable coffee mug, dumped her coffee in it, and after slipping her shoes on and grabbing her shades, walked out the door. The door clicked behind her, and she paused until she heard the automatic lock engage. She walked down the street and headed through an overgrown alley that hadn't seen car traffic in years. The drying grass rustled against her jeans wafting the sweet smell of summer towards her.

The sky was bright blue, uncharitably unmarred by clouds and the sun, already warm even this early, chased away the cold she'd been unable to shake for months even as it intensified the throbbing hangover pain behind her eyeballs. Viv strode through Eden Valley, hoping her determined stride would discourage anyone from approaching her. When she got to Main Street, she looked around from the shadow of the gas station awning; then sure the coast was clear and neither Bev nor Evie were close, she darted across the street, took a sharp turn into the city park, and skirted the trees at the edge of the park until she got to the trail that started in the park and wound its way around Eden Lake. Once she was a few yards down the trail and not visible from either the park or Main Street, she rolled her shoulders and winced as everything and more popped with the release of tension that'd been piling on for far too long.

Viv walked slowly down the trail. It'd been a long time since she'd been to this part of the lake—she usually hung out at Evie's—but she was sure there was a... There it was. A bench, nearly hidden by the low shrubs and high grass that edged the trail. Viv pushed her way through and settled onto the bench. It was clean and afforded a clear view of the Lake with the Cascade Mountains rising dramatically on either side. The air was clear and crisp, and a bit of mist rose from the water.

The sun was warm on her back, but the cool breeze coming off the lake balanced it perfectly. No matter how much she ran, how many times she professed to hate the town she'd lived in since she was nine, the town her mother had grown up in, coming here was coming home.

Viv leaned back and tipped her head up, letting the sound of the waves gently lapping against the shore lull her into an almost meditative state. It'd been a long time since she'd allowed herself to be alone with her thoughts. She'd spent most of the last year either working or drinking, and, if she was honest with herself, the years before that either working or distracting herself with whoever she was dating at the time. When she found herself between relationships, she threw herself into work and exercise classes—cardio classes, Zumba, spinning. She'd stopped running about a year before her trip to hell when the meditative calm she'd always loved became another place for her negative thoughts to clamor for attention.

The one time she'd tried therapy to work through her mother issues, she lasted three sessions before ghosting her therapist who'd insisted she needed to spend time with herself before she could figure out where to go and what to do. He'd had the unmitigated gall to tell her she'd let herself be defined first by the mother she'd spent the last forty-plus years disappointing, then by her friends who she constantly compared herself to, and then by the series of relationships that never seemed to go anywhere and left nothing of herself to be defined by what she wanted. He'd offered up what felt like so much critique of her character, her reactions, and her coping mechanisms—which used to be exercise instead of alcohol—and no guidance or even leading questions about how to begin to heal.

Viv finished her coffee and pushed her shades on top of her head. She winced as the sunlight hit her, bringing a fresh wave of nausea and stabbing pain. She put both feet on the ground, closed her eyes, and did the breathing exercises she'd picked up from a short-lived meditation kick when she thought she could learn to let go of her thoughts and rise above the anxiety, self-loathing, and depression that had dogged her for too long. When the hangover-like symptoms had dissipated to a manageable level, she slowly opened her eyes.

She'd been gone too long—she knew Bev and Evie would be worried about her, and she didn't want to be a bigger jerk than she'd already been. She grabbed her phone, didn't check the messages or voicemail, and dictated a message to Siri letting them both know she was okay.

She hit send and heard the *ping* of an incoming message. Viv shot to her feet and looked around. Adrenaline surged through her body, freezing her like a deer in headlights. Evie was on the trail behind her, baby on her chest, and a disgruntled expression on her face.

Viv watched as her best friend looked around, then plunged through the underbrush towards Viv.

"You are a world-class jerk," Evie huffed. "Not only did you disappear without a note, knowing we were worried about you—alcohol detox is no joke, asshole—you made me go for a freaking hike, carrying a wiggly baby, when I still haven't recovered from pushing this ungrateful demon with her giant demon head out of my body."

Evie collapsed on the bench, and Viv sat down gingerly beside her.

"Sorry," Viv said in a small voice she barely recognized. "It's just a hangover, but I didn't think it through."

Evie blew out a long breath. "It's fine. Really. I get why you'd need some time, and I know why you're here."

"You do?" Viv asked. She'd thought her propensity to hide in plain sight over the years had gone unnoticed.

"Of course. This is the bench where you, me, and Bev swore to be best friends forever, where we became blood sisters." Evie held up her hand. A small, silvery scar on her wrist flashed in the sunlight. Viv held her wrist up to display a matching scar. "But you should've left a note. I didn't tell Bev you were missing—she doesn't need the stress—but I did have a momentary freak-out." Evie looked down at Viv, and Viv couldn't read the expression in her eyes. Evie said, wry grin spreading across her face, "I need to apologize."

"For what?" Viv wracked her brain, but all she came up with were her own shortcomings.

"I pushed you. I used the power I've gotten from Luc and my children to force you into something you didn't want to do. I know I'd do it again, but I took away your choice, and that was wrong."

Viv shifted her gaze to a point over Evie's shoulder and twisted her hands together. "It's okay. I really believe you couldn't have made me do anything I didn't want to, even if that want was buried pretty deep down. Thank you for caring, for not giving up on me."

"Always," Evie said. She pulled Alex out of the baby carrier on her chest and fanned herself. "These baby wearing contraptions are hot."

"May I?" Viv asked, holding her arms out towards the baby. She was grateful for the change of subject and unworthy of having a friend who could read her so adeptly.

Evie handed her over. "Be my guest. If she goes for a boob, let me know and I'll feed her. Hopefully she won't need a change immediately. I didn't bring the diaper bag."

Viv sat down and cradled the baby in her arms. She raised Alex close enough to breathe in the fresh, sweet baby scent of the baby's perfect, if relatively large, head. "She's so big," Viv said, inhaling deeply through her nose.

"She's six months old," Evie said.

There wasn't a hint of censure in her friend's voice, but it didn't prevent a swell of guilt from rising. At this rate, between the waves of guilt and fear and self-loathing, Viv was going to get washed out to sea—she looked over Alex's head at the impossibly blue-green body of water in front of her, or lake, she amended—by a cliché tidal wave of emotion.

Evie, seemingly oblivious to the storm of emotions vying for prominence in Viv's chest, rolled her neck and arched her back. "And she is heavy. I think I know why women in their forties shouldn't have kids. I thought carrying Lily around was bad enough eleven years ago...but I am so much older and stiffer now." She opened her eyes and with a final grimace, sat down next to Viv and followed her gaze out to the lake.

"I still have trouble being close to the lake for too long," Evie confessed. "Knowing that *something* is in there. After almost losing Lily and my dad last year... The only good thing is that for the first summer in as long as anyone can remember, no one drowned last year."

Eden Lake was still this morning, like an unmarred mirror, perfectly reflecting the mountains rising up in a semi-circle around it. "I love it," Viv said. "But I get why you wouldn't. Not saying I want to ever go out on it again—there isn't anything that could ever get me to touch that water—but I spent a lot of hours on this bench growing up. Every time I needed to escape my mom and didn't want to be around people, I came here. I don't like the stillness, though. It's easier to let it pull out all the negative feelings when I can count the waves."

Concentric circles, narrow at first, then widening, appeared in the middle of the lake. Less than a minute later, gentle waves lapped the beach in front of them.

Viv and Evie froze, staring at the waves that hadn't been there before and had no obvious source.

"Um... Wanna go get breakfast at the diner?" Evie asked, putting the baby carrier back on and holding out her arms.

"Abso-fucking-lutely." Viv turned and glanced behind her. The waves were stilling—almost gone—and a pair of emerald eyes appeared above the water's surface in the center of the lake. She blinked, and they were gone. A ghostly image of Bev took its place, hovering above the water and holding something that Viv knew was a body. One more blink, and the lake was once again placid, not a wave marring its surface.

She braced for the spike of pain that accompanied her flashes of knowing, but nothing came. She didn't release the tension in her shoulders, though, until she and Evie were on the trail and headed back towards the park.

NOT IN THE CARDS
ORACLE BAY BOOK 1

Not in the Cards is the first book in the Oracle Bay series—a paranormal romance series set on the Washington (state) coast. It's a separate series but in-world with the folks of Eden Valley (and you might even find the connecting character!).

Welcome to Oracle Bay, the town where the local **psychics were already expecting you!**
Oracle Bay has always attracted the preternaturally clairvoyant. When anyone with seers' blood in their veins steps foot in this quaint coastal town, their powers awaken. They receive a visit from the Psychics Union, and shenanigans ensue.

Sandy Franklin is on the run from her old life and her almost-ex-husband. Lured to Oracle Bay by a too-cheap-to-be-believable apartment with attached tarot reader shop, she has found new friends and a job she didn't know was possible. Hiding from her past while building a new future.

When Vincent, the handsome stranger who owns most of Main Street, announces he's selling Oracle Bay to stave off personal problems, Sandy and the other resident psychics devise a plan to save the town using their divination skills and a little old-fashioned sleuthing.

The one thing Sandy couldn't predict was how hard she'd fall for the one man who could crush Oracle Bay and her hopes for a new life without blinking an eye... Will Sandy get a second chance at true love with the man whose past might be even more dangerous than her own?

TAKE A TRIP TO ORACLE BAY. Come for the scenic Pacific Northwest, stay for the paranormal romance in these (mostly) standalone novels.

Once Sandy has you hooked, check out the rest of the psychics in Oracle Bay.

ABOUT THE AUTHOR

 Amy Cissell is a USA Today Bestselling Author of urban fantasy and paranormal romance novels. She lives in Portland, OR with her husband, her haunted house-obsessed daughter, their three cats, and the murder of crows she's conspiring to turn into her vengeful army.

When she's not working or writing, she's sleeping because that's all she has time to do! There are few things Amy loves more than a well-timed pun, a good book, a glass of wine, and time at the Oregon Coast.

Although she reads anything and everything, her first love is fantasy. Eleven-year-old Amy discovered fantasy when she 'borrowed' her father's copy of The Hobbit and an enduring love affair (mostly with dragons) was born.

facebook.com/acissellwrites
twitter.com/acissellwrites
instagram.com/acissellwrites
bookbub.com/authors/amy-cissell
goodreads.com/acissellwrites

ALSO BY AMY CISSELL

Paranormal Women's Fiction

Eden Valley

Raising A Demon (June 2021)

Devil and the Deep Blue Lake (September 2021)

Valley of Angels (November 2021)

Guardian of Eden (February 2022)

Eden Valley World Novellas

Match Made in Hell (June 2021)

Fall From Grace (September 2021)

Hell's Bells (December 2021)

Heaven Sent (February 2022)

Paranormal Romance

Oracle Bay

Not in the Cards (October 2018)

First Hand Knowledge (November 2018)

Belle of the Ball (December 2019)

Hell and High Water (2022)

Tempest in a Teapot (2022)

Bad to the Bones (2022)

Oracle Bay World Novellas

Wing and a Prayer (January 2019)

Contemporary/Urban Fantasy

The Eleanor Morgan Novels

(complete series)

The Cardinal Gate (February 2017)

The Waning Moon (June 2017)

The Ruby Blade (October 2017)

The Broken World (March 2018)

The Lost Child (June 2019)

The Iron River (May 2020)

The Dark Throne (February 2021)

The Eleanor Morgan World Novellas

The Throneless King (March 2020)